DEAD

'Perhaps I should have warned you that Detective Sergeant Fielding is a tutor on our self-defence courses,' Anderson said to Sealey. 'Were you at the house?'

Fielding seemed to have knocked the stuffing out of Sealey. He just knelt there on the tarmac with the rain bouncing all around him. 'All right. Yes, I was. I went there Saturday night to tell Drax what a bastard he was. I wanted to beat him up, all right?' His head jerked up. 'And I knew if I told you I'd been there you'd try to pin the murder on me, and now that's exactly what you're going to do, isn't it?'

Anderson closed his eyes for a moment. His suit was already soaked. The thin fabric was like a wrung-out crumpled flannel, and there was every chance that the colour would run and ruin one of his favourite shirts. 'Get up,' he said coldly.

A MOMENT OF MADNESS
A Fairfax and Vallance mystery

DEADLY AFFAIRS
A John Anderson mystery

DEADLY AFFAIRS

by
Juliet Hastings
A John Anderson mystery

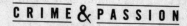

First published in Great Britain in 1997 by
Crime & Passion
an imprint of Virgin Publishing Ltd
332 Ladbroke Grove
London W10 5AH

Crime & Passion series editor: Pan Pantziarka

ISBN 0 7535 0029 9

Typeset by Avon Dataset Ltd, Bidford on Avon, B50 4JH
Printed and bound in Great Britain by
Mackays of Chatham PLC, Chatham, Kent

For Jonathan

Sine qua non

Flaubert's *Salammbô* is quoted from the Penguin Classics edition, translated by A. J. Krailsheimer

PROLOGUE
Thursday

David was always cautious in his dealings with his boss. Eddie Drax, creative director and owner of half of the capital of Drax & Bond, was not a reliable man. However, there was one aspect of his character which was superbly consistent. Sooner or later, Eddie would argue with everyone.

David had managed to avoid arguing with Eddie since he was recruited, six years ago. He thought this was a record to be proud of. If Eddie irritated him, he hid it, and they appeared to get on very well. It was June, and in the long bright evening they played a pleasant nine holes at the Farnham Park Golf Club and then repaired to the bar.

David's wife, Penny, was already waiting for them, cool and elegant in a linen dress, gin and tonic in hand. She welcomed her husband with a peck on the cheek. 'Hello, darling. Hello, Eddie. Good game?'

'Excellent. I won a tenner off Eddie.'

'Fluke,' said Eddie, catching the barman's eye. 'A tenner on nine holes? Pure fluke.' David bristled. It wasn't a fluke. He had played better than Eddie: more consistently, more accurately. But Eddie was a bad loser. 'I was distracted. Now, where's Amanda? She's the whole point of this evening.'

Eddie flitted with alarming rapidity from one relationship to the next, and it seemed that once every six months they were required to meet the latest flame. David glanced at Penny, sharing his amusement with her. He accepted a drink and settled himself comfortably on the big sofa. The club was new and expensive, patronised mostly by wealthy executives, and though he had been a member for three years he still enjoyed the feeling of being at home there.

'There she is.' Eddie left the bar and hurried across the room to meet a woman in the doorway. He caught her into his arms and kissed her hard. David raised one eyebrow as he examined her. A typical Eddie choice, early thirties, tall and statuesque. This one was blonde, the first blonde for some time. Eddie was only about five feet eight and wiry, and in her low heels the woman was his height to an inch. David's eyes lingered on her big breasts and full high bottom, but without interest. He didn't share Eddie's tastes.

'Amanda,' said Eddie, his arm firmly around the blonde's waist, 'let me introduce David and Penny Thompson. David, Penny, Amanda Sealey. David's in charge of the money at Drax & Bond. We couldn't do without him. Everyone needs someone to count the beans.'

David got up to shake Amanda's hand and managed a smile, though as usual he was irritated by the dismissive way in which Eddie introduced him. He was finance director, for God's sake. What was so great about being a graphic designer? 'Delighted to meet you,' he said easily to Amanda, as Eddie headed to the bar for a Pimm's. 'I wonder if we've met before? I seem to know your face.'

'Nice to meet you, Amanda,' said Penny. 'You know, I think I've seen you too.'

Amanda blushed. It suited her. Her ash-blonde hair was bobbed, and her eyes were hazel. She looked classy. A better choice than the last, certainly, though David felt a little guilty even as he thought it. 'Well,' Amanda said in a voice that was slightly tinged with a London accent, 'you might have seen me here.'

'Oh, are you a member?'

'No. But –' She blushed more deeply and seemed to run out of steam.

Eddie barged in, pushing Amanda's glass into her hand and taking charge. 'Amanda's not a member,' he explained as they settled down again into the sofas, 'but her husband Tony is.'

'Oh,' said Penny. David could see that she was shocked.

'He's left home,' Amanda explained, looking up into David's face as if she sought his approval. 'We're getting a divorce.'

What was one supposed to say under these circumstances? 'Congratulations' would probably have been accurate, but it sounded incongruous. He settled for a neutral, 'Ah, I see.'

'Amanda's going to move in with me,' Eddie volunteered eagerly. 'After the weekend. She's off to see her parents, then that's it. Sell their house. A clean break.'

David almost shook his head in disbelief. It was only a week since Eddie had dismissed his last live-in girlfriend. Who did he think he was? He behaved more like a twenty-year-old than a successful businessman of forty-two. David took a deep draught of his gin while Eddie rattled on about changes to the house which Amanda had suggested.

Suddenly Amanda set down her Pimm's unsteadily on the glass table and caught at Eddie's arm. Her face was pale. 'Eddie. Eddie, it's Tony.'

'Where?' demanded Eddie, sitting up straight and looking eagerly around him.

'Oh, no,' Penny whispered, shutting her eyes.

If there was one thing that Eddie loved, it was to make a scene and be the centre of attention. David's stomach clenched with approaching embarassment. He whispered to Penny, 'Oh, God. Not here.'

A dark young man about Amanda's age stalked towards them. He was dressed in a suit as if he had come straight from work. His eyes flickered from Eddie to Amanda and his lips moved as he muttered to himself.

'Hi, Tony,' said Eddie cheerfully. David cringed inwardly. What an insensitive idiot! The newcomer was clearly furious. If Eddie had wanted to pick a fight, he could hardly have started better.

'You bastard, Drax,' Tony Sealey replied.

'Tony,' said Amanda quickly, 'please, don't.'

'Don't what?' Tony pushed his way in among the sofas and stood over Eddie with his fists planted on his hips, staring

3

down and snarling. 'Don't tell Eddie Shitface Drax what a bastard he is to steal another man's wife?'

All around the bar people were looking. Soon the club servants would move in. It was hideous, embarrassing and dangerous. David got reluctantly up and said placatingly, 'Ah, I wouldn't –'

'Please, Tony,' said Amanda, 'just go away.'

She began to get up and Tony's teeth bared in sudden rage. 'Shut up,' he snapped. He pushed her roughly down to the sofa with the flat of his hand.

Amanda let out a little shocked 'Oh.' Eddie's face flamed with fury and he leapt up from the sofa and hit Sealey hard in the stomach. Eddie's slight body was mostly muscle. The force of the blow drove all the air from Tony and he folded over, gasping.

David winced and extended a hand. 'Eddie,' he said anxiously, 'don't.'

He might as well have talked to the trees. Eddie punched Tony hard in the mouth. The younger man fell backwards across the coffee table, scattering Pimm's and gin far and wide. David closed his eyes, hardly able to believe that this was happening.

'That,' said Eddie crowingly, 'is why Amanda was with you and is now with me. All right, Sealey? Want any more?'

'Oh, Mr Drax.' The barman was hurrying towards them, hands flapping. 'Mr Drax, please.'

Eddie flung up his hands and sat down again. 'Amanda,' he murmured, 'darling, are you all right?'

'David,' hissed Penny, 'do something.'

David rolled his eyes reluctantly to heaven then leant down and hauled Tony from the coffee table. Blood trickled from Sealey's split lip and fell on to the patterned cream-and-gold carpet. 'Come on,' David said in a low voice, tugging at the young man's shoulders. 'Come on, that's enough.'

Tony let David guide him almost as far as the door. Then he pulled free violently, wiped his hand across his mouth and waved his bloodstained fist at Eddie. 'Drax,' he yelled, 'see this? It ought to be yours, you bastard! It will!'

Christ, David thought, if I try to make him leave he'll

probably hit me instead. The whole situation was a nightmare. He was profoundly relieved when one of the greenkeepers ran in, no doubt summoned by 'phone, and steered the cursing Tony towards the door. David accompanied them, glad to look as if he was doing something positive. Tony smacked away the greenkeeper's officious hands, climbed into a red Celica, slammed the door and drove off in a screech of tyres.

The greenkeeper returned, shaking his head. 'Dear dear,' he said. 'I doubt they'll let Mr Sealey stay a member after this.'

David nodded. That was certainly true. By rights it should be Eddie who was barred, but Eddie was one of the club's original debenture holders and he was allowed to get away with worse behaviour than an ordinary member. Unfair, of course, but that was what money did for you.

Thank God it was all over. He dusted off his hands and clothes as if contact with Tony might have made him dirty, nodded his thanks to the greenkeeper and went back across the car park towards the bar.

Just as he reached the door he saw a silver Nissan Micra squeezing into a tiny space on the far side of the car park. He frowned. Not Elaine! The evening had gone badly enough already.

His worst fears were realised when a tall girl emerged from the Micra, dressed in leggings, Reeboks and a tight T-shirt. She still looked aggressively fit. Her breasts were big and high and muscles flowed on her long sturdy legs as she came across the car park, jamming her car keys into a little dangling purse. The clothes she wore were, as always, slightly too tight, slightly too revealing. The outline of a narrow G-string was visible underneath her leggings. Had she really meant to come into the club dressed like that? Same old Elaine, still mistaking crudeness for chic.

The girl shook back her permed mane of dark hair and combed her fingers through it nervously. Then she saw him and stopped in her tracks.

'Elaine,' he said awkwardly. He couldn't help feeling some sort of responsibility for her. He had never wanted to be her father confessor, he had always tried to get out of it, but while she had worked at Drax & Bond he hadn't been able to avoid her. The last thing he had wanted was to see her again. 'How are you?'

'I know Eddie's here,' Elaine said, ignoring his greeting. Her voice was strained and slightly adenoidal. After nine months of high living with Eddie she still looked brassy and sounded common. No wonder Eddie was bored with her.

Elaine gestured across the car park to where a shiny red Porsche 944 was parked at an angle across three slots. Its number plate read EDD1E. 'I know he's here. I'm going to talk to him,' she said defiantly. Then she sniffed, spoiling the effect.

'No, no,' David said soothingly. 'Elaine, I really don't think that would be a good idea. Not in the club.'

Elaine's face worked. Tears began to trickle down her cheeks, smudging her heavy mascara into streaks. Her lower lip quivered helplessly. 'It's not fair,' she gulped. 'It's just not fair. He just threw me out. David, it's not fair!'

David shook his head as if he sympathised, which he did, partially. Elaine had thrown herself at Eddie from the day she started work as his secretary, but Eddie had been eager. She had certainly liked the Porsche and the big house in Guildford, but who wouldn't? And that bastard Eddie had thrown her out without compunction the moment he found a woman he preferred. 'Come on,' David said gently, putting his arm around Elaine's heaving shoulders. The sight of her breasts rising and falling was vaguely disquieting. He guided her gently back towards her car, murmuring, 'Another time, eh? Go and see him at the weekend.'

Her tear-streaked face turned to his. 'That bitch Amanda will be there.'

'Actually, she won't. She's going to see her parents. He'll be on his own. Why don't you go to see him then?'

They were standing next to the Micra in the slanting evening sun. Elaine dashed her wrist across her face, smearing the snot from her nose like a grizzling child. 'I might just do that. He would deserve it. I ought to sue him.' Suddenly her face changed and she caught at his arm. 'David, why don't you talk to him? About me? I know he listens to you. You

6

and Julia, you're the only people he takes any notice of. Talk him out of this stupid Amanda woman. Please.'

Elaine had always believed he could walk on water, and he knew how untrue it was. His face contracted in a tight smile. 'I don't think he'd take any notice of me on this issue, to be honest, Elaine.'

'Please.' She was still holding his arm. It made him uncomfortable. 'David, I know I can rely on you. Please.'

He would have to refuse her. He shook his head slowly. 'I'm sorry.'

For a horrible moment he thought that Elaine was going to slap him. She was all of five foot ten and she worked out every day. But she folded over and buried her face in her hands, sobbing.

He let out a long sigh. 'I'm sorry, Elaine. Really.' Then he turned away from her and walked slowly back to the club-house.

ONE
Sunday

The lights were still burning at number 14 Devonshire Avenue when dawn came, but the house was set well away from its neighbours and nobody had been disturbed.

Similarly, nobody noticed when, as the sky lightened with dawn, the car engine which had grumbled all night finally faltered and stopped.

In the afternoon of the same day Detective Chief Inspector John Anderson tucked his big pewter-grey BMW into the side of the road and examined the house from his seat. With a flash of annoyance he registered the little white police Metro pulled up on the block paving immediately before the front door and the police surgeon's Vauxhall beside it, blocking in a bright yellow Fiat Coupé which he did not recognise. They wouldn't have called him unless they had suspected foul play, and they should have known better than to leave cars where there might be evidence.

He got out of the car and took a long breath. He relished the challenge of a crime scene, the need to notice and remember the smallest detail. He was good at it. Many DCIs spent much of the time behind a desk, but he did not.

His suit was slightly creased. He brushed at it, then walked towards the house. Several people were clustered at the bottom of the drive, drawn by morbid curiosity. He looked at them coldly and they made way for him and drew together after he had passed.

A big house, typical Guildford stockbroker belt. The upper windows were dormers, let into long sloping eaves, and the windows were glazed with rustic diamond panes. The wide front garden showed the attentions of a gardener. He ran his eyes over the rose beds at either side of the drive, looking for disturbance, but saw nothing apart from the marks of a hoe and a few excavations by the local cats.

Beside the attached garage one of the PCs from the Metro was standing with a woman dressed in expensive casual clothes. Anderson's eyes flickered over her, taking in glossy, shoulder-length hair, a full body beneath the carefully draped garments, a confident, assertive stance. The owner of the Fiat, no doubt. She saw him coming and made a move towards him, but the PC extended an arm to keep her back. Good. He wanted to examine the evidence without any preconceptions.

The front door of the house was open and another uniformed officer was waiting for him there. He was very young and although he was doing his best to appear calm Anderson noticed his dilated pupils and slightly trembling hands. The older officer would have offered to look after the woman, the witness, leaving this one to secure the scene. As Anderson approached the young policeman drew up his shoulders and swallowed, getting ready to tell this visitor to go away.

'DCI Anderson,' said Anderson briefly. He restrained a smile as the youngster's face suffused with relief. 'I see the surgeon's already here.'

'Yes, sir.' The young officer stepped back, inviting him into the house. He was eager to hand over responsibility. 'This way, sir.'

He should have asked for identification. To remind him Anderson produced his ID and flipped it open. 'And you are?'

The young man's face flamed as he made a business of inspecting the ID, trying to look as if he had intended to all along. 'PC Davies, sir.'

There was no need to rub it in. 'Which way?'

'Round to the left, sir. At the end of the hall there's the kitchen and the garage is beyond it. The door was shut, sir, but we had to open it to get to where the, the body was.'

He stammered on the word 'body'. His first death on duty, perhaps. Anderson hoped that Davies and his colleague hadn't disturbed the surroundings too much. Inexperienced officers could wreak havoc with evidence. He made his way slowly along the chequered Amtico tiles of the hallway, watching where he set his feet. The floor was pristine, as if it had been cleaned yesterday, with the exception of a couple of very faint, dark smears which came and went between the door of what looked like the living room and the kitchen. He dropped to a crouch to examine one of the smears, rubbed his finger delicately over it, nodded and got to his feet.

Beside the door to the kitchen was a big mirror with a birch frame. He stopped, turned to the mirror, and gave his own face a steady, searching glance. He made a minuscule adjustment to his tie, then drew a pair of disposable gloves from his jacket pocket and pulled them on before opening the kitchen door.

The smell of exhaust fumes was appalling. He coughed and waved his hand in front of his face. Into the smog he called, 'Any reason why I shouldn't leave this door open, Fred?'

'No,' called back another voice, followed by a cough. 'Good idea.'

Anderson went through the Smallbone kitchen to the garage door. An overhead fluorescent tube illuminated the big double garage with a cold blue light. The stink of exhaust fumes was even stronger. Fred Edwards, the police surgeon, rose from his uncomfortable crouch beside the open door of the red Porsche. 'Looks straightforward to me,' he said, pressing his hand to his back. 'Oh, God, I'm getting too old for this game. Suicide by carbon monoxide inhalation. Hose taped to the car exhaust. No signs of any force. The woman outside identified him as Eddie Drax, her business partner. This is his house and his car.'

Anderson leant forward and looked inside the Porsche. In the driver's seat sprawled a slender, wiry man in his forties, dressed in chinos and an open neck shirt. His eyes were closed and his face was flushed bright pink.

'Looks as if he's sleeping like a baby, doesn't he?' Fred said. 'Not a bad way to go, altogether. Peaceful, anyway. And quick. No more than ten minutes, at this level of concentration.'

'Any thoughts on the time of death?' asked Anderson, looking at the dead man's face. Clean shaven, but with a five o'clock shadow. Hair rather longer than was fashionable, in what would have to be described as a footballer's haircut. Anderson brushed one gloved hand half-consciously through his own hair, which he kept cropped short. What sort of a man chose to look like that?

'Time of death? I haven't taken the rectal temperature yet, I thought you'd want to see him *in situ*. More or less complete rigor and hypostasis. You know how hard this is, John. Twelve hours or so since he died, I would guess.'

Anderson took one last look at the dead man's face, then stooped further to examine his feet, thrust under the pedals of the car. 'Have you called the ambulance?'

'I was waiting for you. It looks like suicide to me, but if it isn't you'll want the works, won't you? And they must have been worried, or they wouldn't have called you.'

The soles of the dead man's shoes were made of dark rubber. In general the shoes were scuffed and dirty, but the heels and the leather above them were rubbed bright at the very back, as if they had been polished. Anderson examined them for a few moments, then stood up. 'Quite right. I want the team here straight away. Now I'd better talk to the witness.' He walked quickly towards the garage door, stripping off his gloves as he went.

'I'll get out of this poisonous atmosphere, then,' the surgeon called. He wasn't expecting a reply, and he didn't get one.

'How long do I have to stand here?' demanded Julia Bond, fixing the unfortunate policeman with a steely eye. 'Where has that Chief Inspector got to?'

'I'm sure he'll be back shortly,' the policeman replied placidly. Julia didn't feel by any means so certain. The detective had walked past her with scarcely a glance, clearly more interested in the contents of the house. She felt shaky and angry and insulted. She'd just found her business partner dead. Didn't he care?

Little knots of neighbours had begun to advance up the drive in twos and threes and the younger policeman had gone to keep them away. Julia knew that they were staring at her, and she lifted her chin arrogantly, unembarrassed. Life without Eddie – in some respects it would be so much simpler. She could start to run the company the way she had always wanted to. No half measures, no more compromise.

The front door of the house opened and the detective emerged again and came towards her. 'About time,' Julia muttered. The policeman with her nodded to his superior and went away to join his colleague on the drive.

'Ms Bond?' said the detective. 'DCI John Anderson.' He folded up his ID and badge and tucked them neatly into a pocket.

Somehow she hadn't imagined that a policeman would look quite as smart as DCI Anderson, even in plain clothes. She liked to know her enemy, and she took a few moments to compose herself and study him. He was quite tall, and his slim, well-proportioned body was dressed in an olive-green suit which draped in the casually elegant way that only good fabric and cut could achieve. The bulky ID had vanished without a trace, leaving the discreet hang of the jacket uninterrupted. How much did they pay a DCI? Is that where her taxes went? This was expensive taste. Beneath the linen jacket was a cream-coloured shirt in heavy two-fold poplin, and the tie was Liberty cotton in muted, pleasing tones of olive and green and gold, touched here and there with pink. The complete effect could have appeared foppish, but instead looked very masculine. Perhaps this was because his thick, straight dark hair was cut so short, or perhaps it was because below a pronounced widow's peak his lean face was very steady and his eyes were narrow and brighter than a cat's. She had misjudged his age. His hair was heavily streaked with silver, but he couldn't have been much more than forty. So, a good-looking ambitious bastard who dressed beautifully for effect. Well, she could relate to that.

He had been studying her, too, with just as high a level of

attention. She thought that his eyes gleamed. Mutual interest? But now he seemed to have finished his examination. 'I understand', he said, 'that you found Mr Drax's body. I'd be grateful if you could tell me about it.'

A good voice, too, a dark, well-modulated baritone, with a slightly throaty quality, as if he was restraining it. It radiated authority. This was the first time for years that she had come face to face with authority, aimed at her. She felt suddenly threatened. 'That's not exactly right. I came here to pick up Eddie, we were going to go out to lunch. All the lights were on, but he didn't answer the door. And I smelled fumes from the garage and I got suspicious, so I rang 999 on my mobile.'

'How did you get into the house?'

'Eddie was hopeless. Always locking himself out. There's a loose brick in the paving there,' she gestured at a spot on the edge of the drive, 'and he always kept a key underneath it.'

'But you called the police before you went in?'

He sounded almost disapproving. 'Yes,' she snapped, irritated. 'Of course I did. If I hadn't been worried I'd just have gone in. I told you, I could smell the fumes.'

'And what did you think when you smelt the fumes?'

Those steady dark blue eyes were fixed on her face. Her discomfort increased. 'I didn't know what to think. What would you think?' She let the hypothetical question hang in the air, but he ignored it. 'Look, Anderson.' She knew his rank, but she was damned if she was going to trot out 'Chief Inspector' every time. He raised one dark eyebrow at the bald use of his surname. 'I saw Eddie last night for a drink. I left the house about a quarter to eight and when I left him he was as happy as a sandboy and just settling down to watch the telly. What was I supposed to think? I was scared. I called the police.'

'What were you scared of?' he asked in that same quiet, implacable voice.

'For God's sake,' she exploded, 'is this what policemen do, just ask stupid questions? I was afraid that Eddie was dead. And I know Eddie. I've known him for twenty years. He'd never kill himself. Someone killed him.'

Anderson's face contracted in an infinitesimal frown. 'The police surgeon says it looks like suicide.'

'I know it looks like suicide,' she said witheringly. 'Isn't that what a murderer would try to make it look like? The point is, Chief Inspector,' she used the rank this time with heavy irony, 'that I saw Eddie last night and he was like a dog with two tails. He couldn't have killed himself.'

'So what happened?'

She bit her lip. 'After I left last night? I can guess.'

Anderson didn't speak, but his straight brows arched enquiringly. For a moment she hesitated. She didn't want to sound hysterical. But she had to say it, anyway. 'I think Eddie's old girlfriend came round, Elaine Williams. She could have let herself in, she never gave Eddie back her key after he threw her out. She was furious with Eddie. And she's a big girl, too. I don't know what she did, maybe she hit him with something and then stuffed him in the car. Or maybe she just waited until he was sleepy. He was hitting the bottle pretty hard. She could do it, I know she could.'

Still Anderson said nothing. His silence seemed to draw more words from her. 'She used to be Eddie's secretary, you know. But she was just his type, and it didn't take her too long to figure it out. She wanted his money. She probably had one eye on the divorce all the way through.'

'So why should she kill him?' Anderson asked softly.

Julia hesitated. She hadn't liked Elaine, and suddenly she felt that it showed. 'I – Well, he threw her out, and he'd just got himself another girlfriend.' Those eyes! She felt as if she was being scrutinised by some quiet dangerous carnivore, considering whether she would make an acceptable titbit. She had been in business too long to find men in general intimidating, and it was both surprising and slightly annoying to know that there were still some specimens around who could give her a run for her money. Her lips tightened angrily. Eddie was dead and the prospects for life without him looked remarkably attractive. She didn't like this smart copper's slick attempts to interfere with her future.

His mouth moved in a very slight smile. His lips were pale and well defined. 'And you,' he said. 'What happened last night, after you left this house?'

With a shock she realised that he actually suspected her.

14

That was both insulting and inconvenient. She felt her cheeks beginning to redden. It would make her look guilty, and besides, no man ought to make her blush. Anger replaced her discomfiture. How dare he? 'I drove straight home,' she said stiffly.

'And where's that?'

'Lakenford,' said Julia. 'Near Farnham. I didn't hurry. I got home about 8.15.'

'Ah,' said Anderson. 'Well, thank you, Ms Bond.' He seemed to think for a moment, then added, 'You said you had known Mr Drax a long time?'

'Twenty years,' she confirmed. 'Since art college. We studied together.'

'And you were in business together?'

'We've had a graphic design business for ten years. Drax & Bond. We couldn't resist the names. After *Moonraker*, by Ian Fleming –' Christ, why was she telling him that? His eyes were like magnets, pulling words out of her. She set her jaw in silence.

'It must be a shock to find your partner dead.'

No hasty reply this time. If he suspected her, it would make things worse to tell him that Eddie's death was actually a relief. After a moment she said, 'I was very fond of Eddie. But nobody's indispensable, even in business. And he was a – difficult man. That's why I'm sure that somebody killed him.' She let her face show her anger. 'That Elaine killed him.'

Anderson nodded, but made no comment. He glanced beyond her shoulder and she turned and saw more people arriving, police cars with their blue lights flashing, men in white coats, an ambulance. It was quite horrible. She had seen enough TV programmes to imagine them in the house, delicately and methodically taking Eddie's last resting-place to pieces. What would they find?

A thought struck her with macabre humour. She couldn't keep in a little gurgle.

'Something amusing, Ms Bond?'

How did he make that warm dark voice quite so cold? And how did he have the gall to disapprove of her? 'Yes,' she returned icily. 'I was just thinking that Eddie would be pleased that if he had to die anywhere, it was in the Porsche. He loved that car. Whoever killed him had a sense of humour.'

Why had she bothered to explain herself to him? There was no answering amusement on his face. He caught the eye of the young policeman and signalled him to join them. 'Ms Bond,' he said calmly, 'I'd like you to go to the station with PC Davies and make a formal statement. And give a set of fingerprints, too.'

Who did he think he was, assuming she would agree? 'I can't. I'm busy.'

'You were going to go out to lunch with Mr Drax,' said Anderson. 'Since that appointment has been rather conclusively broken, you presumably have the time to spend half an hour at Guildford police station.'

She stared at him, then turned without a word and walked to her car. She was furious. Nobody got away with manipulating her. He wanted to upset her plans, but she would upset his. He was ambitious, just like her. She would revenge herself on him elegantly, by making him fail both personally and professionally. The spark she saw in his eyes showed that she was in with a chance, and she relished a challenge.

A slow, elegant waltz of cars began on the block-paved drive as police personnel continued to arrive and Fred Edwards and the policemen shuffled around to let Julia Bond's Fiat out. Anderson watched until the little yellow coupé headed off down the road, escorted by PC Davies in his white Metro. Then he went back into the house to join the investigation team.

Detective Sergeant Patricia Fielding was waiting for him by the door. She was a slight, dark woman, quietly dressed in fawn trousers and a plain pale shirt, her shoulder-length hair twisted into a neat plait. He nodded to her, satisfied that she was there. They had worked together more than once and he had always found her calm and efficient. It was never easy for him to delegate, but Fielding gave him less cause for concern than many. Women were easier to work with than men.

He wasted no time on pleasantries. 'I think it's murder,' he said. 'Julia Bond insists that it is, but that's not why I think so.

16

Someone dragged Drax through the house to the car. Look.'

Fielding followed him without comment. He did not fail to notice her slightly quizzical look, but he did not need her to remind him that he had a reputation as a ladies' man, nor to point out that Julia Bond was a very handsome woman.

He showed her the faint marks of Eddie's heels on the tiles of the hall. They traced them back to the door of a large, plush living room. Fielding crouched down by the brass bar across the threshold, gazing intently at the carpet. 'Here, as well, sir. He must have been in here, and whoever it was towed him through to the garage.'

'The room has been Hoovered,' he said. 'Over the marks of his heels.'

'A tidy murderer, then,' commented Fielding, standing up. Her dark eyes were intent with concentration. Neither of them entered the living room. They both knew that everywhere the murderer had been there might be traces of his – or her – presence, and that any unnecessary movement might erase them.

DC Hart came past them, carrying the tape which would mark out a path along which visitors to the scene might walk. Fielding instructed him to fit it around the heel scuffs on the floor. Presently the tape was laid. Anderson said, 'Pat, if you would go and keep an eye on things in the garage. I want to look around the ground floor.'

Fielding said nothing, just nodded. One of the things that he valued about her was her abstention from unnecessary talk. He stood in the doorway to the living room for some time, looking in at the place where Eddie Drax spent his last evening alive. The television was still on, playing at a reasonable volume. On the table there was an empty bottle of whisky, but no glasses. The room was furnished in a violently modernist style and hung with original artwork relating to consumer products: a shampoo, a filing system, even a well known tea bag image.

'All my own work,' he muttered, turning away from the door.

He moved gingerly along the marked-out walkway, drawing his gloves from his pocket. The first door he opened was a dining room, all smoked glass and chrome. His eyes scanned it, looking for evidence of occupation on the previous night. But apart from a few free newspapers scattered over the table the room looked polished and unoccupied. Eddie Drax must have had a conscientious cleaning lady.

The next room was a study. In contrast to the rest of the ground floor it was Victorian in style, with heavily patterned dark red curtains and a desk and bookcases of polished mahogany. There was a Filofax lying open on the desk, next to a large workstation with a graphics monitor. He studied the carpet, then walked carefully over to the desk.

The Filofax was open to a page of addresses. The writing was large and flamboyant, with long risers and fluidly curling tails. A note at the bottom of the page read, *Elaine, flat,* followed by a Guildford address and telephone number.

He looked at the Filofax for some time. Then he took out his mobile phone and dialled the number. He let it ring twelve times, then broke the connection.

The books in the bookcase were an interesting collection of dated art-school reference works, more recent books on design and computers, and a number of business books from *The One Minute Manager* to *When Giants Learn To Dance*. Anderson liked books, and he was always interested in the makeup of personal libraries. He studied the spines for some time. Then a thought struck him. He turned back to the desk and with his gloved hand turned the pages of the Filofax to the little transparent ruler which marked Today.

There were no entries for Sunday. The following day, Monday, held one entry only. *Catherine Marshall, 9 a.m. & Lunch.* He lifted his eyebrows and turned slowly back to the address pages. He found Catherine Marshall listed under C, and beneath her name the address of the Guildford office of a local firm of accountants.

The same woman, then. He had met her a little more than a year ago, acting as expert witness for the defence in a fraud case. He remembered her as composed and professional in the witness box, even under considerable pressure from counsel for the prosecution. She had caught his eye, as intelligent women often did, but at the time his marriage had been in its final throes. He had been too preoccupied with his collapsing relationship with Sarah to do anything about seeing Catherine. In the small world of Guildford it was hardly surprising that their paths should cross again, but he contemplated her name and address with quiet contentment.

DS Fielding's voice came from behind him. 'Sir, can you come through to the garage? There's something I'd like to show you.'

They stood together in the glare of the police photographer's lamps, occasionally wincing involuntarily as the flashgun lit up every shadow. Fielding dropped to her haunches beside the tail of the Porsche and gestured. 'Look here, sir. This parcel tape, fastening the hose to the exhaust. I know it's a bit melted, but there are no fingerprints. None. And the car door has prints all over it.'

'Where's the reel of tape?'

'It was lying here, beside the exhaust. Gerry took it to the small prints room. Just an ordinary reel of tape, on a red dispenser.'

He nodded. 'What sort of gloves was the murderer wearing?'

'Marigolds,' replied Fielding promptly. 'A drawer in the kitchen was open, they must have come from there. The pattern on the fingers is easy to recognise.'

The body had been photographed and now Fred and DC Gerry Hart were manoeuvring it slowly out of the car, a tricky task given its rigid condition. Anderson watched them for a while, concentrating on the corpse. Presently he said, 'Pat, could you have hauled Drax around?'

'Yes, sir,' said Fielding without hesitation. 'He's not tall or heavily built. He wasn't,' she corrected herself. Anderson smiled a little. He had a towering reputation as a pedant, and gained a fair amount of private amusement from the care that his officers took to mind their syntactical Ps and Qs when in his presence. 'Mind you, I'd have got him over my shoulders – a fireman's lift, sort of. Dragging a man is hard work.'

He considered Fielding for a moment. She was about five foot four and slender, but he knew her to be both fit and strong. 'You saw Julia Bond earlier,' he said. 'Do you think she was capable of dragging him?'

Fielding shrugged equivocally. 'Maybe, sir. She was quite – well, well built, wasn't she?'

Julia Bond, five foot six of Junoesque softness. His visual recall was excellent, and he could picture her from the top of her impeccable honey blonde hair to the expensive Nubuck shoes on her small feet. 'Yes,' he said, knowing that his face did not show how attractive he found the memory. 'Yes, you could say that.'

'You think she's a suspect,' Fielding ventured. 'Didn't she have an alibi?'

'She didn't even try to have one. Just said that she went home. The last person to see Drax alive and the one who found him dead, she must be a suspect.' Plus, he thought, she went to considerable trouble to try to pin his death on someone else.

'But wasn't he her business partner? What could her motive be?'

'Well, we'll need to find out. Pat, I know I can leave you in charge here. Put a house to house in place. We need to know what the neighbours saw last night: who came, who went, the usual thing. And there's someone we want to interview. Elaine Williams, Drax's ex-girlfriend. Julia Bond told me that they had recently argued and he threw her out of the house. We need to find out where she was on Saturday. Her address is in Drax's Filofax in the study.'

Fred had finished with the corpse. It lay on a stretcher, head and hands bagged in plastic, no longer human. He called across to Anderson, 'Rectal temperature suggests a time of death before midnight last night, given that Drax was short and slight. He wouldn't have taken long to die. He could have been put in the car any time from 9 p.m. and midnight, really.'

'Any signs of violence?'

Fred shook his head. 'He could have been drugged. You'll have to wait for the PM results.'

Anderson went through into the kitchen with Fielding following him. She said, 'The dishwasher was freshly run, sir.

Still drops of water inside it, unevaporated. Whisky glasses in it, but nothing else.' Her dark eyes met his. 'A very tidy murderer, sir. Hoovered afterwards and put the glasses in the dishwasher.'

'Next thing,' he said, 'you'll be telling me that women are more houseproud than men and a woman would have been bound to clean up after her.'

Fielding opened her mouth to protest, then said nothing and looked rueful. He smiled. 'A very palpable hit. You know the way I work, Pat. Don't trust hunches. Trust facts. They speak for themselves.' He took a final look around the kitchen. 'I'm going to speak to Bond, if they've finished with her at the station. Tomorrow you can brief me on the progress of the forensics and the house to house. After I've been to see Drax's accountant. He had an appointment booked with her for tomorrow morning.'

'Her, sir?' Fielding asked, with an innocent gaze.

He met her eyes and was pleased to see that her look of amusement was swiftly quenched. 'Her,' he confirmed icily.

The little Fiat was just skidding into the drive when the mobile rang. She jammed the brakes on and answered it. 'Julia Bond.'

'Ms Bond, it's Anderson here.' He reproduced the tone of voice in which she had spoken his name as accurately as a mimic. 'Are you home yet?'

'Just. This minute.'

'Ms Bond, it seems that you may have been right in believing that Mr Drax's death was murder. I'd like to come and talk to you again, if that's possible.'

So Mr Smooth wanted to visit. This was her chance to begin her campaign. 'By all means. You've got my address, of course. Can you find your way?'

'I believe so. Will twenty minutes be convenient?'

'Only if you drive fast,' she said dryly.

'I do,' said Anderson's sombre voice. 'Goodbye.'

She switched off the phone and sat for a few moments with her hands clutching and releasing the steering wheel. He had found her attractive, his face had shown it. Why not play up to him? Use her face and her body against him?

Yes, that would work. It would be fun, too. She put her foot down and rocketed the car up the long gravel drive to the cottage.

The place was tidy, thank God. She hurled her bag and jacket on to the Edwardian chair in the hall and ran up the stairs. In her bedroom she looked at herself in the mirror, thought for a moment, then began to strip. His dark blue eyes had sparkled when he looked at her, and how would he concentrate if he found her attractive? She would tempt him. It would be a suitable revenge. And he'd find it hard to suspect a seductive woman.

Time to show him different clothes. Any man who dressed like that would admire a woman with taste. Dressed in bra and panties, she pulled open the doors to her huge wardrobe and began to flip her way through the contents, occasionally pulling something out, holding it against her, rejecting it and hanging it back up again.

After a good fifteen minutes she settled on an Escada outfit, white with brilliant appliqué work on the pockets of the trousers and at the collar and cuffs of the matching tunic. She didn't often wear white trousers, but these were so well cut that they made her hips look curvy and desirable rather than just too big for fashion. She was about to pull them on when she looked at herself in the mirror and saw the underwear. Perfectly smart and practical for summer, white flowered cotton from M&S, but not the thing to wear when she wanted to appear seductive. She unhooked the bra, pulled off the knickers, and rifled in her lingerie drawer for something more suitable.

At last she found what she wanted. A delicate body, made in peach-coloured satin, the underwired bra cups decorated with fine spider's web lace. That was more like it. It was an evocative garment. It would give her power over him, even though he wouldn't see it.

The doorbell rang. Christ, he did drive fast. 'Oh bloody hell,' she said, then ran to the stairs and yelled at the top of her voice, 'Just a minute!'

'Damn.' She wrestled with the trousers. 'Damn damn damn.' The tunic was on. She leant forward and brushed violently at her tousled hair, then slid her feet into a pair of elegant sandals. A squirt of perfume, no time for makeup. With a final heartfelt, 'Damn,' she ran for the front door.

Anderson stood in the porch, comparing Julia Bond's house to her business partner's. It could hardly have been more different. Drax's house was all glitz and polish, executive expense no object. This, on the other hand, was the ultimate chocolate box cottage, white-painted and freshly thatched, with a garden that at the height of June was a tangle of colour and scent. The path to the door was edged by tumbling pinks, smelling deliciously of cloves, and the borders were crammed with white peonies. A rose scrambled over the porch, apricot-coloured buds set off by flowers of the most delicate pink. They were beautiful. He reached up to catch one of the fully blown roses and pulled it down to his nose, inhaled its perfume and sighed with pleasure. The sweet, slightly musky scent swam in his brain.

Movement in the hall. He immediately released the rose and let his expression assume its normal impassivity.

'I'm sorry I kept you waiting,' Julia Bond said. 'I was – busy.'

She was wearing an outfit which was well coordinated and expensive, if a trifle glaring for his taste. The smell of her perfume was still sharp, as if it was freshly applied. She looked both sexy and challenging, a heady combination.

Another part of his mind regarded his attraction to her with a disinterested eye and reminded him to be careful. She was a suspect, and suspects were out of bounds. Look, but don't touch.

Looking, however, was pleasant. She led him through into the inevitable farmhouse kitchen and breathily offered him a drink. He declined and watched her pour herself a gin and tonic. She drank deeply, refilled the glass and gave him a small smile. 'Shall we sit down? We could go outside if you like. It's a beautiful evening.'

'Why not.' He wanted to see the rest of the garden.

At the back of the house there was a little flagged terrace, facing westwards and shaded from the still bright sun by a tall

23

elegant tree. Flagstones and fine gravel blended imperceptibly into patches of thyme and other fragrant herbs. Beyond the terrace an undulating lawn swept away into the distance. 'Your garden is superb,' he said, concealing his regret beneath honest admiration. Since his divorce he had had no garden, and he missed the sensual delight that it offered, there to be enjoyed whenever he had the leisure.

'Thank you,' she said. 'The designer won first prize at Chelsea five years ago. It's pretty much mature now. Mind you, it does take a lot of keeping up. My gardener has to come three times a week, this time of year.'

He nodded, concealing his disappointment. He had hoped that she had designed the garden herself, but on consideration it was just too perfect. He should have known better. He sat down on one of the white-painted wrought iron chairs and looked steadily at Julia, whose face was buried in her drink. His baser nature was still keenly interested in her sparkling eyes, the rosy flush on her cheeks, her soft lips. Her perfume had settled now, a heavy sweet scent, *Poison*. She had a slight but undeniable double chin. It reminded him of one of Charles II's mistresses. He would like to see her in fawn-coloured satin and milk-white linen, a carefully disarranged *deshabillé* suspended delicately from one white-skinned shoulder.

She swallowed another gulp of gin, then said quickly, 'So now you think that Eddie was murdered. Why is that?'

He knew better than to betray what clues they had already found to a suspect. 'Ms Bond –'

'Please,' she husked, looking at him from under her eyelashes. 'Julia.'

'Ms Bond,' he repeated steadily. She stiffened and turned her head slightly away from him. The movement showed off her round, white throat. 'Ms Bond, I would like to ask you about your partner. You said that he was a difficult man. What did you mean by that?'

'Oh,' said Julia, leaning back in her chair and gesturing expansively. 'Eddie! What do you want to know about him? I was very fond of him, of course. But he was really a – a nuisance.'

'A nuisance?'

It was always pleasant to see how simply echoing someone's

words back to them could extract just what was needed. 'To be honest, he was a pain in the arse. He was a good designer, I don't deny it. He had flair. And he could get a client really excited about our proposals. To begin with it was always him who won the work. But after a while, you see, he couldn't keep it up.'

'Keep what up?'

'The clients. In the end we got it worked out. Eddie got the work in and then he handed them over to me. I'm not the world's greatest draughtswoman, but I can manage an account, and I know how to keep a client happy. All Eddie knew was how to have rows with them. He rowed with everybody in the end.'

A man who rowed with everybody might well have been killed by anybody. 'What do you mean, rowed?'

She seemed only too happy to talk. Her eyes, which were blue and wide-set, fixed on him as she waved her drink to punctuate her sentences. 'Oh,' she said, 'it didn't matter who it was, in the end Eddie would argue with them. Except me, of course. I've known him –' She stopped speaking, apparently shaken by her own use of the inappropriate tense. She swallowed hard, then went on, 'I *had* known him for a long, long time. He couldn't do anything that would surprise me.'

'Were you lovers?' he asked softly.

He had meant to startle her, and he did. She bridled, sitting back in her chair and drawing in her chin. Her reactions were overt, not subtle. 'What?'

'Were you lovers?' he repeated. Same inflection, same pitch.

'Well,' said Julia, hesitantly now, 'once upon a time, we were. I'm –' she gestured down at her opulent body, then lifted her eyes to his with a certain coyness, 'I'm rather his type of woman. He liked them big, you see. But that was all over years ago. Years ago,' she repeated emphatically.

He regarded her with detachment. Her embarrassment was appealing, but she had a streak of vulgarity which did not please him. 'So,' he said evenly, 'if Eddie argued with everyone, who would have had a reason to kill him?'

Her face twisted into an unpleasant expression of dislike. 'I told you. Elaine Williams.'

'We'll follow that up, Ms Bond, don't worry. But suppose she has an alibi? Suppose she was in –' he considered Julia's description of Elaine before selecting a suitable destination – 'in Marbella this weekend? Who else might it have been?'

She frowned. The expression brought out lines on her forehead and on either side of her full, heavy lips, making her look her age. 'I don't know,' she said after a moment. 'I mean, with Eddie, it could be anybody. Why do people kill people?'

He remained silent. A woman as garrulous as Julia would be bound to answer her own question in the end. After a second, as he had known she would, she ran on. 'I mean, it could be for money, or it could be because he had –' She broke off and looked up at him again from under her eyelids. Her eyelashes were long and darker than her hair. 'Eddie had rather a reputation,' she said, as if it were a terrible confession. 'He – ah – put it about rather, if you know what I mean.'

'You said Elaine had been his secretary,' he commented. 'Do you mean he put it about at work?'

'Well, not exactly. No, at work he wasn't too bad. She just set out to get him, the cow. No, I mean outside work.' She glanced from side to side as if she was afraid that someone would overhear, then whispered conspiratorially, 'Friends' wives.'

'Whose wife in particular?'

'Oh, God knows,' said Julia, rather too loudly. The gin was beginning to work. 'Anyone's. He was particularly bad at the golf club. Perhaps all those bouncing balls made him randy.'

He was not amused, but he concealed his distaste. 'Which golf club?'

'Farnham Park. Eddie had quite a reputation there, let me tell you. If he hadn't been a debenture holder they would have given him the big E for sure. Even when Elaine was living with him he was – mm – active. He had a new girlfriend too, that's why he ditched Elaine. I hadn't met her yet. I got a bit bored with talking to all Eddie's women.'

It was easy to believe that Julia could quickly be bored talking to or about any woman other than herself. He said with disarming casualness, 'And what did you think of all this?'

She gave him a sharp look. The gin had not softened her entirely. 'Me? It was nothing to do with me. It only got to be a bore when it affected business. Which it did, sometimes. But I could cope. As I said, I had known him a long time.'

It was time to shake her. He sat forward in his chair and said softly, 'And as I said, Ms Bond, I am surprised that you are so unmoved by the death of a man you have known for twenty years. I would like to ask you again: where did you go after you left Eddie's house that night? Who can corroborate where you were?'

The flushed skin of her face and throat tensed and paled. 'Chief Inspector Anderson,' she replied, tossing her head, 'I told you where I went. I came straight back here. As you can see,' she gestured around the broad expanse of her garden, 'this house is isolated. Nobody sees me come and go. You have to take my word for it.'

'When did you get home?' he demanded.

'About 8.15. I told you that, too. I came in, made myself a drink, and settled down to watch opera on Channel 4. Do you care for opera, Mr Anderson?'

He couldn't restrain a slight, wry smile. 'Not particularly. I don't believe that it's compulsory.'

'Well, I love opera. It was *Tosca* on the television that night. Have you ever seen it?'

'No,' he said, with a shake of the head. He didn't care about the opera, but he thought that she was going to tell him about it.

He was right. Julia leant forward, her crossed arms pressing her full breasts more closely together. 'It's my favourite,' she offered, licking her lips. 'It's so erotic. I swear it's the sexiest opera ever written. Act 2 is marvellous. The villain, the baritone, Baron Scarpia, has Tosca's lover imprisoned in the next room, and he tortures him. Horribly. Of course, what Scarpia wants is Tosca. To sleep with her,' she added, as if he might have missed the point.

Her wet lips and lifting breasts delivered an insistent message. He preferred her when she was embarrassed. 'And when did the opera finish?'

The cold question brought her up short. She said after a

moment's thought, 'About 10.30, I suppose. It's not long.'

10.30 allowed plenty of time for her to drive back to Guildford. 'And what did you do then?'

'I had a bath and went to bed.' Julia's face contracted with sudden anger. 'Look, what are you suggesting? Are you suggesting that I killed Eddie?'

'You seem to have no confirmable alibi,' he pointed out evenly.

'Why do I need one? I'm telling you the truth.'

So they all say. He raised his brows.

'Who do you think you are?' demanded Julia, surging from her chair. 'Baron Scarpia? Well, it's not that easy, Anderson.' Now her use of his name alone was a calculated insult. 'If you want me, you'll have to do better than that.'

Was she offering herself to him? If so, he didn't like it. But she was splendid, standing over him with her hands on her hips and her eyes and red lips glittering with anger. Perhaps her indignation was real, perhaps not. If she was lying, then she was clever at it. But in either case, he had gleaned some useful information.

He also got to his feet. Standing, he was several inches taller than her. She seemed at once to diminish, to dwindle. Her blue eyes gazed up at him with a look of anxiety which rekindled his interest. 'I have plenty to be going on,' he told her. 'I take it that you told them at the station where you can be contacted over the next few days?'

'I'll be at work,' she said shortly, 'as usual.'

'In that case, I look forward to our next meeting.' He gave her a small cold smile. 'Goodbye, Ms Bond.'

She waited until he had walked to the edge of the terrace before she spoke. 'Goodbye. Baron Scarpia.'

TWO
Monday Morning

The receptionist at Chandler & Cooke, Chartered Accountants, was on the telephone when Anderson arrived. He waited by her desk, looking around the reception area. The chairs and the carpet were in toning shades of blue and grey, and the pictures looked as if they had been bought by mail order. A plastic stand in the corner was loaded with brochures earnestly advising him to consider planning now for his eventual demise, and adjuring him not to forget the appalling penalties for misreported VAT. The chartered accountant's reality was not his. In his reality people died unexpectedly in their cars and Customs & Excise pursued drugs runners, not VAT offenders.

'Can I help you?' asked the receptionist.

'Chief Inspector John Anderson, Surrey Police,' he said, 'to see Catherine Marshall.'

The receptionist's eyes opened very wide. Then she said in a small voice, 'Yes, of course,' and picked up the phone. She cupped her hand around the receiver as if to hide from anyone passing the fact that a policeman was standing at her reception desk. 'Sue, is that you? There's an Inspector Anderson in reception to see Catherine.'

Few organisations like to leave a policeman examining their premises. In a very few minutes a young woman appeared, dressed in clothes that were cheap, but smart: a straight plain skirt and a brightly coloured jacket. She said, 'Mr Anderson?'

He turned from his scrutiny of the brochures and nodded. 'Please come through,' said the secretary. 'Catherine's all ready.'

She led him through a cramped area of desks, computers and filing cabinets, where young people in dull suits tried not to look as though they were staring at him. At the end of the corridor she knocked on a plain wooden door and opened it without waiting for a reply.

Catherine Marshall emerged from behind her desk, smiling and holding out her hand. He knew her at once. He had watched her in court for two whole days on the witness stand, and he could remember every detail of her face. Now her smile was strained and there were lines under her soft hazel eyes. Her plain desk was clear except for a file with *Eddie Drax* written on the cover. It appeared that she already knew the reason for his visit.

'Chief Inspector Anderson,' she said, taking his hand. 'Good morning. It's a pleasure to see you again.'

Her handshake was firm and dry, and despite the receptionist's mistake she had remembered his rank. She sounded as if she meant what she said, too, though God knows an expert witness for the defence should hardly welcome the reappearance of one of the mainstays of the prosecution. He returned the handshake. 'I see you already know why I'm here,' he said.

She looked startled. He nodded at her desk and she glanced at it, saw the file and laughed uncomfortably. 'Oh, I see. Of course. You are a detective, after all.' She ran her hand through her hair, which was mid-brown, cut just above her shoulders, and as unruly as a spaniel's. It contrasted vividly with her clothes, which were neat and almost prim: a white blouse with a small brooch holding it shut at the collar and a restrained, tailored suit in a subdued shade of dark green. There was a taut figure beneath the dowdy clothes, but it was almost concealed. He remembered her hair from court. He had found it endearing then, and he still did.

'Would you like coffee?' she asked. 'It's real. I mean, it's not out of the machine. Sue makes it for me. We have our own little cafetière and things.'

Her volubility made him smile. 'Yes, please,' he said. 'Black.'

'And one for me, please, Sue,' said Catherine. She shut the door behind her secretary and smiled again. Her smile was very vivacious and made her look more in her twenties than her middle thirties. 'I remember you clearly,' she said. 'You wore a different suit every day. I was astonished. How many suits do you have?'

It was a rather personal question, but she hadn't meant to be improper. Glancing at his reflection in the glass of her window he saw himself vivid in teal-blue linen, a pale chambray shirt and a tie in which golds and reds predominated. 'I follow the principle of birds,' he said warmly. 'The male looks the brightest.'

He hadn't actually answered her, but either she hadn't noticed or she didn't mind. 'A peacock policeman,' she said, returning to her desk. She sat down and looked at the file and her face changed. The smile slipped from it and her brows knitted, showing her suddenly as her own age and very sad. 'I called Eddie yesterday,' she said. 'When he wasn't in I called Julia and she – told me about it.' Her eyes lifted to his. 'She told me that the police think it was murder. Is that right?'

He lowered himself into the visitor's chair opposite, watching Catherine's face. Her eyes were intelligent and starred with long lashes. She wore no makeup, and the little lines on her cheekbones proved that she smiled often. He felt sorry for her. He would have liked to have been open with her, but in the course of an investigation he had to stick to procedure. 'It looks suspicious,' he said. 'I know you'll understand that I can't say any more than that at present.'

Catherine dropped her eyes. 'I can't believe it. I can't believe it. Eddie.' Her fingers crept out towards the file and stroked it. She wore no rings at all. 'He's been my client for so long. He was the first client I took on when I joined the firm. I've been working on his account for five years.'

'That's a long time.'

His voice was even, but she looked up at him quickly. 'How much do you know about Eddie?'

He parried the question. 'In what way?'

'Oh.' Catherine swivelled away from him and pushed both

hands through her tousled curls. 'Well, you're bound to hear this from someone, so it might as well be from his professional adviser. Eddie was – given to arguing with people. I always managed to keep on the right side of him. God knows how.'

'Whom did he argue with?'

She shook her head. 'Oh, I don't know. Lawyers, one after another. That's why he came to me for a lot of personal advice, because he could never agree with a lawyer for more than a few months at a time. Friends. Not Julia. Nor David Thompson, either.'

'Who is David Thompson?'

Sue came in, carrying a small tray decorated with a painting of a cat. On it were a cafetière and two bone china cups. She put the tray down, smiled at them and slid out, closing the door behind her.

'David Thompson,' said Catherine as she poured the coffee, 'is the finance director of Drax & Bond. Appointed six years ago.' She passed a cup to him.

The coffee smelt excellent. He drew in the fragrant steam, then savoured his first sip. 'I'd like to know why Eddie was coming to see you today.'

'Yes.' She met his eyes anxiously. 'I was thinking about that myself, last night. You see, I –' Her lips pursed briefly as she wondered whether to go on speaking. 'I was thinking that perhaps, if someone killed him, perhaps it had something to do with what we were going to talk about.' She pulled a loose piece of A4 out of the file and pushed it over the desk.

He drew the paper a little towards him and read, *Agenda. (1) Consider draft will, finalise & sign. (2) Personal tax issues, Revenue investigation. (3) D&B issues, options, articles.*

He looked up at Catherine. 'Why did you think that any of these things might be related to Eddie's death?'

Catherine took a long sip of coffee and pressed her lips together, gazing down at the agenda. Then she said in tones of dull misery, 'It's the will. I can't believe that he died the day before he was due to sign the will.'

'Do you have his current will?'

'That's it,' Catherine said, with more animation. 'He doesn't have one. He's intestate. I'd been ticking him off about it for years. He kept on getting a solicitor to draft it, but then they would argue and we'd be no further forward. So I did it for him. There were some complex tax provisions, too. And he was due to sign it today!'

'Do you have the draft will, then?'

'This is the copy we were going to look at.'

She pushed a document over the desk. He raised his eyebrows. 'It's pretty thick. I've seen wills written on the back of an envelope.'

'As I said, the tax provisions are complicated.'

He picked up the will and flicked through it. The first few pages were preamble. Then came an almost incomprehensible tax planning section. Then came a heading labelled 'Bequests'. He stopped skimming and read properly.

To my mother…to my sister Meg… Large sums, thousands of pounds; but not a lot, compared to the value of that house and half of a successful company.

He read the next entry and stared. *The residue of my estate including my property, 14 Devonshire Avenue, to Amanda Sealey, with whom I have found true love at last.*

'Amanda Sealey?' he asked, looking up.

'Amanda Sealey.' For a moment Catherine buried her face in her hands as if she couldn't bear to think about it. 'I tried to put him off, but he insisted. She's his new girlfriend. He's only known her a few weeks, but he was absolutely head over heels. Eddie was very – immature in some ways, especially about women. He was determined that Amanda should have more or less everything. I told him it was crazy. She's still married. If she had inherited from him before she was divorced, her husband could have ended up with some of the money.' She sighed and made an appeasing gesture. 'Don't blame me, Chief Inspector. I did my best. It was better that he have a will, even a stupid one, than no will at all.'

He took out his notepad and wrote down Amanda Sealey's address from the will. 'Who will inherit now?'

'Eddie's mother and sister. They had no idea about all this. His mother is – well, she's not all there, he paid for her to be in a home. She's got Alzheimer's very badly, he had power of attorney for her. And his sister is in Australia. They haven't seen each other for years. She married a sheep farmer.'

He considered this information as he added the addresses of Drax's mother and sister. Then he asked, 'And what did Amanda's husband think of all this?'

Catherine rolled her eyes. 'Oh, lord. I'm sure he was furious. Eddie told me that –' She hesitated and blushed, then hid her face in her coffee.

'That what, Miss Marshall?'

Without looking at him she said, 'That Tony Sealey caught him and Amanda in bed together.' Her eyes flashed up to his, then away. 'Making love.'

The blush was quite charming. She looked like a governess to whom the master has made an indecent proposal. Her lips were parted, her eyes veiled.

This was not relevant to the investigation. He drank the rest of his coffee and set the cup down on the saucer with a louder than necessary clink to break his mood. 'Who else might have been interested in Eddie's will?'

Catherine replied at once, 'His ex girlfriend. Elaine Williams. She's not very clever, but she's very stubborn. She seems to have got it into her head that because she lived with Eddie for nine months he owes her something, as if rent-free accommodation and use of his gold card wasn't enough. She's been after him for support, the silly girl. She'll expect something from his estate, I'm sure of it.'

'Has she spoken to you?'

'She's tried. But I have to take my client's viewpoint. I couldn't see the advantage to Eddie in speaking to Elaine.' Catherine finished her coffee and poured more. 'I was thinking about this last night. I can't think of anyone else. The Sealey complication and Elaine, that's the best I could do. But I hope it's helpful.'

'It's very helpful,' he agreed. He put his finger on the second agenda item. 'Now, what about this tax business?'

'Purely to do with Eddie. Undeclared income. He was a twit,' said Catherine, with the tolerant affection of an older sister. 'I was doing my best, but the Revenue were on his tail. They'll be after £150,000 out of his estate.'

He thought this through, but could not imagine anyone

34

to whom Eddie's tax problems would be of interest. His finger moved down. 'What about these corporate issues? Can you tell me something about Drax & Bond?'

There was a little silence. Catherine had responded to his other questions promptly, and now he looked at her in slight surprise. She licked her lips thoughtfully, then said slowly, 'Chief Inspector, you must realise that I am in a difficult position. I advise the company as well as Eddie. So if you don't mind, I'd like to restrict myself to generalities. And I'd like your assurance that what I tell you is in confidence.'

'In confidence? This is an initial interview, Miss Marshall. It's not on the record. But I'm involved in an enquiry relating to a suspected homicide. I'll be asking you to make a formal statement. I can't give you any assurances at all.'

'But the information could be commercially sensitive.'

'What information?'

She opened her mouth to reply, then stopped. 'You won't catch me that way, Chief Inspector.'

Her expression was quite calm, almost stubborn. He felt growing respect for her professionalism. 'If it helps,' he said, 'I will give you my assurance that I won't use this information for personal gain, if that's what you're intimating.'

There was a pause. Catherine drank more coffee and looked at him over the top of the cup. Her soft eyes became hard and measuring. She was actually assessing his honesty. It was novel for anyone to suggest that he might be what was usually known as a bent copper. He could have felt insulted, but like him she had a job to do.

She reached a decision. 'All right. I shall have to trust you. The thing is, Chief Inspector, that a plc is considering making an offer for Drax & Bond at the moment. There's nothing on the table yet, but it's in the air. If there was speculation in that company's shares as a result – well, the whole thing might be off.'

'A takeover?' He was surprised. He had gained an impression of Eddie Drax as an entrepreneur, not a plc executive.

'Yes. One hundred per cent. The purchase price would be adjusted for results in the next few years, but it would be bound to make Eddie and Julia very rich.'

Her face was a professional mask. He probed gently, 'What do you think of it?'

The mask slipped, she was personally engaged. 'Me? I think it's the right thing for the company at this point. They're overtrading and the profits haven't been as good as they should be for the last couple of years. A takeover would give them access to new funds and new resources. A real lease of life.'

'Why have the profits been depressed?' he asked, remembering the fraud case in the course of which he had met Catherine.

She clearly remembered, too. 'I don't think it's anything to do with fraud,' she said hastily. 'Their audit reports have been clear.'

He lifted a sardonic eyebrow. All auditors were of limited value, and no doubt the auditor of Drax & Bond was one of Catherine's partners.

'Anyway, you should ask David Thompson about it, the FD. He's very good, he'll know what's going on. I'm just the tax advisor.'

He sat back a little in his chair and laid one hand on the agenda, looking at item 1. *Consider draft will, finalise & sign.* Another suspect to add to Elaine and Julia – the offended husband, Tony Sealey. He said almost absent-mindedly, 'What difference will Eddie's death make to the deal?'

Another long silence. When he looked up Catherine seemed torn, as if she wanted to say something but was too loyal. At last it came out. 'Look, if I'm – if I'm really honest, the fact is that it won't make any difference. In fact it might even make the purchaser more likely to go ahead.'

He frowned. 'Why is that?'

This was painful for Catherine. She refilled her coffee cup for the third time and stared out of the window. 'You know that Eddie was, ah, volatile. Well, he'd already almost put the purchaser off once. Another row and they might have pulled out altogether. The thing is –' Suddenly she seemed ready to confide in him. She put down her coffee and leant forward eagerly. 'The thing is, Chief Inspector, Eddie was the founder. He had half the shares. But what he was good at was getting things going. He had lots of energy, enthusiasm. But no stamina, and such a temper! It had got to the stage where you could say that the company was better off without him altogether.'

'And by the company you mean?'

She hesitated. 'Well, Julia Bond owns the rest of the shares. But,' she went on quickly, 'Julia had known Eddie for years. I mean, I don't believe –' She broke off, embarrassed.

So Catherine didn't want to accuse Julia of Eddie's murder. She might be right. It looked as if a dispute over Eddie's money or his love life had caused his death. There were more questions to ask, but Catherine saw things, quite properly, from her client's viewpoint. He would spread the net more widely if he talked to the finance director, David Thompson.

He put his notepad away. 'Thank you, Miss Marshall. You've been extremely helpful.' He met her eyes. 'One last question. If I might confirm your whereabouts on Saturday night?'

For a moment she stared at him, quite astonished. Then she laughed. 'Good God! You don't think I killed Eddie?'

'Just a routine enquiry, I assure you,' he said, smiling as he spoke, because he had been watching her carefully throughout the interview and he was as sure as he could be that she had not wanted Eddie Drax to die.

She seemed to take comfort from his expression. 'I was at a dinner party,' she said. 'Deathly dull. Business related. It broke up about 1.30 and then I went home. Is that enough for you?'

'Thank you,' he said. 'It would be helpful if you could make a formal statement of what we have discussed, but there's no urgency. I know you understand the procedure.'

'I certainly do,' she laughed. 'I got sick of the sight of Guildford police station last time.'

Her laugh changed the atmosphere in the room. She looked relaxed, approachable. He enjoyed the last of his coffee, then asked with genuine curiosity, 'Tell me, how was it that you were the only advisor who never argued with Eddie?' Although he would refer to the dead man in writing as Drax, it seemed natural to call him Eddie in conversation.

'No idea,' said Catherine, though she seemed flattered to be reminded of it. 'We just got on, I suppose. And most of his other advisors were men. Perhaps he felt that I had a lighter touch.'

'I've often thought that about women,' he commented, quite honestly. He considered Catherine's open, pleasant face beneath her mop of unruly hair and felt a surge of affection for her, not out of place now that the interview was complete. His fingers itched to stroke those shining, dishevelled curls. He replaced his cup on the table and as he did so said, 'I was impressed by you during that trial. I would have liked to have had you on my side.'

She looked embarrassed now. 'Well, thank you. I was glad we won.'

He waited until she looked up, then met her eyes. Quite simply he said, 'I would very much like to meet you outside work, Catherine.'

For a moment she was silent. A blush started on her throat, under the brooch that held her blouse closed, and crept up to her cheeks. Her professional veneer was shattered. 'Really?' she whispered, as if she couldn't believe that any man would want to ask her out.

He could have eaten her. 'Really.'

She hesitated, then licked her lips and said, 'Well, as it happens, I, ah, I have concert tickets for tomorrow. Nothing special, Corelli and Vivaldi. The friend I was going with has let me down. I know it's terribly short notice, I don't suppose you'd be interested –'

Her diffidence was irresistible. He said with a smile, 'I'd love to. Baroque music is my favourite. But I can work very long hours in the early stages of an investigation. I might let you down.'

'That would be a shame,' she said. 'But I would understand. Let me give you my home number. If you'd like to come, I could meet you at the concert hall at 7.30.'

'I'll do my best to make it. And if I fail, I'd like to call you anyway.'

Her hazel eyes were very bright. 'I'd like that.'

David looked out of his office door and saw that his secretary, Lisa Cresswell, was reading a book. This didn't surprise him, since the whole place was in a state of paralysis following Eddie's death and he knew that she wasn't busy, but it didn't look professional. He walked very softly across the carpet between them, intending to surprise her.

Then he looked over her shoulder at what she was reading. His throat tightened and his heart thudded as he read, *She hung above him, gasping with suspense, and suddenly he seized her hips and pulled her down and she cried out as the great smooth shaft slid up inside her, filling her so magnificently that she screamed.*

'Christ,' he hissed, his eyes skidding down the page, 'what on earth is this?'

Lisa jumped and turned her elfin face to grin over her shoulder at him. 'Just a book,' she said, showing him the cover.

He glanced up at the door to the outer office. It was shut. Excitement reared up in him. 'Go on reading,' he said.

Lisa lowered her long eyelashes and opened the book again. David swallowed convulsively. He leant over her and put one hand on her shoulder as he gaped at the page. She was wearing the clothes he liked, a tight ribbed top and a wraparound skirt, showing off her little high breasts and offering tantalising flashes of her long, slender legs. Her nipples were visible through the top, small, tender buds of flesh. He licked his lips and hitched at his trousers, making room for his engorging cock. His left hand slid down Lisa's body, found her breast and cupped it.

'Mmm,' Lisa whispered, though she never took her eyes from the book.

The heroine was being conclusively shafted, front, back and sideways. He was astonished. He had no idea that women enjoyed reading such explicit material. His cock was hot and aching and trying to find its way out of his boxers. He took hold of Lisa's spare hand and guided it back to rest on his fly.

'Mmm,' she said again as her fingers began to explore the stiff length of his penis. He glanced again at the door, feeling a rush of excitement at the danger. Then he put his hand back on her breast and began to tease her nipple. It stiffened beneath his fingers. He leant further forward, swept her long fair hair from her neck and brushed his lips against her nape. With his right hand he tugged gently at her skirt until the wrap fell open, revealing her bare legs. His fingers rested on her thigh, then crept upwards.

Lisa sighed and shifted slightly in her seat. Her smooth tanned thighs fell a little open. Her panties were white and lacy. He swallowed hard, then stroked his fingers against the crotch of the panties, feeling the soft resilience of her sex beneath them. She was warm, like a sun-kissed peach. His left hand clutched more tightly at her breast as he gently eased back the panties and slipped his finger inside them.

She was already very wet. Reading that dirty book was really turning her on. He squeezed her nipple, then slid his exploring finger up to the front of her slit. Her clitoris was engorged and protruding, easy to find. He flicked his fingertip against it and Lisa moaned aloud and spread her legs wider apart.

'Hush,' he hissed throatily. He could hardly speak. 'Someone will hear you.'

Lisa folded her lips tightly together. Her right hand clutched the book, her left was stroking steadily up and down the imprisoned length of his cock. She lifted her hips a little off the chair, thrusting herself towards him. He teased her clitoris a little more, then slowly, juicily slid one finger into her moist, tight vagina.

'Oh.' Lisa couldn't keep in a little smothered cry of pleasure. She began to hump herself against his hand, urging him to finger her harder. He had never seen her so excited. Her body was quivering, her nipple was like a pebble, the velvety rings of her sex opened and closed on his penetrating finger. He pushed another finger into her and slid both fingers in and out, quick and hard, as his thumb stimulated her trembling clitoris. Her loins jerked spasmodically and suddenly she was coming, eyes closed, lips parted, belly and thighs quaking.

He drew his hand away. 'Into my office. Come on.'

Lisa gasped, slid the book into her drawer and got unsteadily to her feet. She followed him into his office without a word. He closed the door and locked it, then altered the angle of the Venetian blinds so that nobody could see in from the outside.

What now? He would have liked her to suck his cock,

down on her knees in front of him, but he knew that if she did he would come in her mouth and then he wouldn't be able to fuck her. He wanted to fuck her. She was so deliciously young, slender and petite, and he wanted to put his cock inside her. She was watching him with soft heavy eyes, licking her lips. She looked like Lolita. 'Bend over the desk,' he said hoarsely. 'Take your skirt off.'

Lisa smiled at him. 'Whatever you say.' She unfastened the skirt and drew it off. The white knickers were almost transparent, wet with her juices. A few strands of pale wispy pubic hair escaped from them. She turned her back, looking archly at him over her shoulder, and then bent forward over the desk.

Her long legs curved beautifully into the round moons of her small high buttocks. Between them the white line of her knickers drew his eyes. He came up behind her and pulled the knickers down to cling around her slender thighs, then stepped back. The tender downy mound of her sex gleamed with her juices. He ran one hand appreciatively over the curve of her arse, then reached for his fly.

The telephone rang. He said quickly, 'Don't answer it,' but Lisa shook her head and reached out to lift the receiver. 'David Thompson's office,' she said calmly.

He shuddered with tension as she dealt with the call. 'Eleven thirty? Yes, that will be fine. I'll make sure he knows. Thank you.' She put the phone down.

'Why did you answer it?' he demanded.

'You don't want it ringing through to the main office and someone wondering what we're up to,' Lisa said, reasonably enough. She arched her back, thrusting those wonderful pert buttocks up towards him. The tightly-clasped lips of her sex shifted like the petals of a flower. 'Come on, David. Fuck me.'

He growled with lust and flung open his desk drawer. At the bottom of it was a packet of Durex. He wrestled one out of its wrappings, tore open his fly and pulled the condom on. Then, with a snarl of satisfaction, he drove his erect cock deeply into Lisa's warm wetness.

She gasped as he penetrated her, then clutched at the desk to hold herself steady as he withdrew and plunged into her

41

again. He held tightly to her flanks and slammed his body against hers, relishing the feel of her round arse fitting perfectly into his loins. She had had her fun, he'd made her come with his finger, and now he didn't care whether she came again or not. He was focused purely on his own pleasure. He thrust his cock in and out with delirious energy, shafting her as hard as he could, and when he felt the surge of hot seed brimming up and bursting it was all he could do not to bellow like a bull.

After only a few moments he pulled out of her. There was a packet of tissues on the side table and he extracted a couple so that he would not have to touch the condom. As Lisa straightened and reached for her skirt he wrapped the condom up and put it in his confidential wastebasket, then wiped his hands on another tissue.

'All right?' he asked Lisa perfunctorily.

She tidied the skirt and her hair. 'Mmm,' she replied, smiling. 'I thought you'd like that book.'

'You're a temptress. What shall I bring you for a present?'

Her eyes widened. 'Ooh. It's my mum's birthday tomorrow and she loves Elizabeth Arden's *Beautiful*. Will you buy me a big bottle?'

'I'm sure I could manage that.' What was a bottle of scent compared to what Penny and the kids cost him? He deserved some relaxation, and it was cheap at the price. He checked that his clothes were all in order, sniffed cautiously at his fingers, then sat down at the desk and straightened the papers which Lisa's dangling breasts had disarranged. 'Oh, who was on the 'phone?'

'A policeman,' said Lisa, with a mischievous grin. 'Detective Chief Inspector Anderson. He wants to come and see you before lunch. I thought it must be about Eddie, and everyone's supposed to help the police with their enquiries, aren't they? So I said all right.'

'Fine,' he said evenly. Something else was required, and as Lisa turned to leave the room he called after her, 'That book. Which bit do you like the best?'

Lisa looked over her shoulder. 'The bit where you put your fingers up my cunt.'

She closed the door and he stretched his legs out under the desk. His eyes fell on the picture next to his computer, Penny and Thomas and Louise all smiling on last year's holiday in Provence. For a moment he felt guilty. Then he shook his head. He needed the release. And Penny didn't have to know.

The telephone rang and he lifted the receiver wearily. Lisa's bright voice said, 'David, it's Mr Marchant from Dacre & Co.'

'Put him through,' David said.

The policeman appeared promptly at half past eleven. David inspected him warily as they shook hands. They were both a fraction under six feet tall, but Chief Inspector Anderson seemed smaller, perhaps because he was slim and his movements were economical and as precise as a dancer's. David felt clumsy and unwieldy in comparison. And why was a policeman wearing a petrol-blue linen suit? David examined Anderson's cropped hair with dislike and decided with satisfaction that the Chief Inspector was probably gay.

'I hope this won't take long,' he launched in at once. 'I'm sure you can imagine that I'm very busy.'

'Has Mr Drax's death caused a great deal of difficulty?' asked Anderson.

David made a face. 'Paralysis, more like. The staff are all shocked, they can't get anything done. Julia's not come in today, either. I have to compensate for it. Especially as, well, there are things in the air at the moment.'

'Things?'

Was it safe to tell a policeman about Dacre & Co.? Well, most public servants were wholly ignorant of the business world. He said, 'It's possible that a plc may be about to make an offer for Drax & Bond. Obviously that means a lot of work.'

'Obviously. And will Mr Drax's death affect that offer?'

'Not at all. In fact, it will make it easier. He was a key man, you see.'

Anderson frowned slightly. 'A key man?'

The way Anderson echoed his words was almost comic. David leant back in his chair, feeling more comfortable. He was always pleased when other people did not share his knowledge of the arcana of the business world. 'A couple of weeks ago we took out key man insurance on the lives of the directors. That's Eddie, creative director, and Julia, marketing director, and me, the finance director. The insurance pays directly to the company in the event of the director's death, to cover loss of profits and recruiting a replacement and so on. Not in the event of suicide, mind you. I hope this is a murder investigation.'

'How much is the insurance worth?' asked Anderson.

'Five million. Cash, straight into the bank account. It's just what we need at present. With that injection, Dacre & Co. won't be able to resist us.' He hadn't meant to let the name of the potential purchaser slip, and he made a little moue of annoyance, then straightened his face. To conceal his mistake he asked again, 'And do you suspect murder? Julia said you did?'

Anderson didn't seem to have caught his discomfort. 'All I can say at present is that the circumstances surrounding Mr Drax's death were suspicious.' David made a face at the official language, but Anderson went straight on, 'That's a lot of money. I thought Drax & Bond was a successful company. Why should you need that cash?'

'Any company can make good use of cash. And our funds flows haven't been everything they could be recently. We're bumping against our overdraft limit.'

'Any chance of fraud?' asked the policeman, with an innocent look.

David laughed aloud. 'What do you think I am? I'm the bloody finance director, for God's sake! If I thought there was a fraud going on, I'd call the auditors straight away for spot checks, and then I'd be on the 'phone to you boys in blue.' He gestured with one hand at Anderson's vivid suit and laughed. 'Of course I don't suspect fraud. We've just been overtrading slightly.'

'So,' said Anderson, ignoring the joke, 'who would you say most directly benefits from Mr Drax's death?'

'The shareholders,' said David, after a moment's pause.

'Not the directors?'

'No, the shareholders. I'm a director, but I can't get my

hands on that five million. It belongs to the company, not to me. Dacre & Co will up their offer to take it into account, and the shareholders will benefit.'

'Who are the shareholders?'

'Julia Bond and whoever inherits from Eddie.'

The policeman nodded slowly. Then he said, 'Do you know who will inherit Eddie's shares?'

David pursed his lips, then shook his head. 'I imagine it will all be set out in his will.'

Anderson said in his cool measured voice, 'I spoke to your tax advisor this morning, Catherine Marshall. Apparently Mr Drax was intestate.'

This was a surprise. David lifted his brows and whistled. 'Phew! That's bad news for somebody. Good news for his family, I suppose.'

'Did Miss Marshall know about the key man insurance?'

'Catherine?' The question was puzzling. 'No, probably not. As I said, we only took it out a couple of weeks ago. I think there are some tax complexities when we get around to the corporate return, but there wasn't any reason why she should have known. Unless Eddie told her.'

Anderson regarded him for a few moments in silence. David looked back at him, stiff with dislike. Would women find this slender, dapper man attractive? Or would they also think him effeminate? He hoped so. He reflected with satisfaction on his recent encounter with Lisa. Anderson probably didn't get the chance to screw anybody over a desk, let alone a luscious, eighteen-year-old secretary.

'Just for completeness,' said Anderson, 'I'd like to know where you were on Saturday night, Mr Thompson.'

David gaped, then scowled. 'I hope you're not suggesting that you think I have any involvement with Eddie's death.'

'It's routine,' said the policeman, his voice quite expressionless.

'I don't have what I suppose you would call an alibi.' He didn't bother to hide his hostility. 'I met an acquaintance on business at the golf club until about eight that night. Then on the way home I stopped by Beacon Hill. It was a lovely night, a beautiful twilight, and later there was a full moon. I wanted to take a little air and think. I suppose I got home about eleven.'

'And you were at Beacon Hill all that time?'

'That's right. Walking.'

'You drove there?'

'How else would I get there? There is a car park.'

Anderson appeared to be absorbing this. After a moment he said, 'Who do you think killed Eddie Drax, Mr Thompson?'

'Good God, I don't know. That's your job.'

Anderson stared at him for some time, then got up from his chair. 'Thank you, Mr Thompson. I trust I can come back to you if we have any further questions.'

'I suppose so,' said David. Anderson's coolness was infuriating. 'I just want this cleared up soon. I spoke to the insurers today and they won't pay out until after the coroner has delivered his verdict. Until then what can I say to Dacre & Co.? When will the verdict be?'

'There has to be a post mortem,' said Anderson unsympathetically. 'And there are a number of forensic tests to complete. They can take a week or more.'

'A week! What am I supposed to do?'

'Excuse me,' said Anderson, apparently unmoved. 'I'd like to talk to a few more of your staff, if you don't mind.'

'Must you?' David asked sharply. 'They're finding it hard enough to work as it is.'

'If the company needs a verdict of murder, Mr Thompson, I'm sure you won't want to obstruct the police in the course of their enquiries,' said Anderson.

Bloody smart Alec policeman! David folded his lips angrily. 'Oh, I suppose not. But just don't take up too much time, all right?'

Anderson left David Thompson's office stone-faced. He had taken a thorough dislike to the finance director. Snide remarks and dismissive comments would always lift his hackles, and Thompson made it quite clear that he considered any mere policeman to be his inferior.

However, this was not germane to the enquiry. He could see no reason for Thompson to have killed Eddie Drax, but he still had reservations about the company. There had been an element of bluster in David's dismissal of his suggestions of fraud.

To David's secretary he said, 'I'd like to talk to Mr Drax's secretary, if that's possible.'

The pretty girl, who looked hardly old enough to be out of school, shook her head. 'I'm sorry, she's not in today. She was so upset to hear about Eddie.'

He nodded. 'In that case, perhaps I could speak to Mr Thompson's number two, whoever that is.'

'You want Sam,' said the girl, gesturing through the door. 'Samantha Smith. She's the girl with dark hair, at the desk over there. Sam!'

The girl with dark hair lifted her head, revealing a pale face set with eyes as vivid and cold as jade. He walked over to stand by her desk. She looked up at him with a hostile, defensive expression which could not conceal the fact that she was stunning. Did beautiful women congregate in graphic design businesses? Samantha appeared to be in her mid-twenties, and the half of her body that showed above her desk was shapely, with rounded arms, big breasts and a narrow waist. Her eyes were phenomenal, pale clear green without a ring around the iris, as transparent as glass.

'Good morning,' he said, reaching for his ID. 'I'm DCI John Anderson. I'm investigating the death of Eddie Drax. I'd like to talk to you for a few minutes.'

Her face stiffened and became even paler. 'I can't,' she said, turning her head away so that he could see only her hair, a dark shoulder-length tumble of curls that clustered around her head like a halo. 'I'm much too busy.'

'Another time, then.' She was nervous, and that was almost certainly important. 'Whenever suits you.'

'I'm always busy,' said Samantha, suddenly turning back to stare at him as if the ferociousness of her glare might scare him away.

'I'll come to your house, if it's easier. When will you be home from work?'

Her lips parted. For a moment she didn't seem able to speak. Then she said in an odd clotted voice, 'I'm busy tonight.'

47

'Tomorrow then,' he insisted. The more excuses she made, the more important she seemed.

Samantha closed her lips suddenly and scowled. 'Oh, if you must,' she snapped, with a fierce dismissive gesture. 'All right. Tomorrow evening. Six o'clock.'

'Thank you. What is your address?'

She looked as if she was going to curse him, but instead wrote a few words on a scrap of analysis paper and thrust it towards him. 'Don't be late. I'm going out.'

'I'll be there,' he said.

Anderson felt satisfied. He had discovered that Julia Bond might have had a strong motive to rid herself of a business partner who had become an encumbrance, and unearthed an accounts assistant who was distinctly unwelcoming. Her reluctance to speak to him might well suggest guilt over something. That seemed sufficient for the day. Other officers from the investigation team could continue the interviews at Drax & Bond.

'Are you finished?' asked David Thompson's lithe young secretary. 'Let me show you out.'

As they walked towards the door he asked casually, 'Did Samantha know Eddie well?'

'Sam?' The secretary looked amazed. 'No, not at all. Why?'

'I just wondered.'

'No, Eddie was going out with his old secretary, Elaine. Until a few days ago, anyway. And Sam's got a rich boyfriend.'

He noticed the sly implication. 'Has she?'

'Ask her, if you're going round to her flat. Everyone knows about him and nobody sees him. He keeps her in Versace T-shirts and cars, though.' The girl's face was a picture of jealousy. 'She got a new sports car last year. It's gorgeous.'

'Thank you.' He opened the door of the offices and walked across towards the BMW, wondering about Samantha Smith. She appeared to be living above her income.

He did not gain a hopeful picture of Drax & Bond. Had he been given to imagining possibilities, he might have linked Eddie and Samantha in a web of fraud and deception that would lead inevitably to Eddie's death. But he prided himself on being grounded in fact, and he thought that the explanations were probably simpler in themselves and separate. If Sam were committing fraud to support her lifestyle, there was no reason at present to suppose that it had anything to do with Eddie.

The complexities of the case pleased him. He had no interest in simple crimes, where the outcome was obvious from the start. It was the challenge that entertained him, the chance to solve a tough intellectual puzzle, followed by a pursuit that was as exciting as any blood sport. Like a hunter, he enjoyed the chase, and he hoped that his quarry would be fit enough to offer him a good long run. But his object was always the same. Pursuit, while thrilling, was not enough. He loved to be in at the kill.

THREE
Monday Afternoon

Detective Sergeant Fielding was waiting outside the station when Anderson's grey BMW appeared. Anyone who had worked for Anderson, even once, knew better than to keep him waiting. His punctuality was legendary. As the big car pulled to a halt she was already almost at the door, ready to climb in.

As she fastened her seat belt he nodded to her, then gunned the engine. She relaxed back into the BMW's plush upholstery, ready to enjoy the ride. DCI Anderson drove himself whenever possible, and she could understand why. He did it so much better than most people. In some respects his driving was very like his whole character. Controlled, adept, precise, and frighteningly quick.

'Know where we're going?' he asked her as they shot past a line of stationary Guildford traffic on the inside lane.

'Yes, sir.' This was as close as he ever got to coaching her – firing direct questions and expecting direct answers. There were other chiefs who were easier to like. In fact several of her colleagues hated Anderson cordially. But all of them had made mistakes and received a bollocking as a result, and nobody ever forgot an Anderson bollocking.

She took a deep breath and glanced at the sharp profile beside her. Her stomach was antsy with apprehension, but she was excited too. She didn't exactly like Anderson, but she did respect him. She had already learnt a lot from him, about observation, about detail, about reserving judgement until she had the all the facts. And he got good cases, high-profile cases. Case experience wasn't supposed to make any difference to promotion prospects, but it couldn't hurt, could it?

'I doubt that Amanda Sealey knows about Drax's death,' Anderson said. 'None of the people I've met would have bothered to tell her.'

'OK, sir.' At least with Anderson she wouldn't just be there to break the bad news and provide tea and sympathy. He'd always been scrupulously fair to her, treating her just as he would have treated a man, and that meant letting her get her hands dirty as well as giving her the opportunities she sought.

An unusual chief altogether. Other women at the office were almost indecently curious about him. Only this morning she had been standing by the coffee machine with Carrie, one of the few other women in CID, and Jan, their secretary, and Carrie had said with a broad grin, 'You ought at least to get him in to bed this time, Pat.'

'I'd give him one,' was Jan's comment. 'Tomorrow, given half a chance.'

'He's not my cup of tea,' Pat replied. 'Too thin. And what would Charlie say?'

'Too thin? What about those eyes?' demanded Jan. 'He came second in the Copper Most Fancied, after Gerry Hart.'

'I wonder what he's like in bed?' Carrie said. 'He's such a control freak. Do you think he ever shouts and yells? or does he just nod and say "Good"?'

The idea had sent them all into fits of giggles. Her lips twitched as she remembered. Anderson glanced at her and she looked quickly away from him. She didn't blush easily, but she knew he would notice. He always noticed everything. She thought that he would ask her what she was thinking about, but he just smiled as if he already knew and returned his attention to the road.

They left the centre of town and headed out towards one of the small executive developments about twenty minutes' drive away. As they entered the estate Anderson slowed down and she realised that he wanted her to tell him where to find the road on which Amanda Sealey lived. Fortunately she had checked the map before leaving the station, and she gave him the crisp instructions he expected.

The house was a smallish detached homette, depressingly like all the others. There was a blue Golf in front of the garage. Anderson parked on the road and they got out of the car.

As they approached the house a couple of small children raced along the pavement towards them, carrying ice creams and shrieking. They were just boisterous and excited, and Pat stood still and lifted her arms with a smile as they dashed past her. Anderson stepped back off the pavement to get out of their way. He would probably cope better with the threat of violent physical assault than with the prospect of a stain on one of his beautiful suits.

He caught her eye as he rang the bell. 'Look around as much as you can.'

She nodded, but didn't speak. Someone was coming to the door. It opened, revealing a tall, opulent woman with ash-blonde hair in a blow-dried bob. She was holding a long-stemmed lily in one hand in a gesture that looked more than a little artificial. Her eyes jumped from Anderson to Pat and back to Anderson. 'Yes?'

'Mrs Amanda Sealey?'

'Yes.' Now she was worried. The flower drooped in her hand. Pat watched the woman's pretty face with the utmost concentration, looking for signs that their news was unexpected.

'Chief Inspector John Anderson, Surrey Police.' Anderson held up his ID. 'And Detective Sergeant Fielding. May we come in?'

'Oh, God.' Amanda opened the door for them and stepped back, clutching the flower to her large, shapely bosom. 'What's happened? Is it Tony? What's happened?'

'We are investigating the death of Eddie Drax,' Anderson said gently.

For a moment Amanda stood in frozen silence. Then she dropped the lily and folded forward with a disbelieving cry. Either she was a formidable actress, or she hadn't known.

Anderson put one hand on Amanda's shoulder and steered her into the lounge. Pat followed him, looking carefully around. A man's coat was hanging on the stand in the hall, and a washing basket full of dirty cricket whites protruded from the recess under the stairs. If Amanda's husband had left home, he hadn't come back for his things yet.

The lounge was painted white with a hint of pink and furnished with a suite in rose-coloured Dralon. Anderson sat on the sofa beside Amanda, his hand resting on her shoulder as she sobbed. Pat regarded him sardonically. He did it very well, but then he always handled women well, as if he was really concerned. It took another police officer to know how manipulative he could be.

'I thought he would call me today,' Amanda wailed, lifting her tear-stained face to Anderson's. He nodded, his expression full of sympathy. 'I've been away for the weekend, I went to see my parents to – to tell them about us!' She buried her face in her hands as if overwhelmed. Distress, or deceit?

'I can see you're very upset,' Anderson said easily. He looked up, bright-eyed. 'Sergeant Fielding, perhaps you would be kind enough to make Mrs Sealey some tea. For the shock.'

Pat nodded and left the lounge, still looking around. She heard Amanda Sealey wail, 'What happened? Tell me what happened!'

She found her way to the kitchen, restraining a smile. Anderson wanted to stay with the woman and watch her reactions. Fair enough. There would be information in the kitchen, too.

The kitchen was as characterless as the rest of the house. There were no pictures. The sink was full of flowers, and on a pinboard by the back door was a programme for the Surrey County Show flower arranging competition.

She set the kettle going and examined the pinboard. A note read, 'Tony's new work number.' Yes! She pulled out her notebook and wrote it down, then looked on.

The Sealeys' Barclaycard bill was enormous, with a big balance carried forward and a hefty interest charge. Very bad money management; much better to pay it off every month. They must be pushed for cash. No wonder Amanda was upset to hear of Eddie's death. If her idea of fun was staying at home and arranging flowers she would have been a damn sight better off with Eddie than her husband.

The kettle boiled. Pat found a teapot and tea bags. There was no sugar anywhere, so presumably the Sealeys didn't take it. She looked for cups, which Anderson preferred, but there were only mugs. Making a wry face, she arranged mugs, tea and milk on a tray, then carried it deftly through to the lounge.

Amanda was sitting with her head buried in her hands, weeping. 'What am I going to do?' she wailed. Pat reflected sourly that she seemed a good deal more concerned about herself than the dead Eddie Drax.

'Where is your husband?' Anderson asked softly.

'Tony?' Amanda lifted her face, red and puffed with crying. 'He's – not here. He's left.'

'Have some tea,' said Pat, offering Amanda a mug. Anderson's eyes flickered up again to hers. She caught a look in them that she had seen before, an eager look. It meant they might be on to something. Well, they were. Sealey had one hell of a motive.

Amanda took the mug, gasped, and drew in a long gulp of tea. Pat offered the tray to Anderson, who looked at the mugs and shook his head. She didn't insist.

'I understand', Anderson said, 'that Tony and Eddie had a disagreement over you.'

Amanda lifted her eyes, swimming with tears. 'Oh, it was awful,' she gulped.

'What was awful?'

Pat watched Amanda swallow hard and dash her hand over her face as she tried to bring herself under control. She was actually making an effort to respond to Anderson. How did he do it? What was it about his gentle, probing questions that made people want to answer them? All he did was repeat people's words back to them, like an echo. He was a living example of Investigative Interviewing techniques.

'It was at the golf club,' Amanda managed to say. 'I went there with Eddie to meet some friends of his, David and Penny Thompson, do you know them?'

She sounded as if she expected some social connection. It

was absurd, but Anderson smiled and nodded, encouraging her to go on. Amanda sniffed hard. 'We were just having a drink, you know? And Tony came in, straight from work, and he called Eddie such foul names, and Eddie – hit him –'

She was sobbing again. Pat felt a surge of scorn. This big, strong woman, crumpled and crying and leaning against Anderson's supporting hand as if she would collapse without it. It was pathetic.

'He hit him?' Anderson repeated.

'He hit him. He knocked him over and then he laughed at him. And Tony was so angry, I've never seen him so angry.'

There was a pause. Then Anderson said, 'Where is Tony now?'

'Tony?'

'Tony. Where is he?'

Her wet eyes were wide. 'I – don't know. He hasn't been home for a week.'

Anderson glanced over towards Pat. She frowned, uncertain of what he wanted. His eyes narrowed slightly. Then he took hold of Amanda's shoulder, quite gently, and said, 'Mrs Sealey, I'm sorry to ask you this under these distressing circumstances. But I'm sure you understand that we need to ask your husband about Eddie's death. No doubt he can give us a perfectly good explanation of where he was. It would be much easier if you told us where we could find him.'

'He couldn't have hurt Eddie,' Amanda gasped, staring into Anderson's face. 'How could he? You said Eddie was at home. Why should he have let Tony in?'

'If you tell us where Tony is,' said Anderson reasonably, 'we can ask him.'

There was a long silence. Amanda gulped hard and wiped her face again. 'He,' she said hesitantly at last, 'he's staying with some friends of his. Bob and Diana Toomey. In Burpham. I'm sorry, I can't remember their telephone number.'

Anderson smiled at her. Again Pat wondered how much of his warmth was real and how much was calculated. 'Don't worry,' he said. 'We can find it.' He had what he wanted, but he seemed unhurried. And besides, there was one question left to ask.

This time, when he glanced at her, Pat knew her cue. 'Mrs Sealey.'

Amanda looked up as if startled to hear her speak. It was bloody irritating that even a woman assumed that a female detective was just there to listen and make the tea. 'Mrs Sealey, Chief Inspector Anderson will have told you that we believe that Eddie Drax was murdered.'

'Yes,' wailed Amanda, in fresh floods of tears. 'It's so horrible –'

'If you have any thoughts about who might have killed him,' Pat ploughed on, 'please tell us.'

Amanda fell silent and stared first at her, then at Anderson. Her face was a blank apart from the blotchy tear stains.

'Was there anyone with a grudge against him?' Pat prompted her. 'Anyone who might have benefited from his death?'

'No,' moaned Amanda, hiding her face again. 'I don't think so. No.'

Well, she would say that, wouldn't she? Her husband was the prime suspect. Pat caught Anderson's eye and shook her head. He stepped smoothly in. 'Now, Mrs Sealey, I'm worried about leaving you. Is there someone we can call to come and look after you? Will you be all right?'

She didn't lift her head. 'It's all right. I'll call a friend.'

Anderson nodded to Pat and they made ready to leave. Amanda Sealey followed them through to the hall, picking up the corpse of the lily *en route*. She held it between both hands, turning it round and round. She was in shock. Pat was glad when Anderson touched Amanda's arm and said gently, 'Let me call someone. You don't look well.'

Amanda shook her head, staring at the carpet. 'No. No. Please.'

Anderson's mouth twitched. He met Pat's eyes and she gave an infinitesimal shrug. What more could they do?

On the way down the drive Anderson said, 'See if one of the neighbours is in, Pat. You know the drill. Then back to the car.'

When she climbed back into the BMW he handed her a

piece of paper from his notepad. 'Here's her parents' address. Up in Yorkshire. Check that she was there this weekend.'

'Yes, sir.' Ask a neighbour to look after someone and then go straight back to the station and check out her alibi. A funny business, policing. Pat fastened her seat belt and leant back, thinking about her own notepad. I know something you don't know, she thought with quiet satisfaction.

Anderson glanced at her face and smiled slightly. 'Well, Pat,' he said, 'what did you find?'

He could read her like a book. She laughed, half ruefully, and confessed. 'Sealey's work telephone number, sir. Pinned to the noticeboard in the kitchen.'

'Good,' Anderson said shortly. Pat felt a hot glow of satisfaction. A simple *good* was Anderson's highest form of praise. 'I'll take you back to the station, you can try to get hold of him. Get the computer going, too, see if he's got any sort of a record. I'm going to go back to Devonshire Avenue and have a look at the forensics.'

The case against Sealey was just what she wanted. A quick arrest would look brilliant on her record. But Anderson was wasting his time by going back to the scene. 'There was nothing much there this morning, sir,' she reminded him.

'So you said. But I want to have a look for myself.'

Damn him! He trusted her to look for a suspect, but not to check a crime scene. He might as well not have praised her at all.

She relapsed into a gloomy silence, which she maintained until Anderson let her out at the police station twenty minutes later. If he noticed that she was sulking, he didn't show it. He drove off at speed as soon as she closed the door.

'Bastard,' she said to the retreating boot of his car.

Devonshire Avenue was about two miles from the police station, but the traffic appeared to be suffering from an early afternoon rush hour and it took Anderson fifteen minutes to get there. Just as he arrived Fielding called him in the car. 'I've tried to get Sealey, sir, but no luck.' She sounded as if she had overcome the discontent which had been visible in her face and body for the whole of the journey back to the police station. 'He's a salesman for a drugs company and he's on the road at the moment and his mobile's switched off. His patch includes Hampshire and Dorset. His firm are expecting him back in the office tomorrow. Can it wait, sir, or should we get the other forces on to it for us?'

'No, not yet. If he doesn't turn up at the office when expected it will look suspicious and we can launch a manhunt. Until then it would be premature. Anything from the computer?'

'Not yet, sir. I'll keep you posted.'

'Good.'

He pulled the car on to the block paving and looked at the house for a moment. The diamond-paned windows glittered in the bright sunshine. Many people would find it highly desirable – a big, ostentatious property in a smart road. Sarah would have found it desirable. He did not.

There was blue and white Police tape tied between the oak pillars of the porch. He ducked carefully underneath it. The door was stained white here and there with aluminium fingerprinting powder.

Within the house the scene of crime officers were beginning to clear up. The photographs had been taken, the prints had been lifted, and soon the house would be left to its ghosts. He walked through to the kitchen, where a row of small objects, bagged in polythene, was neatly laid out on the tiled work surface.

Berriman, the scene-of-crime specialist, was also in the kitchen, tidying his equipment. He glanced up as Anderson entered and acknowledged him with a nod. 'Afternoon, John. Not much to see here.'

'Disappointing.'

Berriman made a face. 'Less than we normally expect, to be honest. A good palm print off the door and loads of prints, but they're mostly the householder's. Some belong to his cleaning lady, and a couple to that woman, Bond. One print doesn't match any of those, but it's smudged. Whoever made it went to wipe it out and just missed a bit.'

'Where was that?' Fielding had told him all this, but she might have missed something. She was reliable and she had flair, but he liked to see things for himself.

'Here, on the kitchen drawer.' Berriman pointed it out. 'The killer took a pair of rubber gloves out of this drawer and wore them when he put Drax in the car and then cleared up afterwards. It's a bugger, to be honest, John. He Hoovered the whole bloody ground floor wearing those gloves and then put the glasses in the dishwasher. No fibres or hairs anywhere, and no prints on the glasses. These dishwashers are far too effective.'

'And the print doesn't match any of the others? Not even the palm print?'

'The palm print doesn't have fingers attached. It looks as though someone was banging on the door with the heel of his hand.' Berriman demonstrated on a kitchen cupboard.

Julia's fingerprints were everywhere: but then she had never denied that she had been at the house. The unidentified print could be good news for her, if it belonged to the murderer. Or not. One print, and a smudged one at that, was thin evidence to secure even a prosecution, never mind a conviction. 'Could that single print have been left some time ago?' he asked.

'I suppose so,' said Berriman equivocally. 'Unlikely, given that the drawer front was wiped clean, but possible.'

Hardly any forensic evidence. This was not good. These days juries assumed that there would always be forensic proof, and sometimes without it they were unwilling to convict. It would be even more important to get sound evidence from reliable witnesses to prove who was with Eddie Drax the night he was killed. He would need to check the house to house enquiries.

He went over to the kitchen counter and considered the objects in their transparent resealable plastic bags. The keys to the Porsche, parcel tape from the car's exhaust, the tape dispenser. 'Are these going back to the lab?'

'That's right. The tape needs to be treated with gentian violet, and you need a fume cupboard for that.'

He frowned at the tape dispenser. The parcel tape was not lying smoothly around the roll. Its end was wrinkled. The asymmetry irritated him. He wanted to lift the end and replace it smoothly.

And how had it become disarranged in the first place? To Berriman he said, 'This parcel tape has been lifted and replaced. Have you looked under the end?'

Berriman came over and scowled down at the tape in its bag. He gave Anderson an aggrieved look, then extracted a fresh pair of disposable plastic gloves from his pocket and pulled the bag open. Gently he took hold of a corner of the tape and peeled it back to show Anderson the upper and lower surfaces. 'Nothing,' he said, in tones of accusation and offence. 'I did look, you know. I have done this before.'

'I'm sure you did. But the tape was pulled back further than that. There's a mark there, Stuart, I'm sure.'

Slowly Berriman peeled the tape away from the roll. After another couple of inches he stopped and drew in a breath.

Stuck to the upper surface of the tape were two or three long, brightly coloured fibres. 'Cotton,' Berriman said, leaning closer. 'Blue cotton. From a sweater, maybe.'

Drax had been wearing a mulberry-red polo shirt. Anderson couldn't restrain a smile. They would have found the fibres at the lab in any case, but it was always pleasant to beat the experts at their own game. 'Well,' he said, 'thanks, Stuart. I'll see you again when the tests are completed.'

He let himself out of the house and called Fielding from the BMW. 'Any news on the house to house, Pat?'

'Afraid not, sir,' Fielding responded. 'Gerry and Rick and Bill have been to pretty well every house on the street, but no luck at all. The neighbours at number 16 were having a barbecue and the people from most of the other houses were invited.'

'And not Drax?'

'He'd argued with his neighbours not long ago, sir,' said Fielding, with a certain ironic satisfaction. 'Some people saw the yellow Fiat arriving, Julia Bond's car. She turned up about 6 p.m., apparently. But by 6.30 the barbecue was in full swing. The road was full of cars coming and going. Nobody noticed the Fiat leaving, or anybody else arriving. They would have assumed that cars were going to number 16.'

'Nobody?' Experience told him that the average person was slack and hopeless about observing details, but it never failed to disappoint him.

'Nobody, sir.'

There was a pause. He frowned into nothingness. The case was becoming distinctly unsatisfactory. If it was a burglary or an assault he would crash it now, without hesitation: give up, file it, stop wasting time and resources. But he couldn't crash a murder, no matter how barren it looked. So with no witnesses and insufficient evidence for an arrest, what could he do? Could he provoke a confession somehow? Julia Bond at least looked determined to maintain her innocence. She looked determined altogether. She had challenged him, and then stared him out with her wide blue eyes. She would be hard work, though working on her might prove enjoyable.

'One piece of good news, sir,' said Fielding's voice. 'We've made contact with Elaine Williams. She's at her flat now, if you want to go around and talk to her.'

He glanced at the dashboard clock. Five thirty. 'Give me the address.'

It was a long, irritating drive through rush-hour traffic to Elaine Williams's flat, on the other side of town and in an unfashionable area. He searched for a parking space in the crowded streets for some time and finally slid the BMW into a space only just big enough for it under the nose of another driver, who mouthed obscenities at him over the steering wheel.

Not a flat, but a maisonette. The upper floor of a 1930s house. The front garden was dry and dishevelled. As he walked up the cracked concrete path a dead narcissus grazed against his trousers. He stooped down and carefully swept away the traces of yellow pollen.

The paint on the front door was peeling. He brushed again at his jacket and then rang the upper doorbell.

There was no entryphone. After a few moments he heard quick footsteps on the stairs, then the door opened a crack. 'Who is it?'

His ID was ready. 'DCI Anderson, Surrey Police,' he announced, holding the badge to the crack. 'Investigating the death of Eddie Drax. I'd like to speak to Elaine Williams.'

The door opened fully. The girl who opened it seemed

several inches taller than him. He concealed the fact that he was taken aback by her sheer size. 'I'm Elaine,' she said. She pushed back a mass of dark curling hair from a face that was pale and slightly strained. Her eyes looked pink. Had she been crying?

When he stepped up into the gloomy hall he realised that in fact Elaine was an inch or so shorter than he was, five feet ten perhaps. She was a strapping girl, broad-shouldered and muscular, a real Amazon. The singlet and Lycra shorts which she wore revealed every part of her splendid body. Eddie Drax had liked big women. No wonder he had not been able to resist this one.

'Upstairs,' she said, and turned to lead the way. Her round, high buttocks undulated as she climbed, and the muscles moved smoothly on her tanned calves. She was big all over, and all of it was fit. There was no doubt in his mind that she could easily have dragged Eddie from the drawing room to the car. She could probably have carried him with one hand.

At the top of the stairs was a plain white fire door with a Yale lock. The lock was on the snib and Elaine pushed it open and went through. He followed her, his eyes scanning from side to side. There was a dark patch on the ceiling above the door, as if the roof was leaking, and the flat smelled of air freshener. Elaine must be trying to conceal the smell of the damp. What a comedown from the executive comforts of 14 Devonshire Avenue. No wonder she looked miserable.

Was she miserable enough to have killed a man?

'Please sit down,' said Elaine, leading him into the lounge and gesturing at the faded tapestry covered sofa with one hand.

He considered the sofa. Elaine appeared to have a cat; the tapestry cushions were thickly sprinkled with pale shiny fur. 'I'm fine,' he said.

'Would you like some tea?' Elaine asked.

Her hands were moving nervously and she was shifting from foot to foot. He would have expected a more grounded stance from someone with an exercise bike and a rowing machine crowding out the space in her small lounge. The place was tidy, but soulless, as if she was camping in it, not living in it. Perhaps she had been hoping that Eddie would ask her to come back to him.

He didn't admit to many superstitions, but one of them was a dislike of accepting hospitality from suspects. 'No, thank you.'

'Do you mind if I have one?'

She was watching him with apprehension. He thought that she wanted to have something to do. 'Please, go ahead,' he said, and moved smoothly over to the door to the kitchen so that he could talk to her while she prepared the tea.

The kitchen was small and tatty. Washing up was arrayed neatly on the draining board and Elaine had rigged up a little washing line from the hot water heater to the window. Tea towels were hung on it, and a pile of underwear was soaking in suds in the sink. Was that a pair of men's briefs among the Marks & Spencers knickers?

'I understand,' he said as Elaine wriggled the kettle between the washing and the tap, 'that you used to live with Eddie Drax.'

'That's right,' she said, switching on the kettle. 'Until not long ago, actually. He was so unfair. He said he wanted to marry me, and then that Sealey woman turned up and he just – dumped me.' She sounded utterly defeated, not vindictive.

'How did that make you feel?'

'Livid,' she responded instinctively. Then she glanced over her shoulder at him, her face stiff with anxiety. 'Well,' she said, 'well, no, not angry. I was fond of him. I mean, I loved him.' Her voice carried no conviction. 'I was upset, like I said. Really upset. He had promised me so much, you see. He promised to marry me.'

'Were you engaged?'

Her lips twisted. 'No. I mean, he hadn't bought me a ring. But he was going to. Everybody knew about it.' She sniffed wretchedly. 'And now he's dead, and look at me, stuck in this dump! I gave up my job for him, you know. I haven't worked for nine months. It's not so easy to find something else after that long. There's always temping, but I hate it.' She set her jaw and met his eyes. 'I deserve something, you know. He

63

made me promises. I'm going to ask his accountant what's in his will.'

Julia Bond had called Elaine a shameless gold-digger. He wasn't convinced. She had been lying when she said that she loved Eddie, he was sure of that, but that didn't mean that she had been manipulating him all along. That would have taken brain, and Catherine had been spot on when she described Elaine quite simply as not very clever. She didn't stand a chance of getting any of Eddie's money, and her hopefulness was really rather pathetic.

But she didn't strike him as a suitable candidate for a murderer, either. She was too simple and not good enough at lying. Whoever killed Eddie Drax had kept a very cool head, and had covered his or her tracks most thoroughly.

None the less, he needed to establish where she had been when Eddie died. 'I'd like to check,' he said as she stuck a tea bag into a mug, 'what you were doing on Saturday night.'

Her body gave a slight jolt, as if something had shaken her. Why the shock? He internally revised his previous opinion of her innocence. She made a business of dunking the tea bag in the hot water, and without looking at him she said, 'I went to the cinema.'

'Whom did you go with?'

She gave him a scared look and hesitated. Then outside the window a cat mewed and Elaine's face suffused with relief. She leant over the sink and called, 'Frosty!'

Frosty. Good God, what an imaginative name for a cat. The animal appeared, a big white cat with one black ear, prowling towards its mistress with its back arched and its tail stiff with welcome. It must have some feline route up to the first-floor window.

Elaine scooped the cat up and held it clutched to her chest. Its squeaky purr sounded like a creaking door. For a moment she buried her face in the thick fur. 'I rescued him,' she volunteered. 'From the cats' home. He was thrown out too.'

He did feel sorry for her, but there was no doubt that she was trying to avoid the question. 'With whom did you go to the cinema?' he asked again.

His voice was gentle, but she flinched. 'On my own,' she said, still not looking at him. The cat began to wriggle and she set it gently on the ground, then extracted the tea bag from her cup and balanced it on the teaspoon to put it in the bin. The spoon exaggerated the shake of her hand.

'Which cinema?'

'The new multiplex.'

'What did you see?'

Her eyes lifted to his, then quickly moved away. She licked her lips. '*Sirius Rising*. With Alec Baldwin.'

'What time did you get there?'

'About –' She waved one hand uncertainly. 'I don't remember. Early. About half past seven, I suppose. I wanted to get some popcorn and the queues are often bad.'

'When did the film start?'

Again that uncertain wave. 'I'm not sure. About half past eight?'

He didn't believe that she'd been to the cinema at all. 'What did you think of the film?'

Her lips parted and she stared at him like a rabbit in the headlights. After a few false starts she managed to say, 'I, I, didn't like it much. But I do like Alec Baldwin. That's why I went. He's so cute. I go to see all his films.'

This wasn't the way he would have chosen a film. His own preferences leaned towards Peter Greenaway and Jean-Paul Renoir. He raised his eyebrows and said nothing.

Elaine turned to face him, holding her cup of tea. She managed a nervous smile. 'You, you look a bit like Alec Baldwin yourself, actually. You know, with the dark hair, and the blue eyes, and everything.'

He could almost have laughed aloud. Was she trying to be seductive? Perhaps not, her face looked quite innocent. But at the least she was trying to flatter him, and her attempts at flattery were almost as clumsy as her attempts at lying.

She looked hopefully at him for a moment, then sighed. The cat wreathed around her legs, then darted into the lounge in a flash of white. She followed it and he moved away from the door to let her through.

'So,' he summarised, 'you went to the cinema on Saturday

night to see a film that started at about 8.30. And when did you get home?'

The cat jumped on to the sofa and circled round several times, then settled on one of the cushions and began to wash. Elaine leant against the exercise bike, then glanced at it. A sweatshirt was hung over its handlebars. She flushed, then tried awkwardly to push the sweatshirt out of sight. He barely restrained a rueful shake of the head. She was a tall enough, big enough woman for the sweatshirt to be hers. Why prove that it was a man's by blushing and trying to hide it?

In her confusion she had not answered his question. He repeated, 'When did you get home, Miss Williams?'

'Oh,' she stuttered. 'About − about − I don't know, about eleven, I suppose.'

'Still alone.'

'Yes. Oh, I remember now. I needed to go to the bank machine and the first one I went to wasn't working, so I had to find another one. It took ages. But I didn't have any money left.'

'So you found a machine to make a withdrawal.'

'Yes. Barclays. I had to drive right into the middle of town. So I was later home than I should have been, you see. I can't have got back until midnight.'

A collection of such ill-assorted lies would be easy to dis-assemble, so easy that he felt no inclination to do it. Another time would suffice. He looked at Elaine as she leant against the exercise bike. She was a magnificent specimen, but he didn't find her attractive. She couldn't compare to Julia Bond, whose blue eyes and swift acid challenge had set his teeth on edge.

He said, 'I understand that you have a key to Devonshire Avenue.'

Elaine jumped and spilled her tea. 'Damn! Who told you that?'

'I can't tell you.'

'I bet it was Julia. Oh God, she's such a bitch!' For a moment he thought Elaine was going to burst into tears. 'She's always hated me. What else did she tell you?'

'I would like to know if you still have the key,' he insisted.

'No,' said Elaine, jutting out her strong golden jaw. 'I gave it back to Eddie.'

'Are you sure?'

'Yes, of course. Why should I want it? He threw me out.'

Her eyes avoided his and she looked as if she wanted to cry. He said in his coldest and most official voice, 'Miss Williams, this could be extremely important. Do you know where that key is now?'

'How should I know what Eddie did with it? He probably gave it to Amanda Sealey.' But she still didn't look at him.

'You're sure you have no idea? Could the key have been taken from you? If someone else had got hold of it, they could have used it to get into Devonshire Avenue.'

'I don't know where it is,' Elaine insisted. At last she glanced up at him, and there were tears on her cheeks. 'Why are you being so horrible to me? I don't know, I don't know!'

People often became distressed when they were lying and he put them under pressure. But there was no need to push her now. In any case, if he was going to break her story it would be better to have another officer with him as a witness, Fielding, perhaps. 'All right,' he said. 'I don't need to ask you anything more at this stage. But I'd like you to come down to the police station when it's convenient for you and make a statement and let us take your fingerprints.'

She brightened up at once, which was puzzling. 'Fingerprints? Do you have the fingerprints of the person who killed him, then?'

It was almost as if she thought that the prints would prove her innocence. He said evenly, as he always did, 'It's just a necessary procedure.'

'I'll come down tomorrow,' said Elaine. She wiped away a tear and leant back on her hands. Her big breasts thrust aggressively out in front of her. He wasn't sure whether the movement was conscious or not. 'Will that be all right?'

'Yes,' he said without a smile. 'I suggest you ask for Detective Sergeant Fielding. In the mean time, Miss Williams, if you think of anything else, or if you realise that anything you have told me wasn't quite right, call me.' He took a card from his wallet and handed it to her.

She took the card from him, looking down at it so that she did not have to meet his eyes. She seemed terrified. What was she hiding?

'Thank you for your time,' he said. She made no move to show him out.

By the time he eased the BMW out of its tight parking space it was nearly seven o'clock. He thought about returning to the station, but decided in the end to go home.

As always in the early stages of a case, his mind was filled with his impressions of the victim. He was certain that if he had met Eddie Drax alive he would have disliked him very much indeed – despised him, even, as the immature, temperamental self-made man he seemed to have been. Nothing about Drax's taste or behaviour appealed to him.

However, that did not give anyone the right to murder him. And it was slightly chilling to review the interviews of the last two days and realise that nobody seemed to be grieving for the loss of Eddie Drax. Julia was apparently somewhat relieved, Elaine was hiding something, and even Amanda seemed much more concerned about herself than about her dead lover. The possible exception was Catherine Marshall. He would have liked to give Catherine the benefit of the altruistic doubt, but deeply ingrained cynicism, born of experience, reminded him that Catherine had just been deprived of a valuable source of recurring fees.

Of all of them, Julia's reaction surprised him the most. She had known Drax for twenty years. However infuriating he was, was twenty years' acquaintance not worth a little grief?

He tried to keep his mind on Catherine and their forthcoming meeting. He liked Catherine and thought her very attractive, but he couldn't concentrate on her. His thoughts kept sliding back to Julia Bond. He hadn't exactly liked her, in fact he hadn't liked her at all, but he had found her fascinating. Their conversation had been barbed, spiced with danger.

He decided to call in at the squash club on his way home to see if anybody was there who could give him a really challenging game. He wouldn't normally go to the club on the off chance, but he needed something to take his mind from the case.

To take his mind from Julia.

FOUR
Tuesday Morning

A bright low sun hovered beneath a veil of cloud. Anderson's shadow stretched out in front of him, lying along the towpath like the outline of a corpse, and his regularly falling feet pounded it into the ground.

He ran like a machine, his usual four miles, two miles up the towpath to the bridge and back. The fresh air should have cleared his brain, but the morning was close and heavy. There was no wind, and once the sun lifted behind the clouds it would become intensely humid. He tried to concentrate on his breathing, but within half a mile of home he lost it. There was Julia Bond, licking her lips. Damn! He put on a burst of speed, dashing for home in a sprint that made his heart hammer.

Every time he saw the Mill he thought himself lucky. It was an old warehouse, converted recently into apartments, and at the very time when he and Sarah split up the penthouse had been on the market. It was exactly right for him. The location was excellent, the riverside site provided some compensation for the garden which he no longer had, and the whole building exuded a pleasant faded look from its mellow bricks and the white wood of the windows and doors. He liked natural materials.

Running up the stairs was part of the morning routine. The sprint had upset his usual easy bound, but he refused to give in and walk, or worse, take the lift. Four floors up he stopped on the landing in front of his apartment and tilted back his head, gasping. That unplanned sprint had revealed his limitations. He would have to run an extra mile the next day. Then he let himself in and headed straight for the shower, slotting a CD into the player as he passed it. Monteverdi's *Vespers* filled the air with joy and glory.

After the shower he ran a comb carefully through his hair and shaved. There was positive pleasure in the neat, predetermined movements of shaving, peeling away the stubble and watching his own dexterity in the bathroom mirror. He never cut himself. His moisturiser stung slightly, a refreshing sensation.

Then he padded barefoot through the apartment to the kitchen. He did not take his surroundings for granted. The space and light of the apartment continually pleased him. It was the entire upper floor of the old building, a wide living area floored with polished birch and with large windows looking out over the river. Beyond the windows was a balcony, running the whole length of the building and facing south and west into the evening sun. The kitchen at one end was also made of birch, with work surfaces of polished dark grey granite. At the other end of the flat was the bathroom and the bedroom. The whole place was uncluttered and spacious and contained several very beautiful objects, and he was entirely satisfied with it.

He had primed the espresso machine and put the croissants on to warm before he set out, and now he poured a double espresso into a white cup with a gold rim, arranged two croissants on a matching plate with mathematical exactitude, and carried his breakfast out on to the balcony.

There was a small teak table and matching chair at the left-hand end of the balcony, set so that he could watch the sun rising while he ate his croissants. This morning, unfortunately, the sun was already half obscured by the veil of thin cloud, and as he sat down it vanished completely. The light became diffuse, threatening. He loosened his thick dressing gown to let what breeze there was caress his naked skin.

He lifted the coffee to his lips and let his eyes focus on the trees on the far side of the river. They were willows, and their dense narrow silvery leaves formed a pleasing shape, restful to the mind. Some people would find all sorts of pictures and imaginative patterns in the abstract complexities of the trees. But why? They were natural things. When he looked at them he saw the strong bare skeleton of trunk and branch and twig. The leaves concealed it, but not from him. It was revealed by the apparent chaos of the leaves. What existed and could be seen betrayed what was hidden.

The coffee was excellent. He held the cup between both hands and closed his eyes for a moment, luxuriating in the taste and smell of the coffee and the hot smoothness of the porcelain cup beneath his fingers. Then he sat up and began to disassemble one of the croissants preparatory to eating it.

This was a good time to think. Now he focused on the suspects in the Drax case. Tony Sealey was the obvious choice, a man with a well developed grudge against Eddie Drax. But suppose Sealey had an alibi? Then came Elaine. But despite Elaine's lies he couldn't really believe in her as a murderer, at least not a murderer as neat and organised as this one seemed to have been. Julia, on the other hand, was £2.5 million better off since Eddie's death, and had he lived he might have obstructed a transaction which would make her even richer. Julia was small for a Drax woman, only about five feet six, but she struck him as exceptionally determined. And Eddie had been dragged.

Then there was Samantha Smith. She too had something to hide. What if Eddie had discovered that she was defrauding his company? That could be reason enough to kill him. Her eyes had been pale and cold and green. She had looked both angry and afraid.

He was sitting at his desk considering the post-mortem report on Eddie Drax when the phone rang. He lifted it and tucked it between his shoulder and his ear so that he could go on comparing parts of the report. 'Anderson.'

'John, it's Graham.'

Detective Superintendent Parrish. He put down the report and sat up. 'Yes, sir.' His voice didn't show his annoyance, but he was annoyed. Parrish should know better than to chase him up at such an early stage of the case.

'John, I've just had the local press on the telephone about this Drax case. They wanted to talk to you.'

'There's nothing to tell. I'll talk them through the post-mortem results if they want to be ghoulish. Drax was very drunk, and he was killed by carbon monoxide inhalation. There are no signs of any violence. It won't make much of a story.'

'But you're sure he was murdered.'

'Yes, sir. He didn't walk to his car, he was dragged. And if you read between the lines of the post-mortem, Drax really was very drunk indeed. Almost certainly too drunk to walk, never mind to tape a hose to the car exhaust so neatly that he left no fingerprints.'

'Who's your prime suspect?'

Parrish had had an inital report already and he should have known who the suspects were. Anderson said patiently, 'Sealey, sir, in that he has the most immediately apparent motive. However, there are others. In particular, we can't discount Bond. By her own admission she was at Drax's house on Saturday evening, and she reported his death.'

'Have you spoken to Sealey?'

'Not yet, sir. DS Fielding is tracking him down.'

'As soon as possible, then, John. I'd like to have a result before the coroner's court sits. It would look good.'

Parrish was always concerned about looking good. He talked about clear-up rates to outsiders and 'getting a result' to his officers. Anderson found himself believing, not for the first time, that Parrish would rather have a quick conviction than a just one.

'If that's all, sir,' he said evenly, 'I'd like to get back to it.'

There was a silence. Then Parrish said, 'You've got Pat on this one, then.'

What now? 'Yes, sir.'

'How is she getting on?'

'As usual, sir. She's doing fine. I asked for her.'

'She's applied for DI again,' Parrish said. 'I'd like her to make it this time. What do you think we can do for her?'

There wasn't any helpful comment to be made. Promotion to Inspector was always a thorny issue, with many more candidates than opportunities. He had managed it himself entirely without patronage, and it was typically old-fashioned of Parrish to believe that patronage could help. Or did Parrish think it would reflect well on his political correctness if Fielding made DI? It made no difference. Pat had to fight her own battles, and the truth of it was that despite all the recent changes women still didn't get promoted easily.

'Look, John,' said Parrish after a little silence, 'don't be dense.' Dense! How dare Parrish accuse him of being dense! He still said nothing, and Parrish went on, 'Let Pat take a lead role. When the breaks happen, pass them her way, hmm?'

Her role in the investigation would make no bloody difference. Parrish was living in the past. Anderson controlled his still simmering anger and spoke quite calmly. 'I've got her on Sealey's track, sir. She couldn't do much better than that.'

'John, if you were more of a team player I would congratulate you on your sensitivity. But you're not, are you? A DCI ought to be in the office managing his team, not out getting his hands dirty. But you can't leave it alone. I only put up with it because you catch the villains. So if you've got Pat running after Sealey, it's because it suits you. The other suspects aren't women, by any chance, are they?'

He knew perfectly well that the other suspects were women. What was he getting at? Did he think this was a joke? 'Sir, all I want to do is secure a conviction. I know Pat feels the same.'

'Absolutely,' Parrish said smoothly. 'Getting a result, that's what it's about. Good luck with the rest of it, then, John.'

Anderson set down the phone with exaggerated softness. Criticism from Parrish was almost too much. Oh, the old fool was sometimes acute, but the accusation of being dense – *dense!* – was utterly unfounded. It was maddening. He got up from his desk and went over to the window. He pressed his palms against the cool glass and rested his forehead on it for a second, allowing his anger to seep away.

Then he called DS Fielding and offered to show her the PM report. What would she think if she knew that Parrish was trying to push her through to Inspector? She would probably despise the idea of assistance. She was a very determined woman, and she treated anything smacking of paternalism with scorn.

But then again, she did want promotion. When there was more time, perhaps he would talk to her about it and find out how she felt.

'Sealey's employers have heard from him, sir,' Fielding offered as soon as she entered the room. 'He called in first thing. He's expected back in the office just after lunch, about 2 p.m., they think.' She slid into the chair opposite him and grinned. She was wearing her usual quiet clothes, pale tailored trousers and a white top that skimmed her body, but she was much more animated than usual. 'I think we may have put him in an awkward position. No employer likes to have the police sniffing around one of their people. And Sealey has a bit of a past to live up to.' She was holding a computer printout, carefully placed against her abdomen so that he couldn't see what was on it.

'He's got a record?'

Fielding nodded. 'Oh, yes, sir.' Her dark eyes were sparkling. She seemed excited by the prospect of a villain to chase. And so was he; but she showed it and he kept it to himself.

He approved of her enthusiasm. It made her look very attractive. He hadn't always appreciated how pretty she was. They looked at each other in silence and there was a second of stillness, of spark. Then Fielding dashed her hand across her smooth dark hair and looked away, saying officiously, 'He's behaved himself for a few years, sir, but he was a bad boy when he was younger. Started off with glue sniffing, then vandalism, then assault. He did six months in a short-sharp-shock when he was twenty. Seems to have kept to the rails after that, apart from the usual traffic convictions: speeding, parking, that sort of thing. He is a salesman, after all.'

Business as usual, then. He held out his hand for the report and passed her the post-mortem in exchange. 'That's more interesting than the PM. Nothing more in there.'

'And still nothing from the house to house,' Fielding

volunteered. She kept her eyes firmly on the PM report. Was she trying to deny that moment of electricity? 'We've tried even the street behind, though the gardens are so long there's really no chance of anything from there. People are so unhelpful.'

She was right to concentrate on work. There was always a tension between male and female officers, but it wasn't professional to acknowledge it, never mind act on it. 'And all the neighbours were so interested once they knew that Drax was dead,' he remarked sourly, skimming his way through Sealey's record. Tony was not a local boy. He was from Essex originally. Perhaps after he came out of prison he had decided to try for a fresh start somewhere else.

Fielding put the PM report down on Anderson's desk. She had pulled herself together. 'Gerry went through Drax's clothes,' she said. 'To look for threads that might match those ones you found on the parcel tape.' Her voice was cool, but there was admiration below the surface, and perhaps a little irritation too. After all, he had spotted something she had missed. 'There's nothing, sir. Drax didn't seem to like blue, apart from denim, and those fibres aren't denim. So it looks as if they might be from the killer's clothes.'

'Have the lab finished the analysis?'

'No, sir, not yet. But I went and had a look and I reckon I know what they are.'

'Without analysis?' She had a streak of rashness that led her to make these snap judgements. He'd warned her about them before, but she would do it.

'It's just the colour, sir. They look like a sweater my boyfriend has, from one of those American catalogues. I haven't ever seen many things that colour, sort of lapis blue.' He said nothing, and she seemed emboldened to continue. 'The catalogues are very widely distributed, sir, but they're not cheap. Definitely ABC1 sort of clothing.'

He didn't want to quench her enthusiasm, but she had to be realistic. 'That's interesting, Pat. But we have to wait for the lab results. If you go around looking only for a man with a sweater like your boyfriend's, you might miss something. Stick to the facts.'

She looked at him in silence for a moment. Her face showed her disappointment. 'Well, all right, sir. But I thought you might want to know.'

'Yes. Thank you.' He glanced again at Sealey's criminal record. 'What else is there, Pat?'

She took a long breath, then said, 'I called the secretary of the golf club. I wondered if he might be able to tell us anything more about Drax's little foibles with the wives of other members. He said he would be prepared to talk, but he asked for you.'

'Why?'

She sat back and laced her hands in front of her, pressing them away from her to stretch her shoulders. Presumably she meant to conceal the fact that she was annoyed, in which case she failed. She lifted her linked hands above her head and stretched again. 'Apparently,' she said, 'there is a certain element of gender discrimination at the Farnham Park Golf Club. Ladies only play when the gentlemen don't, that sort of thing? The secretary was quite clear that he would rather discuss this with a male officer, and preferably my superior.'

Her lips were thin and the rims of her nostrils were white. He could understand why. If he had to deal for an hour with the sort of thoughtless bias that a woman officer encountered every day it would send him mad. He said, 'If he's going to cooperate, he talks to whichever officer I choose to send.'

She shook her head. 'He sounds like an old buffer, sir. I'm sure that he would be more open with you. I'd get nothing out of him. He'd be too busy asking me what a pretty little thing like me is doing in a dirty job like the police.' Her voice was heavy with resignation. Then she shook her head and flashed him another bright grin. 'Go there for lunch, sir. The Farnham Park's supposed to have one of the best chefs around. Make the sexist old shit give you something on the house.'

The grin was infectious. Thank God she could laugh at situations like this. 'Hardly proper,' he suggested, returning the smile.

'Why?' she demanded. 'It's only against regulations if it affects your conduct of the enquiry. And you know it won't.'

'He may not offer.' He glanced at his watch. 11 a.m. 'Time to go,' he said, 'if I'm going to meet you at Sealey's office after lunch.'

Fielding's eyes blazed briefly. She was certainly getting excited about this case. 'What time shall I be there, sir?'

'Two thirty. Let's give him a chance to get his feet under the desk.'

The secretary of the Farnham Park Golf Club did offer him lunch, but hardly out of hospitality. Anderson thought it was because it enabled him to be shoehorned into a tiny table in the corner of the massive dining room, where there was no risk of anybody overhearing what was being said.

The club was only a few years old, and its decor still looked pristine. It had obviously been planned by some expensive interior design consultant, and everything was in such ostentatiously good taste that it made him wince. All the carpets had been specially made to fit the rooms, with ornate borders to prove it, and the walls were hung with early paintings of racehorses and dogs which must have been worth a small fortune. The club must be very sensitive about its *nouveau* origins. Otherwise why should it bother with its chauvinistic regulations, and why should it have appointed a portly retired major type as its club secretary, when a single glance about the dining room revealed that nearly all of its members were businessmen in their thirties and forties?

'Wine?' asked the club secretary brusquely. 'Or are you really not allowed to drink on duty?' He examined Anderson minutely, as if he found it hard to believe that a representative of the Crown might actually appear at the club dressed in pale olive green superfine wool and a chamois-yellow shirt.

'No wine for me, thank you.' Anderson saw no need to explain whether adherence to regulations or personal preference caused him to refuse. 'Sparkling mineral water will be fine.'

'What does Jean-Paul recommend today?' the secretary demanded of the waiter.

Today the chef recommended bouillabaisse or stuffed courgette flowers, followed by rack of lamb or Dover sole.

Anderson ordered the sole, plainly grilled, with new potatoes and a salad. The secretary, whose name was Muir, gave him a look which suggested that a real gentleman didn't need to take care of his figure, and ordered the lamb and a half bottle of Burgundy.

'Now,' said Muir, when the wine waiter had poured and gone, 'this business about Eddie Drax. It's terrible, of course, and if there's anything we can do to help we will, but I do hope that you won't see any need to drag the club into it. If people got the idea that we were that sort of a place, well, it would be terrible.'

'I can see that it could have difficult implications.' Anderson broke open a roll. 'But I'm not sure why you believe that the club might be under investigation.'

Muir sat back, startled. 'But your young lady called and asked me to see her. Obviously I assumed –'

He broke off. Anderson continued to split the roll into bite-sized pieces. It was warm, and it smelt wonderful. He looked forward to his lunch. 'Why did you think it might have something to do with the club?'

The secretary looked from side to side as if to reassure himself that he was out of earshot of the nearest tables. Then he leant forward conspiratorially. 'I have to tell you,' he hissed, 'that Eddie Drax was becoming a sad trial to the Committee.'

Well, that was no surprise. Anderson raised his eyebrows.

'If it wasn't one thing it was another,' the Secretary ran on. 'He was badly behaved on the course. Do you play, Chief Inspector Anderson?'

'No,' Anderson replied shortly.

'You should,' the secretary burbled.

Anderson said nothing. He didn't like golf. He had tried to play once or twice not long after he had married Sarah. Her family was wealthy, and all the male members of it seemed more at home on a golf course than anywhere else. So, in an attempt to please her, he had picked up a club or two. And the fact was he had simply not been very good at the game. So he had never played again. He could not bear incompetence, in himself most of all.

The waiter brought their entrées and for a little while

they sat in silence while dinner plates and kidney-shaped vegetable dishes were arranged in front of them. The secretary requested mint sauce for his lamb and a flunky was dispatched to fetch it. Then there was a further silence while Muir tackled his meat, hacking it from the bone with eager enthusiasm. It was still pink, and next to the ribs the flesh oozed blood. Anderson deftly lifted a fillet from his sole. It was tender and delicious. If only he didn't have to ask Muir questions, it would be a perfect lunch.

'Anyway,' said Muir, once he had managed to consume a few mouthfuls, 'as I was saying, he was a nuisance on the course. He'd play through without asking, cut in, and make a hell of a row if someone did the same to him.'

No doubt this was irritating to a golfer. But it hardly seemed like sufficient cause for murder.

'And then of course,' Muir went on gloomily, 'there were the women.'

There had, it appeared, been several: too many to remember without notes. Muir dolefully recounted tale after tale of Eddie Drax' amours, and page after page of Anderson's notebook filled with neat, spidery writing. There were enough affronted husbands to keep an entire investigation team busy for weeks. Not all of them had been full-blown affairs, but the ones that weren't were in some respects even more fertile ground. Drax had been unable to resist temptation, however it presented itself. Muir worked himself up into a lather as he described one incident in which Eddie was discovered actually attempting to copulate with the wife of a business colleague in his Porsche in the club car park.

'I would have thought that was rather cramped,' Anderson commented.

'It was,' mourned Muir. 'Her legs were sticking out of the driver's side window. It was dark, but even so her husband recognised her shoes.'

'No wonder the Committee found Drax such a trial.'

'We had privately agreed,' Muir confided, 'that one more incident after last week's would be enough to make us take action. It wasn't going to be easy, with the debenture and everything, but enough is enough.'

'What happened last week?' Anderson asked. Catherine and Amanda had both told him already, but it was good to view every incident from as many sides as possible.

Muir shook his head, then glanced around surreptitiously before mopping the last of the lamb juices from his plate with a piece of bread. 'Ah, that was excellent. We did a good day's work when we recruited Jean-Paul.' He caught the waiter's eye and relaxed back in his chair as the plates were removed. 'Can I offer you some pudding, Chief Inspector? What's best today, Daniel?'

'There's white and dark marble mousse,' Daniel suggested, 'and Jean-Paul has made a treacle sponge. Or anything from the cart, or cheese, of course, Mr Muir.'

'Treacle sponge!' Muir enthused. 'Let me recommend it to you, Anderson. Jean-Paul does an amazing job on puddings, for a Frenchman. And his custard –' He waved a hand in the air, indicating that words failed him.

Why did so many people rave about the food that reminded them of school? Anderson did not eschew sweet things entirely, but neither did he suffer from a lingering nostalgia for suet. 'I'm sure it's excellent,' he said politely, 'but I'll try the mousse.'

'Please yourself,' sniffed Muir. 'Coffee to follow?'

'Certainly. Espresso, please.'

Daniel slithered away in the direction of the kitchen and Anderson reminded Muir gently, 'So last week?'

Muir rolled his eyes. 'Oh, God. Last week. Mr Drax obliged the club by indulging himself in a little fisticuffs in the bar one evening. Even for Eddie that was going too far.' The secretary's rheumy blue eyes kindled with anger. 'And as if that wasn't enough, the person he chose to send sprawling over a table was another member and one that he had particularly sponsored. If I'm being entirely honest with you, Chief Inspector, we would not normally have considered Tony Sealey for membership of this club. But Eddie was most insistent. And then this!'

'What was the matter with Sealey?'

'Oh,' Muir sighed, then fell silent as the puddings appeared. He dived into his treacle sponge with cries of glee, seemingly determined to immolate himself entirely in custard. Anderson admired the exquisite arrangement of his marbled chocolate mousse, immaculately displayed on a pool of mango sauce. Since Muir seemed utterly absorbed, he concentrated for a moment on the food. Like the sole, the mousse was excellent, and the sauce provided a pleasingly piquant contrast. He had to agree with the club secretary's assessment of the club chef.

'Sealey,' said Muir at last with his mouth full. 'Oh, he was just a little *infra dig,* if you know what I mean. A salesman. And rather a rough customer to boot. But with a sponsor like Eddie we couldn't really say no. Well, that's all over now. He won't be playing here again.'

He could have felt sorry for Sealey, but that would be inappropriate for a man suspected of murder. 'What exactly happened?'

Muir scraped the last of his custard from his bowl and licked the spoon clean. 'It was quite appalling,' he said. 'Eddie was having a drink with David Thompson, another of our members. Not a founder, but a very reliable chap. He's helped us out with the finances once or twice. And Thompson's wife Penny was there, and, well, Eddie's latest conquest, who happened to be Sealey's wife. Name's Amanda. Nice looking girl. Something to get hold of.'

The secretary's face was flushed. He looked as if he was about to succumb to an apoplexy. It was just as well that Fielding hadn't come. This lascivious old trout wouldn't find it easy to talk to an attractive woman in her early thirties about the misdemeanours of club members.

'And in walks Sealey,' went on Muir, 'cursing like a trooper, practically challenging Eddie to a fight. But that was the thing about Eddie, you see. He wasn't a big chap, but he was frightfully fit. Skinny, you know, and packed quite a punch. Probably needed to be fit, too, to cope with all those women.'

Muir appeared to be getting a little out of hand. Thank God, it was nearly two o'clock. Anderson finished his coffee as quickly as was decent, thanked Muir for the lunch and made his excuses.

'You'll keep this out of the news?' Muir asked again as he accompanied Anderson to the door of the dining room. 'Can't stand bad publicity.'

'If there's anything in the newspaper, Mr Muir,' Anderson assured him with quiet irony, 'it won't have come from us. But we may well need to speak to more of your members. One of my team will be contacting you for names and addresses, if you have no objection.'

'Oh, bloody hell,' Muir grumbled. 'Well, if you must. Have to cooperate and all that.'

He smiled at the receptionist on his way out and she returned the smile with enthusiasm. 'You're the policeman, aren't you,' she said.

He nodded, approving of her vivacity and her elegantly styled short hair. 'Well,' she said, 'good luck. Poor Eddie! I know he could be a bit of a pain, but what a thing to happen!'

'Did you know him well?' he asked, leaning easily on the desk between them.

'I wouldn't say well,' said the receptionist, sparkling up at him. She paused to greet another member on his way in. Her role seemed to involve nothing more than smiling at people, but she was well suited to it. 'No, not well. But, you know, we had, once or twice.'

After nearly twenty years in the police it still amazed him that when an investigation was in train people would spontaneously offer information relating to their most private encounters. All he said was, 'Really?'

'At the club barbecue last year,' said the girl, 'and then at the Christmas party. He had Elaine with him both times. He was so naughty! But I thought he was really sweet.'

So the footballer haircut hadn't put women off. Amazing. 'Did Elaine find out?'

'Oh, I hope not!'

This was an opportunity to ask a question that had been bothering him. 'Tell me,' he said, stooping confidingly towards the girl, 'what exactly was it that women saw in Eddie Drax?'

She hesitated and fluttered her eyelids at him in a parody of naughtiness. Then she gestured for him to lean further down and, when he obliged, whispered hoarsely in his ear. 'He was *enormous*.'

83

She certainly wasn't referring to Drax's height. The suggestion was distasteful. Was that all it took? 'Well,' he said without expression, 'now I know.'

FIVE
Tuesday Afternoon

As Anderson was about to leave the club it occurred to him that after he had finished for the day he should go back to the station and set up the rest of his team to start interviewing the men whom Muir had mentioned as victims of Eddie's popularity with women. Delay was always a bad idea, as memories faded with distance from events. However, this would make it impossible for him to get to the concert in time. His face twisted briefly in annoyance. Then he located Catherine Marshall's card in his wallet and called her.

Her secretary answered the 'phone. 'Catherine Marshall's office.'

'It's John Anderson here. May I speak to Catherine, please?'

'Just a moment, please, Mr Anderson. She's got someone with her.'

There was a silent electronic pause. It drew out. He looked at the telephone in irritation, then returned it to his ear as he heard Sue's voice. 'Just a minute, I'll put you through.'

'Hello?' said a diffident voice. 'Catherine Marshall here.'

'Catherine, it's John.'

'Oh,' she said, her voice suddenly husky as she registered his use of first names. 'Oh, hello. How are you?'

'I'm fine. But I'm afraid that it's just as I expected. I won't be able to make it to the concert tonight. I'm very sorry to let you down.'

'Oh, that's such a shame. Are things difficult?'

'No, not exactly. I could be free by 8.30, I imagine. But that's too late, isn't it.'

There was a little silence. Then, as he had hoped, she said nervously, 'A bit late for the concert, but not too late to meet.'

'Well,' he suggested, 'perhaps I could ask you to dinner instead, since I'm causing you to waste two perfectly good tickets.'

'They won't be wasted. One of my staff is keen, he always sweeps up after me. And I'd love to come to dinner.'

'What sort of food would you prefer?'

'I'm not fussy,' Catherine said. He could hear her smile. 'I'll eat anything except birds all in one piece. I can't bear looking at their little legs.'

He liked it when the choice was left to him. 'Italian, then. Do you know the Ristorante La Barca?'

'Yes,' she said, and he could hear that she had expected him to choose something less expensive. La Barca had opened recently in the middle of the town. Its sparse, easy elegance suited him very well, as did the quality of its cuisine. It was absurdly expensive, but he did not like compromise, and if the restaurant that he preferred stretched his pocket he would simply go less often. 'Yes,' Catherine said again. 'In fact, it's just around the corner from my house. I live up by the castle.'

'That's good,' he said. 'I'll be able to walk you home.'

There was a drawn-out silence. He could sense Catherine blushing above her closely-fastened blouse.

At last he said, 'What time shall I be there?'

She hesitated. 'I don't know. When would suit you?'

'Nine p.m.,' he said definitely. That would give him a chance to go home and change. Just supposing he did walk her home, and just supposing one thing led to another, he would be able to appear for work without worrying about wearing yesterday's clothes.

'Well,' said Catherine, 'that would be lovely.'

'Nine p.m., then,' he confirmed, 'at La Barca. I am looking forward to it very much. And I apologise again for missing the concert.'

'Another time,' Catherine said. 'See you tonight. Goodbye,' she took a breath, 'John.'

'Goodbye,' he said, and hung up.

Patricia Fielding waited in her car in front of Tony Sealey's company offices. Like many new drugs companies, this one was situated on an out-of-town 'industrial park', surrounded by blighted trees and tarmac. A belated sense of sympathy for Sealey made her reluctant to go into the building without Anderson. It would be bad enough for Sealey to have a visit from the police at work, without one of them waiting for a colleague on his employer's premises.

She was very pleased that Anderson had invited her to this interview. Sealey was the prime suspect, and she had expected Anderson to keep the interview to himself. Even if she only got to take the notes, it would be interesting. And it was fair, too. She had done a lot of leg work to find out about Sealey.

Anderson's big BMW swept into the car park and slid neatly into a place near the door. Pat got out of her car and went towards him. She could see him sitting in the driving seat, talking into the radio, his silvered head matching the car's pewter-grey bodywork.

What had happened between them that morning? She had thought she was not susceptible to the famous – or infamous – Anderson charm, but he had looked up at her with a glinting smile and those sparkling dark blue eyes and suddenly she had felt weak at the knees. She knew that she wasn't interested and she didn't think he was. So what was going on? It was as if for a moment he had invited her to share a secret, and because she knew just how private he was she had felt incredibly flattered, honoured, even. Everyone talked about the sexual chemistry between male and female officers working together, but normally they meant the sort of obvious banter which went without saying. Not this, this shock.

Well, it had been interesting. But now she was on her guard. She knew enough about Anderson to be certain that she did not want to become involved with him. It was unprofessional. And as if that wasn't enough, he was self-centred, arrogant and vain. She had her promotion to think about, never mind Charlie.

Anderson nodded to her as he locked his car, then led the way to the door. She would have liked to ask him what role he expected her to play, but somehow she didn't.

The receptionist looked askance at them as she rang through to the sales office. They stood in the open-plan area, looking around at the breezeblock walls, the plants, the industrial-quality carpet underfoot. On the wall was a board showing the Employee of the Month. Pat walked over to look at it. Two months back the lucky winner had been a young looking man with strong dark hair and a fierce grin, who according to the nameplate underneath was Tony Sealey.

The door to reception slammed open and she turned to see the man in the flesh. He was tall, perhaps six feet two, and his white shirt was stained with sweat at the armholes and down his back. His dark eyes were hot with anger. He stalked towards them, snarling, 'Did you have to come to the bloody office, for Christ's sake?'

Beside Sealey Anderson looked small and neat and almost insignificant. 'We wanted to speak to you as soon as possible, Mr Sealey. You could have suggested another time.'

'I bet.' Sealey stood in front of Anderson with his hands on his hips, louring. Pat noticed that his nose and lip were bruised and slightly swollen, a relic of his argument with Eddie Drax, no doubt.

'I'm DCI Anderson,' said Anderson coldly. 'My colleague Detective Sergeant Fielding.'

Sealey glanced across at her and started in surprise. 'Bloody hell!' he said. 'You're too pretty to be a WPC.'

'Detective Sergeant,' she said steadily. One of the first things they taught you in the force was not to let anyone make you angry, however much of a prick he seemed to be.

'Would you like to talk here, Mr Sealey?' Anderson asked with imperturbable courtesy. 'Or is there somewhere else you would prefer?'

Sealey glared at him, then muttered, 'I've got a meeting room.' He stamped away from them and kicked open one of the double doors. Anderson looked at Pat with his dark brows arched and an expression of ironic enquiry. She stifled a laugh as she followed him. He never told a joke, but you couldn't accuse him of having no sense of humour.

The meeting room was bare, furnished only with a round table, four chairs and the regulation plant. Sealey did not offer them coffee. 'I suppose,' he said, 'that you're here about that bastard Drax.'

Amanda must somehow have got hold of him and told him what to expect. Pat drew out her notebook and sat down quietly on a chair, ready to listen.

'Is this a formal interview?' Sealey demanded. 'Are you charging me?'

'Should we?' Anderson asked quietly. Pat smiled to herself as she began to take notes. Anderson was more adept at parrying a question than any other officer she knew.

'No you bloody shouldn't,' stormed Sealey. He seemed determined to perform an imitation of Mr Angry And Innocent Of Guildford. 'Do you think I'm a bloody murderer?'

'We think, Mr Sealey, that you are the man who had a violent and public argument with Eddie Drax last week at the Farnham Park Golf Club.' Anderson's voice was icy. 'Since Mr Drax is now dead and we suspect murder, it is not surprising that we should want to ask you where you were on Saturday night.'

Neat. Anderson had indicated that the police only suspected murder. Sealey had suggested that he knew it was. Anger was not the best recipe for avoiding incriminating mistakes.

'Listen,' said Sealey, 'you've got the wrong man. Bloody police! You can't leave anyone alone. Did you look up my record?' He flung accusing looks first at Anderson, then at Pat, and seemed to see enough to reinforce his view. 'I knew it. Christ! Does it occur to you that I've been a respectable citizen for ten years? Not good enough for you, is it? Once a villain, always a villain, eh? Eh?'

'Mr Sealey,' Anderson said, not attempting to keep the weariness from his voice, 'all I am asking you is where you were last Saturday night.'

'All you're asking me is whether I killed Eddie fucking Drax,' Sealey corrected him viciously. Pat wrote down every word. She wasn't surprised that Sealey's shirt was so sweaty. He seemed determined to seize on every opportunity for rage. She could smell him from where she sat, a hot, ferocious male smell. The contrast with Anderson's pristine coolness was stark. She could smell Anderson, too, or rather she could smell his fragrance, a crisp masculine scent that seemed to embody his unruffled control. Down, girl, she said to herself sternly.

'Well? Did you?'

'No, I didn't.' Sealey raked one hand through his thatch of dark hair. 'He deserved it, damn him, but I didn't kill him. I'd have liked to, believe me!'

'And where were you on Saturday night?'

'I was sitting,' snarled Sealey, 'in the lounge of the house in Burpham where I've been staying since my darling wife decided she preferred Mr Eddie Bastard Drax to me. I was drinking whisky and watching the telly. Football, to be precise.'

'Were Bob and Diana at home?' Anderson asked quietly.

Sealey took a step back. 'Got their names already, have you? Who gave you those, then? Amanda?'

'Were they there?' Anderson insisted.

'No they fucking weren't.' Pat wearied of the expletives and contented herself with a dash on each occasion. 'They were out, weren't they. So I was on my own, moping. I didn't know it was illegal to mope.'

'Can anyone corroborate that, Mr Sealey?'

'Bob and Diana came home about one. Is that enough time for you to pin Eddie on me? That's what you plan, isn't it?'

'How do you feel about his death?' asked Anderson.

'Bloody delighted. Over the moon, Brian.'

'Your wife was distressed.'

'I bet she was. She was expecting him to keep her in the lap of luxury from now on. Well, she's out of luck, isn't she?'

'Will you go back to your wife, Mr Sealey?'

Pat looked up. Why had Anderson asked this particular question? It didn't seem to have any bearing on their enquiry. Perhaps he was just curious.

It seemed to startle Sealey, in any case. He stared at Anderson for a moment, breathing hard. Then he said, 'No, I won't. The bitch. I came home from work two weeks ago and found her humping Drax in our bed. In our bed!' The dark face twisted with what looked like genuine pain. 'Christ, why? Just because he was rich? I was doing my bloody best.'

Pat remembered the characterless box on the executive estate and felt suddenly sorry for Tony Sealey and for his wife. Something inside her told her that Eddie Drax had deserved to die. She fought it down.

'So, Mr Sealey,' said Anderson, 'last Saturday you were in Burpham the whole evening.'

'That's right,' said Sealey. Thoughts of Amanda seemed to have calmed him slightly, but now he looked shifty. Was all that anger just bluster, harder to see through than a simple lie?

'In that case, I'm sure you won't object to visiting the station and making a statement. And giving a set of prints.'

'You've already got my prints,' said Sealey sulkily.

Pat took a quick breath, ready to remind Anderson how unreliable old records were, despite the computer, and how important it was that they should obtain a palmar. She need not have worried. Anderson said, 'Just for completeness.'

'I'm not going anywhere,' said Sealey. 'You haven't charged me. I don't have to do anything.'

'You don't,' Anderson agreed. 'But non-cooperation with the police always looks bad, don't you think?'

Sealey glared at Anderson and subsided into silence, gnawing at his thumbnail. He flung one furious glance across the room at Pat. His narrowed eyes and clenched jaw looked dangerous.

Anderson let the silence draw out. He watched Sealey steadily. At last the salesman made a vicious face and said, 'All right. I'll come to the station some time. Is that good enough for you?'

'Thank you for your cooperation,' Anderson said, without a trace of irony.

In the car park they passed a red Celica. Pat glanced at the number plate and said, 'That's Sealey's car, sir.'

Anderson stopped and gave the car the once over. 'Hmm. Any news on the house to house?'

She simply lifted her brows and shook her head. Then she glanced across at the building they had just left and said, feeling bold, 'What do you think, sir?'

Anderson narrowed his eyes as if he was surprised to have been asked his opinion. 'What do you think, Pat?'

It was irritating that he applied the techniques he used for suspects to her, but she found herself responding almost before she had registered the question. 'I think he's not being straight with us, sir. He doesn't look right.'

'But perhaps he just doesn't like the police,' Anderson suggested.

This was possible, of course, given Sealey's history. 'Even so, sir, wouldn't he control himself a bit better, with a murder charge in the offing?'

'Maybe. But we haven't got any evidence. At least, not until he comes and gives us a fresh set of prints.' Anderson lifted one eyebrow at her. 'Was there a palmar on the computer?'

'No, sir. Fingerprints only.'

'That bloody machine,' said Anderson mildly.

'Should I ask permission for a search warrant, sir?' As she spoke she realised that she desperately wanted Sealey to be the murderer, and she wanted to be the one who went into his house and found a lapis blue American cotton sweater in his cupboard. It meant a lot to her.

Anderson frowned. 'You can try, if you like, Pat. But it's just circumstantial evidence for now. I would be inclined to wait until after we have the chance to check the palmar.'

He was right, of course, but she felt ridiculously chastened. She took a long breath, then said, 'All right, sir. What now?'

Anderson glanced at his watch. It was nearly 3.30. 'Time to go and catch up with the paperwork,' he said, and it was not a suggestion.

Many police officers hated paperwork. Anderson did not. He saw it for what it was, a necessary concomitant of catching criminals. The need for thoroughness, rigour and completeness appealed to his own sense of organisation. As a young detective sergeant, still full of enthusiasm undimmed by cynicism, he had seen an undoubtedly guilty man released without charge because of sloppiness on the part of the officer in charge of the investigation. He was determined that this would never happen on one of his cases.

At 5.15 he assembled the papers on his desk into neat stacks for storage overnight and called Fielding to remind her that when he had finished interviewing Samantha Smith he wanted to check on the allocation of the golf club addresses to members of his investigation team.

'Yes, sir,' she said. There was a little expectant pause. He waited, and then Fielding said very tentatively, 'If you'd like someone to take the notes for this visit, sir, I'd be –'

'Thanks, Pat,' Anderson replied easily, 'but I'll handle this one on my own. It may well prove to have nothing to do with Drax's death. There's no need to tie up two members of the team at once.'

As he walked out to the car he reflected on that refusal. Fielding had wanted to come. Why had he turned her down? She was mature enough to know how to manage her own time, and she had the routine aspects of the investigation well under control. He could have let her come with him. What he had told her was true, of course, but did he really believe it? Or had he simply wanted an opportunity to be alone with Samantha Smith, one of the more striking women he had ever seen, and one whose antagonism he found intriguing?

He drove to Samantha Smith's flat on autopilot, still trying to analyse his own motivation. It was odd how the razor-sharp logic which dissected other people like a surgeon's scalpel became blunt and rusty when he attempted to use it on himself. Not until he parked the BMW in the private car park of the block did he focus properly on the purpose of his next interview.

What did an accounts assistant at a company like Drax & Bond earn? It might be in the region of £25,000 a year, depending on her qualifications, of course. Certainly not enough to gain her a mortgage sufficient to buy a flat in this prestigious, expensive block, or probably even to rent one.

Perhaps she had family money, or perhaps, as Thompson's secretary had suggested, she had a keeper. She was certainly attractive enough.

Or perhaps she was stealing.

He checked the time, slammed the door of the BMW and walked across the car park, looking around him at the evidence of expense. Allocated visitor spaces; hanging baskets of a size and magnificence fit for Wisley; smoked glass windows on the ground floor of the block revealing a gym and a small swimming pool, in which some residents were disporting themselves.

He looked at the list of flat numbers beside the entryphone and raised his eyebrows. Samantha lived in the penthouse. Almost as soon as he pressed the button her voice snapped out at him. 'Yes?'

'DCI Anderson,' he announced.

'Come up. Top floor.'

The door clicked silently open. No tawdry buzzers in this elegant building. He entered the waiting lift.

The door of the flat was open when he emerged and Samantha was standing in it, striking in high-heeled sandals and a short white slip dress that did not hide her svelte figure. Loud music poured through the door, a heavy racing beat and some meaningless caterwaul of vocals. Samantha glared at him, dislike naked in her face. 'At least you're on time. Come in, if you must.'

His polished shoes whispered on the thick cream-coloured carpet. He paused in the hall, looking around him into lounge, kitchen and dining room. The flat was expensively furnished, but in the sort of anodyne taste that belonged to a show flat, purchased ready-made. Only the pictures seemed to express Samantha's preferences. He rather liked them. They were an eclectic combination of representational modern art, Warhol and Hockney mostly, and reproductions of lush Victorian paintings in which opulent women found increasingly absurd excuses to dispose their white bodies naked before the viewer.

'In here,' shouted Samantha over the raucous music. He cast his eye approvingly over a last Victorian siren, then walked through into the lounge.

Sam was stooped over the CD. The racket diminished slightly. Her posture showed off her bare legs almost to the buttock, but his gaze was drawn not to her, but to a second girl who sat on a large velvet sofa, her legs curled beneath her, regarding him with enormous solemn eyes. She looked much younger than Sam, not much more than a schoolgirl, and her petite body accentuated her look of fragility. She had auburn hair, a pre-Raphaelite mass of tresses, and the pale gold-freckled skin of a redhead. A short flared skirt showed off slender legs, and a delicate little jersey top outlined the curves of her small pointed breasts. Something in her expression reminded him of a victim. She said nothing, just looked up at him with her full lips slightly parted, but he was gripped by a sudden ferocious urge both to protect her and to despoil her.

'Emma,' Sam said, turning from the CD and standing with her arms folded, 'this is Detective Chief Inspector Anderson. Anderson, this is Emma. Emma lives with me.'

For a moment he didn't quite appreciate what Sam was saying to him. Then everything became very clear. Sam stalked over to the sofa, moving like a panther, and Emma turned her huge eyes from him and gazed up at the older girl with a look of absolute adoration. Sam sat down on the sofa beside Emma and crossed her legs. Emma watched her earnestly as if she was waiting for instructions. Sam licked her lips, then smiled and said, 'Come here, sweetheart,' and held out her hand welcomingly. Emma immediately snuggled up beside her, nestling trustingly in the crook of her arm, her coppery head resting on Sam's shoulder.

Sam's green eyes were fixed on him, vivid and challenging. For a moment he was disconcerted. She was treating that child like a pet. Then with a hidden shudder he imagined, as Sam had no doubt intended him to, the two of them naked together, slender limbs entwined, lips meeting and parting, hands delicately exploring tender secret hollows of flesh.

He quickly reasserted his normal rational control. If Sam was living with a girl, then the chances of her having a rich boyfriend prepared to pay for her lifestyle were very small.

Unless, whispered his fantasy, the boyfriend likes to watch

the two of them together. Or maybe have the two of them together. He pushed this thought aside. Most men, he knew, were much more orthodox in sexual matters than they would have liked to admit. And somehow he couldn't see Sam taking orders from a man, no matter how rich.

'May I sit down?' he asked at last, since Sam said nothing.

'Please yourself,' said Sam abruptly.

He sat on a chair made in velvet to match the sofa. It was deep and comfortable. He allowed himself to relax back into it and crossed his legs, consciously mirroring Samatha's body posture. 'Well,' he said, 'thank you for allowing me to talk to you.'

Sam's face twisted in a sneer. 'Don't give me that. You're investigating Eddie's death, aren't you? I bet someone at Drax & Bond told you I was worth talking to. I can bet who it was, too.'

'Who would that be?' He was genuinely curious.

'Oh, never mind,' snapped Sam. She tightened her arm around Emma's shoulders and brushed her lips gently against the younger girl's hair. Emma closed her eyes and made a little sound like a sleeping baby.

Samantha owned her. What was it like? Sam was silent, and he had time to realise that the feeling bothering him was jealousy. It wasn't that he wanted Emma, in particular. She was too young and too naive to attract him. It was the sense of ownership, of possession, that he craved. The two girls were completely absorbed in each other.

Then Sam said, 'So, come on, let's get it over with. What do you need to know?'

'I'd be interested to know what you think about the death of Eddie Drax,' he suggested.

'You wouldn't. You've got your own ideas.' Sam sucked in a long angry breath and dug her fingers into Emma's hair, stroking her the way a person might stroke their pet, to calm herself. 'You policemen are all the same. I bet you think I'm disgusting, don't you?'

'No,' he said, calmly and quite truthfully.

'Then you're probably one of those prurient bastards who'd just love to watch two girls getting it on.'

He couldn't help smiling at her. She was so self-consciously aggressive, she was trying really hard. He could remember what it was like to have to assert himself and struggle for position, though he had never gone to Sam's extremes to achieve it. 'You don't seem to have a very high opinion of sexual tolerance in the police,' he commented. He wished now that he had brought DS Fielding along, just to see what Samantha would make of her, a pretty, feminine woman who chose to achieve through being a police detective.

'Sexual tolerance? Jesus! You're a load of misogynist homophobic bastards, aren't you? Sexually assaulting female colleagues on duty and saying it's stress? And don't think I believe that you're different. You're just a bit better dressed than the rest of them. In fact, you're so well dressed I might feel tempted to introduce you to some of my gay male friends, if you'd be interested.'

'Would they know where you were on Saturday night?' he asked. He was actually rather enjoying Samantha's attack. It suggested that she perceived him as some sort of threat.

'They might,' Sam said sullenly.

Emma's big eyes flashed quickly from Sam to Anderson and for a moment he thought that she was going to speak, but she lowered her white eyelids and snuggled more closely into Sam's side, making herself small and vulnerable, like a nestling kitten.

'Then I'd be interested to meet them,' he said. 'Where were you, as it happens?'

'I was at a party,' Sam said. 'Emma and I were at a party, weren't we, darling?'

Emma lifted her head and smiled up at Sam, then looked at him. 'That's right,' she said. Her voice was entirely suitable, sweet and breathy, a little-girl voice. 'It was a rave party. There were lots of people there. Everyone saw us.'

'Everyone saw us both,' Sam said, smiling into his eyes. 'It was a gay party. A friend of mine gave it. Emma and me put on a bit of a floor show for them. Know what I mean?'

He had seen enough of the gay and lesbian scene to have a reasonable idea of what Sam was describing. He looked at Emma, at her pure, wistful face, and found his imagination straining. Sam had enough control over this girl to get her to perform in public; and something obscene, if Sam's bright challenging look was to be believed.

'Emma,' he asked suddenly, 'how old are you?'

'I'm eighteen,' Emma said earnestly.

'So you can get stuffed, copper,' suggested Sam with a grin. 'She knows what she's doing. Or rather, I know what she's doing.'

'Tell me, Samantha,' he said, 'how can you afford this flat, and your nice car, and a girlfriend as pretty as Emma, and no doubt tabs of E, all on the salary of an accounts assistant?'

Sam flung back her dark head and laughed. 'There's the question he's been longing to ask! Don't worry, Chief Inspector, it's all perfectly above board. I'm just very good with money.'

'So it seems.' The fierce look on her face showed that she intended to tell him nothing. Well, it could wait. Perhaps this was an investigation he could pass on to Fielding, once the murder case was solved. He got to his feet and drew out his wallet, extracted a card from it and handed it down to Sam, who examined it as if it might be contaminated with an unpleasant disease. 'Look,' he said, 'Samantha, I really would be interested if you have any thoughts on how Eddie Drax died.'

'Everyone at work thinks Elaine Williams did it,' said Sam casually.

'What do you think?'

She shrugged. 'That's as good an explanation as any. Me, I reckon it was Julia.'

'Julia? Julia Bond? Why?'

Sam buried her nose and mouth in Emma's hair for a moment. Then she lifted her head and said, 'I know about the Dacre & Co. takeover. Nobody else in the office does. I was taking financial data in to the meeting they had with one of the top men at Dacre, and I saw how Eddie was treating him. If that had gone on they'd never have got to a sale agreement. But selling out to a plc is how a small businessman makes a very great deal of money. Eddie was in Julia's way.'

She didn't mention the key man insurance. Perhaps she didn't know about it. She saw sufficient motivation in Eddie's obstruction of the takeover deal. 'That's very interesting,' he said. 'When you make your statement, I would be grateful if you would mention that.'

'Statement? You want a statement from me? What for?'

'It's routine. But I do want one from you. And I want you to say which of your friends, gay or otherwise, can corroborate where you say you were on Saturday night.'

Sam looked up at him, brilliant green eyes narrowed. She seemed to be assessing him against some inner measure. At last she said, 'Emma, show the homophobic misogynist policeman out, there's a darling.'

Emma uncoiled herself sinuously and got to her feet. She was no more than five feet two and tiny. He said carefully, 'I can see myself out.'

'Oh, but Emma's such a good girl,' said Sam mockingly. 'I look after her, and she always does what I tell her. Don't you, Emma?'

And Emma looked round at Sam with a smile of such love and trust that he felt his heart lurch.

Emma closed the door and came back into the flat, shaking her head. 'Why were you so horrible to him, Sam?'

'Like I said,' Sam said, 'he's a policeman, and therefore homophobic and misogynist. Bad news.'

'I rather liked him,' Emma said, with the shadow of a pout.

Sam smiled. 'You would do, darling. You like people who know what they want, and if ever I saw someone who knows what he wants Mr Chief Inspector Anderson is one. I saw the way he looked at you. He'd love to have you. I wonder if he realises?' For a moment she was absorbed in thinking about Anderson. She, too, had found him likeable, but when he entered the flat he had brought with him an air of authority and physical control which she found intolerable. Hence her rudeness and aggression. And he had seemed to enjoy it! The swine.

Suddenly she realised that in her abstraction she was paying insufficient attention to Emma. She got up quickly and frowned. 'Emma, I noticed how much you were looking at him.'

'I didn't!' Emma exclaimed, with a look compounded of guilt and excitement.

'Are you arguing with me?' Sam demanded.

'No, Samantha,' said Emma, looking down.

'I should think not. You were looking at him. You know the rules. You don't look at men until I tell you to.'

Emma's big eyes flashed upward once, then fell again. She was breathing fast.

'Go and get changed. And you can make me a drink. I've got to make a phone call, and it's private.'

Quickly Emma ran off. Sam watched her go, alert for further misdemeanours, but she saw nothing that gave her cause to call Emma back and chastise her. Instead she walked over to the telephone, lifted it and dialled.

'Oh, hello, Penny,' she said when the phone was answered. 'It's Sam, Samantha Smith. How are you? Is David there? I wonder if I could have a quick word, unless I'm interrupting dinner or something?'

There was a short pause, then David's voice said gruffly, 'Sam, what do you want?'

'I just had a visit from Chief Inspector Anderson,' she said with a feline smile.

Silence. Then, 'Well, what's that got to do with me?'

'He's interested in our arrangement.'

'Shit,' David hissed.

She imagined him leaning forward, clutching the receiver, whispering into it in a combination of fury and terror. Serve you right, you bastard, she thought. Serve you right. You used me and abused me and now it's my turn. I hope Mr Chief Inspector Anderson makes you shit your pants.

'Christ! What did you tell him?'

'Nothing, of course,' said Sam. 'Do you think I'm stupid?'

'Why are you ringing, then?' demanded David, aggressive now.

'He's investigating Eddie's death,' she purred. 'Now of course we both know that neither of us had anything to do with it, but it looks as if there might be quite a few police around for a while. And so I thought that if you want me to keep quiet, this would be a good time to put up the fee.'

'You're an idiot,' David snapped.

'Perhaps. But even to an idiot £2,500 a month has a nice ring, don't you think?' Silence. 'Don't you think, David?'

Again there was silence. Then David said, 'This can't go on.'

'Of course it can,' she said happily. 'It's gone on for a year, hasn't it? Who'll know the difference? It's all signed and sealed. And it's no skin off your nose, is it, David? Drax & Bond pick up the tab.'

Anderson was waiting at the bar when Catherine slipped in through the door of La Barca. He got to his feet and smiled at her as she approached. She looked cool and elegant in a tight-fitting white body and a dark blue silk skirt. Her bright eyes were brightened further with a little subtle makeup. Only her hair was wayward, as fluffy and rumpled as if she had just got out of bed.

'Hello,' he said. 'I'm so glad you could make it.' She looked anxious and uncertain. He took both her hands, leant forward and gently but firmly kissed her cheek. Her skin was warm and very faintly perfumed. Beneath his lips her cheek grew hotter and he realised that she was blushing. Touched by her shyness, he drew back, held on to her hands for a fraction of a second, then let them go.

She was indeed blushing, but she kept her head up. She was used to dealing with awkward situations. 'Hello, John,' she said. 'This is very kind of you.'

'Not at all,' he assured her. 'Now, would you like a drink?'

'If it's all right with you,' she said apologetically, 'I'd really like to go straight in and eat. I just had a sandwich on the hoof at lunchtime and I'm starving. And I have an early start tomorrow.'

'Of course.' He nodded to the waiter and stepped back to let Catherine walk in front of him. When they were established at the table, napkins spread and menus placed, he said, 'You look lovely.'

She laughed and tossed her head. 'Well, I knew I would

risk being shown up by the peacock policeman if I didn't make an effort.' She lifted her chin at his immaculate shirt and tie. 'And I wasn't wrong, was I?'

'Well, I'm glad you got dressed up for all the right reasons. But I mean it, you look wonderful. That body really suits you. It would look great under the suit you were wearing yesterday.'

She looked down at herself, apparently startled. 'What, this? For work?'

'Why not? Under a suit it would look perfectly respectable.'

Her eyes lifted to his. She was frowning slightly. 'Good grief,' she said. 'Here we are on a first date, and you're already telling me what to wear.'

'Just commenting on what I see,' he said disarmingly. 'Did you manage to find a home for the concert tickets?'

Music and musicians, art and artists, film and theatre lasted them through the ordering and the first course. The food was excellent as always, the service attentive, but so subdued as to be almost invisible. They discovered enough tastes in common to exclaim together pleasantly about shared experiences, and enough areas of difference to keep the conversation spirited. Catherine appeared very happy to talk and chattered away gaily, but she was still nervous. After the main course was served she almost knocked over her water glass with an injudicious movement. He reached out quickly and caught it.

'I'm sorry,' she said, drawing her hands back into her lap and shaking her head. 'I'm a nervous wreck.'

Her eyes begged to tell him more. He looked attentively at her. 'Why is that?'

'At this point,' Catherine said, 'I always wish that I smoked. It would give me something to do and conceal how awful I feel.' She stopped, but he knew that there was more to come. His eyes never wavered from her. 'Confession time,' said Catherine nervously. 'Did you know that I'm divorced?'

'No, I didn't.' His voice was very gentle. 'If it makes it any easier to confess, so am I.'

'Are you? Really?' She seemed reassured. Then she met his eyes and said with a rueful shake of the head, 'Oh, it's stupid how comforting it is to know that somebody else has made mistakes.'

He reflected on his marriage. 'We all make mistakes.'

'I was too young,' said Catherine. She picked up her glass of wine and held it in front of the candle, looking through the golden liquid at the little glowing point of light. 'But it was all so horrible. He had an affair with someone at the office. I can't tell you how it felt when I found out about it. Under my nose. I was so angry, and I felt so stupid.'

If she asked, he was prepared to tell her about what had happened between him and Sarah. But he didn't want to volunteer his story while she was still finding the strength to talk about herself. She was still staring into the glass of wine, and her face showed that she was afraid. He said quietly, 'What happened?'

'Oh, you don't want to hear the whole sordid tale,' Catherine said lightly, taking a gulp from the wine and setting it down. 'The usual gruesomeness. Anyway, that's not the point. The point is that I've been single for five years and in that time I've hardly gone out with anyone.' She smiled at him. 'They're all married, or so determined to talk about their own experiences that they won't listen to anything I say. Or they just want to go to bed with me. Or they don't dare to ask me out. Or –' Her words had become a torrent. She closed her lips, shut her eyes tightly and bowed her head. He felt suddenly sorry for her, the successful young woman professional. He laid his hand over hers and squeezed gently.

'You see,' she said, lifting her head, 'all I want to say is, I'm rather out of practice at this.'

Tears were glittering in her eyes. He would have liked to kiss her then, but the table separated them. Instead he lifted her hand and held it, stroking his thumb gently over the back of her fingers. She was tense. He drew her hand to his lips, turned it over and very softly kissed the white skin of her wrist.

Her pulse hammered against his open mouth. He closed his eyes and just touched her with the tip of his tongue. She smelt warm and sensual and the taste of her skin was salty. Her arm tightened as if she would pull away, then relaxed again. He let the moment draw out as he absorbed her closeness. When he was ready, he lowered her hand gently and met her eyes.

Her pupils were so dilated that her eyes looked black, not hazel. She swallowed hard and moistened her lips with her tongue, but her swift breathing quickly dried them again. She was trembling, and the little fine hairs on her forearms were standing up. Every line of her face and her body showed that she was aroused, and the fear in her eyes showed that she did not know what to do about it.

He smiled at her. He felt calm, poised and very happy. Catherine was bruised and fragile and she did not know how to ask for what she wanted. But he knew that she would not have to ask him. He said, 'Would you like to go home now?'

Yes, her eyes answered him. But she looked down at her half-eaten meal and protested, 'I've hardly touched this, and it's delicious. And I'm the one who said I was hungry! My eyes are bigger than my stomach. I mean, what a waste, to come to the best restaurant in town and not finish your food.'

'Methinks the lady doth protest too much,' he said, and she gave a shamefaced laugh. 'Don't do anything you don't want to do,' he counselled her. 'I'll get the bill.'

In only a few moments they were standing outside the restaurant. The air was warm and humid. He said, 'May I walk you home?'

'It's only a step,' she said apologetically.

He could have taken this as a refusal. But he just offered her his arm. She hesitated, then rested her hand on his elbow. 'Just up the hill,' she said.

It was, indeed, just a step. They walked in silence. Her hand trembled on his arm and he resisted the temptation to embrace her and reassure her. She was used to being alone, it would be easy to overwhelm her.

At the door Catherine reached in her small neat purse for her key, then looked up at him with an uncertain smile. 'It seems absolutely ridiculous for me to ask you if you'd like to come in for a coffee – but would you?'

'I'd love a coffee,' he responded solemnly.

She opened the door and switched on the hall light. The house was small and old, a little gem of a town house, Georgian-fronted and medieval inside, white-painted and punctuated with heavy beams. As soon as she came through the door Catherine became very animated. 'Just through here to the kitchen,' she chirruped. 'Loo's on the left if you need it. I'll just stick the kettle on.'

The house was like her, neat and restrained. Anderson turned into the cloakroom and freshened up. The towel was scented with lavender. He looked at himself in the mirror over the basin for a long moment, and his dark blue eyes looked steadily back. He knew that he was tremendously excited, aroused by Catherine's attractiveness, by her shyness, by the prospect of leading her by the hand through all the pathways of pleasure. But his face looked calm, composed, unruffled. Catherine did not know him well enough to see the glitter in the depths of his eyes, a sparkle like sunlight on deep water.

Catherine was busying herself in the kitchen, lining up cafetière and cups, milk jug and sugar bowl. 'Nearly ready,' she said as he came and stood behind her. 'I'll just —'

The first time he saw her he had wanted to run his hands through her tousled hair. Now he did so, and it was just as he had imagined, soft as silk, slipping through his fingers like moonbeams. Catherine took a long, sharp breath and stood very still. Then she swallowed convulsively and turned to face him, jerking away from his hands. Her lips were quivering. 'John, I — I don't —'

Those soft lips begged to be silenced. He took her shoulders between his hands and lowered his head to kiss her. She gave a little cry, but she did not pull away.

Mouth to mouth, a gentle, open kiss, hinting at more, but not granting it. He let his hands move from her shoulders to her soft hair, cradling her head between his palms as his lips caressed hers. Their bodies were very close, close enough for him to sense her warmth, but not touching. He opened his eyes to watch her face and saw her rapt, relaxed, every line smoothed out, every anxiety gone.

At last he released her, and at once she was nervous again.

She stepped back, clasping her hands in front of her. 'I told you,' she whispered, 'I'm out of practice.'

He smiled at her. 'Then I'll remind you.'

She was standing with her back against the refrigerator. He came closer to her. She tried to retreat, but he lifted his arms on either side of her so that she was trapped. Then he leant slowly towards her, watching her eyes slip shut.

This time he kissed her properly, his lips firm and hard on hers, his tongue entering her mouth, exploring. She was shy, hardly able to touch her tongue to his, but he persisted and at last she moaned and reached up to clasp her arms around his neck and cling to him. Her breasts pressed against him. He passed his hands gently over her back, easing away the tension he felt there. Catherine whimpered and dug her fingers into his hair, stroking it as she would an animal. Her breath came uncertainly and her body tightened.

He drew away from her and put one hand to the shoulder of her top. Slowly he eased it downwards, revealing white skin and the strap of a pale pink bra. Catherine caught a little sobbing breath, then said, 'Not here. Please, not here.'

He stooped forward to kiss the naked shoulder. Then he looked up at her, smiling. 'Where?'

The bedroom was in the eaves, the shape of a giant letter A. Like the rest of the house, it was neat and tidy. The bed was large and made up with white linen and countless pillows. It looked comfortable and commodious. Anderson went over to the bedside table and switched on one of the small parchment-shaded lamps, then walked back to Catherine, loosening his tie.

She stood against the wall of the room, breathing fast. She looked frightened, as if she knew what was coming and knew that she was powerless to prevent it. 'What's wrong?' he asked her gently.

'Nothing.' She turned her head away, as if she couldn't lie to his face. 'Nothing.' He put his hands on her arms and lifted her towards him. 'It's all right,' he told her. 'Trust me.'

She lifted her head and looked into his eyes. He could see that she wasn't used to trusting people, not with herself. He smiled at her again, reassuringly, then kissed her and as he did so placed his hand gently over the swell of her breast.

Her nipple was hard beneath his palm. He chafed it a little and she moaned. He closed his eyes, concentrating entirely on the sensation of experiencing her sensations, drowning himself in the pleasure he was giving her. Slowly, as he kissed her and stroked her breasts, he undressed her. He unfastened her skirt and let it slip down her thighs, pushed the stretchy body off her shoulders and guided it, too, downwards to the floor. Catherine did not protest, but allowed him to remove her clothes like a child being put to bed. She stood before him now naked except for her pale pink bra and panties, and when he stepped back to look at her she closed her eyes and turned her head away.

'You're beautiful,' he said, meaning it. Her breasts were high and her waist slender, and beneath the tuck of her waist she blossomed into fullness, rich smooth curves at thigh and hip, like a classical Venus.

She opened her eyes then and managed a smile. 'I'm scared.'

'Don't be.' He took her hand and pulled her towards him. She came obediently. He backed slowly away until his legs met the bed, then sat down on it. 'Come here.'

'Turn the light off,' Catherine whispered, resisting.

'No, I want to see you.' He pulled a little harder and this time she obeyed him, letting him guide her down on to the bed beside him. She lay very still, her eyes shut, her breath whispering though her parted lips. Her hands were spread wide, as if she were on a cross. His breath caught in his throat. He leant gently forward, poising his body over her, and softly kissed the pale skin between her breasts.

Catherine let out a long sigh that was half a moan. For a moment her body lifted towards him, then subsided. Her response was enthralling. He began to kiss her, slowly, languorously, firm lips and gentle tongue exploring every inch of her arms, her shoulders, her ribs. She lay quiescent, shivering at each touch. When at last he very gently pulled away the fabric of her bra to reveal her nipple she gave a long shudder, and when his lips closed upon the tender point of flesh she cried out aloud and arched up towards him, saying urgently, 'Oh God, John, please, please.'

At once he lifted himself over her and caught hold of her wrists, pinning her down. She opened her eyes and stared up at him, gasping. 'Please,' she whispered.

'There's no rush,' he corrected her quietly. He drew her wrists together above her head and held them with one hand so that he could stroke the other hand down her half-naked body. She shuddered again and closed her eyes. His fingers fastened upon her exposed nipple and pinched it, first gently, then, as she moaned and writhed, harder and harder. When her white throat twisted with delicious agony he released the swollen peak of her breast and kissed her again, still holding her wrists.

'John,' she whispered, arching against him. 'Oh God.' She pulled her head away from his and looked up as if she had only just seen him. 'Oh God, you've still got all your clothes on, oh God –'

'Hush,' he whispered, placing his lips back on to hers. He kissed her until she was calm again, then slowly, slowly moved down her body, rubbing himself against her, touching her, kissing her, teasing her in unexpected places and then returning to her stiff nipples and sucking them until she moaned. He reached behind her, unfastened her bra, and released her wrists so that he could pull it from her and drop it off the bed. Her breasts were naked, exposed to his caresses. Her nipples were the colour of a rosebud, long and stiff.

Nothing gave him so much pleasure as pleasing a woman. All his senses were engaged, every part of him concentrated wholly on Catherine, on her body, on her responses. Every turn of her head, every lift of her loins was imbued with deep erotic significance. His cock was fully erect, hard and throbbing within the prison of his trousers, but he ignored it. His own satisfaction could wait. Catherine came first, Catherine's beautiful body to be teased and stimulated and caressed into helplessness. She was sensitive, responsive, sighing at his slightest touch, and it felt almost as though he was within her mind, experiencing the pleasure he himself bestowed.

He kissed her soft belly and his fingers slid beneath her

panties, gently easing them away from her white flesh. She lifted her bottom slightly to make his task easier, then suddenly tensed. 'The light,' she moaned, 'the light.'

'I like the light,' he told her. She whimpered again, but said nothing more. He slipped the panties slowly down her thighs, admiring the contrast of the pale pink fabric with her pale flesh. Then they were off and he stooped to kiss the hollows of her thighs, the delicate hollows next to the soft curling fur of her pubic mound.

Catherine moaned again, a helpless, quivering sound. He slid off the bed to kneel at her feet, still fully clothed, delighting himself with the anticipation of what he was about to do. He put his hands on her ankles and gently, deliberately pulled them apart. Catherine gave a little protesting cry and put one arm over her face.

'Catherine,' he whispered. He leant forward to admire the tracery of her sex, complex and curled as the inside of a shell, moist and soft and swollen with longing. She smelled sweet. For a moment he hung back, teasing himself and her with the promise of pleasure. Then, still slowly, still unhurriedly, he put his mouth on her.

She cried out, then smothered the sound into a whimper. Her legs tensed as if she would close them and push him away. He quickly set his palms to the inside of her thighs, pressing them apart, holding her open to him. He kissed, licked, sucked, very gently and slowly, searching out the rhythms of her body.

'Don't,' Catherine moaned. 'Don't, don't, don't.' Each time she moaned he repeated exactly what it was she was begging him not to do. She began to cry out, twisting beneath his caresses, her hungry loins lifting towards his working mouth. For a moment he slowed the pace, teasing her; and then, when she whimpered and writhed, he drew her clitoris into his mouth and sucked at it, harder and harder. Catherine let out a panicky sound that was almost a scream. Her hips began to jolt, thrusting upwards, and he knew that she needed to feel something within her, and just as she began to climax he slid one finger deep into her and twisted it and Catherine cried out, 'Oh God, oh God, oh God,' and her whole body convulsed into orgasm, buffeted by such strong spasms that he had to hold her quite hard to keep his mouth upon her.

When she was still he kissed her clitoris very gently and then lifted himself and lay down beside her, looking into her face. Her eyes were closed and she was panting. The skin of her throat was flushed scarlet with desire. He leant forward slowly and kissed her mouth, knowing that she would taste her own perfume on his lips and tongue, that his face was slippery with it.

She did not protest. Her response was languid, as if he had exhausted her. But when he moved away from her she grabbed at him, clutching at the fabric of his shirt and pulling him closer to her. 'Don't go,' she whispered frantically. 'Don't go.'

'I'm not going anywhere,' he said with a smile. She slumped back on to the bed, her hands above her head, eyes shut, breath coming fast.

He got up off the bed and began to undress. He did not hurry. He hung the shirt over the handle of the wardrobe, draped the tie around its collar, took his wallet out of his trousers, removed a condom from the wallet and laid it on the bedside table. Then he unbuttoned his trousers and unzipped the fly. Catherine heard the whine of the zip and pushed herself up on to her elbows, watching him open-mouthed. He unlaced his shoes, pulled them off, put one sock neatly into each shoe, then removed his trousers, folded them and laid them carefully on the dressing stool. His shorts followed them, and he was naked.

He turned to face her, his penis thrusting forth from his body, eager and erect. A tear of fluid glistened on the scarlet glans. Catherine rolled over on the bed and held out her hand to him, her expression soft with longing.

Before she had been afraid. Now she was satisfied and eager for more. He knelt down beside her and she reached out to him, lifting her shining mouth to his. They kissed, sharing her taste. Her tongue was active now, meeting his thrust for thrust, even daring to move towards his open lips. Her hand slipped down his body, feeling for the rigid shaft of his cock. She found it and gave a little sigh of delight as her hand explored its length and hardness.

Then, suddenly, she pulled away. 'Oh God,' she said helplessly, 'oh God, I haven't got one, I haven't got a condom. I didn't mean to do this.' She grabbed his hands and clutched them, saying earnestly, 'I'm sorry, I'm sorry. I don't usually go to bed with people on the first date.'

'It's all right,' he said, 'I've got one.' He nodded to the bedside table. 'As you see.'

She stared at him, then reached out and lifted the little packet. Her fingers moved hesitantly, as if she was not sure what to do. Slowly she tore open one corner and extracted the condom. Then she looked diffidently up at him.

Her uncertainty enthralled him. 'Like this,' he said, guiding her hand. Her fingers trembled as she rolled it on to his cock and he closed his eyes, breathing shallowly as he brought himself back under control. Then, when he was prepared, he pulled her close to him and laid her back upon the bed.

It was hot in the room. Catherine's limbs were slick with a sheen of sweat. His naked skin pressed against hers, sometimes gliding, sometimes sticking. She sighed and pushed herself against him, arching her hips upwards as if she invited him in. He held back, although the soft flesh between her legs was slippery with welcome. He wanted her to know what it was like to want him.

His cock slid between her legs and rubbed against her sex, stimulating her and teasing her. She dug her nails into his arms and pressed her breasts against him, gasping urgently. He let his erection rub against her labia until she was moaning and baring her teeth with need. Then, and only then, did he penetrate her.

As his penis entered her she clung to him. He thrust gently at first, testing her, finding out what gave her the most pleasure. His hands explored the curves of her breasts, his fingers stroked at her swollen nipples. She began to heave and sigh rhythmically and he went with her rhythm, pacing her, understanding her, and then when he knew the lift and fall of the waves of her body leading her, driving her onwards until she opened her eyes and stared at him in wild disbelief and flung her arms apart as if she was falling, helpless, tumbling naked through empty air.

The soft embrace of her sex tightened on his thrusting cock and the knowledge of her pleasure filled him with glory and he pressed his mouth on hers and kissed her as he came.

She tugged at his arms, pulling him down on top of her. He lowered himself gently, revelling in the feel of her body soft and relaxed beneath his. She clung to him, burying her head in his shoulder, and as she fell asleep he held her close and let his hands stray to his heart's content through her tumbled, sweat-streaked hair.

SIX
Wednesday Morning

Catherine had forgotten to set her alarm clock, but habit woke her just after six. At once, even before she opened her eyes, she relived the previous night. Just for a moment she was afraid that it had all been a dream, and she turned over quickly in the bed and sighed with relief when she saw John asleep beside her.

She relaxed back into the bed, her head pillowed on her arm, watching him sleeping. His face was very calm, his short silver-streaked hair hardly disarranged. She might have known that he would be as controlled, as poised sleeping as awake.

All night it had been hot. They had flung off the duvet, and lay naked on the bare bottom sheet. With a feeling of guilt and stealth she examined his body. In some ways he was unremarkable, neither particularly tall, nor particularly broad, nor particularly anything; a slim, fit, well cared-for man in his early forties. But he exuded a sense of physical rightness, of comfort and confidence in himself. She was not confident about herself, especially about herself naked, and she felt a surge of envy. How wonderful it must be to be like him, so certain, so assured –

– Such a good lover. She felt herself blushing. She had gone to bed with him on their first date, something she had never done in her life. All right, she had wanted him. She had enjoyed their meal as she had scarcely ever enjoyed a meal with a man. He seemed to be really interested in her, he wanted to listen to her, he even seemed to understand her. And after they got home – For a moment she wondered how on earth she would tell him that last night was the best sex she had ever had. Then she decided that she didn't have to tell him. If he was the mind-reader he had seemed to be, he would already know. And if he wasn't, she didn't want him to get complacent.

She glanced at the clock and gasped as she saw the time. She was just swinging her legs off the bed when behind her John stirred and reached out to catch hold of her arm. 'Where are you going?' said his warm, velvet voice.

'Hello.' She turned, embarrassed now that his brilliant eyes were seeing her naked in the early morning light. 'I'm sorry, John, but I've got an early meeting. I have to get ready.' She leant forward to kiss his cheek.

He caught her face in his hand and steered her mouth to his. He kissed her as he had done last night, so searchingly that it took her breath away. He did not touch her body, but she was uncomfortably aware that his penis was already hard, glistening with morning eagerness. Then he lifted his mouth and said, 'I usually go for a run at this time. Some sort of exercise is essential.'

'I can't.' He was smiling, but he looked very determined. She remembered how he had held her wrists to the sheets last night, strong and insistent. 'John, I can't. I'm really sorry. Tonight perhaps.'

'I quite agree that we shouldn't hurry,' he said. His hand lifted to her hair and began to stroke through it, teasing out the night's tangles. 'So,' he went on calmly, 'why don't you just do something for me, and we'll call it quits?'

'What?' She stared, staggered. What was he suggesting?

His eyes narrowed, but his face was quite still. He didn't seem to think that this was anything out of the ordinary. He certainly didn't look as if he expected her to refuse. 'Use your mouth on me,' he said, his pale lips framing each word like a kiss.

She shook her head. How could he ask her in such a matter of fact way? Of course she'd sucked men before now, but not just like that, not first thing in the morning, waking up and having a bit of fellatio just for the hell of it. It was something that happened, well, in the throes of passion.

Even so, the idea had a sort of indecent appeal. She couldn't stop herself from glancing down at his penis, and as she did so it twitched, jerking up towards her as if it would ask her itself if only it could talk. Her mouth was dry, and she realised that she wanted to know what he tasted like. But she was acutely aware of the time, and if she let him interfere now with her morning routine and her work she would be setting a precedent that she would regret later. 'John,' she said, adopting a bright no-nonsense tone, 'I can't. I've got to get up.'

She began to move away, but suddenly he caught hold of her arms and spun her around and pressed her down to the sheets, his naked body heavy on top of hers. The heat of his erection seared against her belly. He looked down into her face and said with a smile, 'Catherine, you have to get your priorities right.'

Before she could reply his lips pressed to hers. Now his kiss was hard, fierce, demanding. It made her gasp and jolted her body into a state of sudden expectant readiness. Her breasts ached and the muscles of her sex clenched together, a quick, tight spasm of need. She moaned, and suddenly her meeting didn't seem important.

He wrenched his mouth away from hers and dug his strong fingers into her hair, then lay back comfortably on the pillows and the rumpled duvet. 'Now,' he said, and he steered her head towards his loins.

She let him guide her. A delicious sensation of wickedness made her shiver. How self-indulgent, to make love first thing in the morning! And his penis was beautiful, very smooth and hard. He smelt of warm male and last night's sex. His legs were spread slightly and she tentatively put her hand on his thigh, then slid it up to cradle his taut balls. He sighed, then tightened his fingers in her hair.

Obeying his silent command, she licked her lips, then drew her tongue along the length of his cock from the root to the tip. As she did so she felt a shudder of urgent desire. She would like to feel him inside her, as she had last night, filling

115

her and stroking her to a pinnacle of such pleasure that she had beaten her head upon the pillows like a madwoman.

He tasted exquisite, and the tip of his cock was softer than thistledown. With a little whimper of pleasure and need she let the shining glans slip between her lips and began to suck, sliding her mouth rhythmically up and down his shaft. He took a long breath, then said softly, 'That's good.'

As her lips moved he began to breathe deeply and steadily, tensing his buttocks in time with her caresses so that his cock slid a little into her mouth and then withdrew. Her lips tingled and ached and her vagina clutched at emptiness. The tips of her breasts were hard, scratching teasingly against the hairs on his thighs. Her whole body was sensitised, aroused. After a few minutes she had to touch herself. It felt dirty, lewd, but she slid her hand between her legs, feeling for the swollen stem of her clitoris, finding it, stroking it.

Then he was gripping her arm, pulling her hand away. His other hand was still in her hair, holding her head steady. 'Don't,' he said in a soft stern voice. 'Concentrate.'

She wanted to protest, but she couldn't. Her mouth was full of his cock. He held her wrist tightly and her whole body began to fill with a warm ache of desire, exacerbated by the lengthening thrusts of his hard shaft between her lips. His fingers dug into her scalp, holding her still, making it impossible for her to move away. He gasped and began to move faster, and she realised that he was going to come in her mouth. For a moment she strained against him, tense with resistance. Then suddenly she couldn't resist any more. He was fucking her mouth, thrusting his cock into her throat so deeply that she almost gagged, and it was blissful. It was like freedom. She moaned with delirious pleasure and sucked greedily at his shuddering cock and felt the semen rising in it, throbbing right through the shaft and spurting at last into her mouth. She swallowed again and again, then gently, diligently licked him clean.

Now her whole body was softened with desire. She remembered how beautifully he had caressed her with his mouth and she rolled over on the bed, holding out her arms to him. 'My turn,' she suggested.

He raised himself on one elbow and smiled at her, a smile creamy with satisfaction. 'I'm afraid not. You were in a hurry, as I recall.'

And without another word he got up off the bed and walked confidently into the bathroom. She couldn't believe it. 'John,' she called, 'John! That's not fair!'

Her only answer was the sound of the shower.

'My God,' said Fielding, 'I wish the Plain English campaign applied to forensic reports.'

Anderson did not find complex English a problem. Normally he would have made a sharp response to Fielding's complaint, but this morning he was sleek and relaxed, a full-fed predator. Like a cat adjusting its fur with one or two lazy licks, he smoothed the lapels of his jacket and smiled at her. 'The gist of it,' he said, 'is that neither the palmar nor the unmatched thumbprint belong to Elaine Williams.'

Fielding frowned at the report, then set it down. 'You saw her on your own, sir. What was she like?'

For a moment he considered Fielding's concentrated, earnest face. Some women were enhanced by smiling, and Fielding had a cheerful, cheeky grin, but her face when thoughtful had an intensity and focus which was just as attractive, though in a quite different way. This morning, sated and replete, he could look at her without a spark of that electrical force which had flowed between them yesterday. In fact, the night with Catherine had done him a vast amount of good. He had been sitting at his desk for most of the morning, and Julia Bond's wide eyes and wet lips had not appeared to him once.

He needed to respond to Fielding. 'She's not bright,' he said. 'A spectacular woman physically, strong and fit.'

'Typical Eddie,' commented Fielding, with a wry face.

'Quite. She lied to me about several things, and I think there's a man living with her.'

'Really? Already?' Fielding looked surprised and disapproving. 'But she told you that she gave the key back to Eddie.'

'I think she was lying.'

'Well,' said Fielding after a moment, 'sir, you know I think that Sealey is probably our man, but if Elaine has a boyfriend, is it possible that she gave him the key? She wanted revenge on Drax, after all. Maybe, I don't know, maybe she sent her boyfriend round to the house to steal a few things, and Eddie was there, and one thing led to another.'

'Pat, that's pure speculation,' Anderson said chastisingly.

Fielding made a face. 'It's possible, though, isn't it?'

He looked into Fielding's brown eyes, letting his mind run again over the suspects. It was untidy to have so many people in the frame. Why couldn't Sealey or Julia Bond have had a reasonable alibi, something worth attacking? 'You're right. It's time we got the truth out of Miss Williams. It'll be better if there are two of us.'

'Oh, what fun,' grinned Fielding. 'Do we get to play nice and nasty?'

'You make it sound like a party game. Which do you want to be?'

Fielding took a quick breath and put back her shoulders. 'I'd like to be nasty, sir, if it's all right with you. Women always get to be nice. I need to expand my range.'

'Whatever you like.'

Elaine rolled over in bed and ran her hand down Alan's brown muscled back. She smiled, watching him sleep. They had known each other for years, since they were kids. Even when she had been living with Eddie Alan would come round to the house on his free days and take her out. She had felt guilty, but she could never say no to him. He had made love to her, too, and she had done it knowing that she was two-timing and knowing that Eddie would be angry. But what could she do? She loved Alan, and she hadn't loved Eddie. She had been with him for the money.

If Eddie hadn't found out about Alan, he might even have married her. He had been all set to propose. If only he had! After a few months she'd have caught him with someone, that little receptionist at the golf club, maybe. Then the divorce, and half of Eddie's money, and Alan would never have had to carry another hod.

She sighed deeply and sat up in the rumpled bed, rubbing her eyes. Alan was fast asleep, his head buried in the pillows. For a moment she admired his back. He was already tanned a deep mahogany brown, and his wide shoulders were smooth and rippled with muscle. If only he had a bit more discipline, a bit more patience, he could really work at the body building and get himself a job as a Chippendale. It would make her jealous, but it would beat labouring. But he was too lazy.

She looked at the clock and rolled her eyes. Eleven already! Who was she calling lazy? Well, Alan wasn't working, and there was no rush. She slapped his taut bare buttock and said, 'Want some tea?'

'Mmph,' Alan responded. Elaine swung her long sleek legs out of the bed and stretched. There was a full length mirror on the wall, and she examined herself in it with close attention. With her build she'd never be a model, but she was determined that every inch of her was going to stay as firm and strong as she could make it.

She went through to the kitchen to make the tea. She heard Alan in the bathroom and clinked the mugs together encouragingly. When he appeared in the kitchen, naked and frowsty and rubbing his hand through his long blond hair, she said, 'You awake?'

'Dopy.' He licked his finger and stuck it in the sugar bowl. Elaine shook her head. She tried to make him eat well, but it was like rolling a stone uphill.

'I still can't believe I cocked up that interview yesterday,' she said, stirring the tea. 'I'll never get out of this dump unless I get another job.'

'Never mind, love,' Alan said. That was one reason she loved him. He was very good natured, and he always saw the bright side. 'Plenty of jobs left in the world.'

She turned round into his arms. 'You're sweet, Alan.'

He hugged her and muttered into her ear, ''Cause I love you, that's why.'

He always sounded as if it was embarrassing to admit it. She laughed and kissed him on the mouth. He growled and held her more tightly.

119

Then a sharp ring on the doorbell made them both jump. 'You expecting anyone?' Alan asked her.

'No.' The doorbell rang again and she frowned and went over to look out of the window.

Below her on the doorstep stood two people, a man and a woman. The man had dark hair streaked with grey and he was wearing a pale green suit. She clutched at her suddenly cold stomach. 'Christ! it's the police, back again. It's that Inspector Anderson.'

'God almighty,' Alan said, 'what'll they say if they find me here?'

'Quick, get dressed. You can go out the door, they'll think you came from downstairs. I'll tell them –' She pushed the window open and leant out and yelled, 'Hang on, I haven't got any clothes on! I'll be down in a minute.'

Alan dashed into the bedroom and threw on the T-shirt and shorts he had worn yesterday, then ran to the door. "'Bye,' Elaine said, waving to him as she stuck her head into a Lycra cropped top. It never hurt to look attractive, even if Anderson had brought a woman with him this time.

A few minutes later she sauntered down the stairs and opened the door, trying to appear cool. 'Hello,' she said, giving Anderson her very best smile.

He smiled back. He was a real looker, if you liked them his size. His smile was warmer than she remembered. 'Hello,' he said. 'Back again, as you see. My colleague Detective Sergeant Fielding. Can you spare us a few minutes?'

Elaine glanced at the woman. She was smallish and slight and she didn't look friendly at all. Her pale face was set in an expression not far short of a scowl. Why had Anderson had to bring her? 'Sure,' she said, returning her eyes, and her smile, to Anderson. She knew where she was with men. 'Come on up.'

'D'you want a cup of tea?' she asked as she opened the front door.

'We're on duty,' the woman snapped.

'Actually, I'd love one,' Anderson said.

Elaine brightened, pleased, and went through to the kitchen. 'I went and gave a statement, like you said,' she told him. 'And

120

they took my fingerprints. It was quite exciting really, like a TV show.'

'Miss Williams,' said Sergeant Fielding, 'it's your statement we've come to discuss.'

Elaine swallowed hard. The pit of her stomach was hollow. 'Really?' she managed, hearing her voice shake.

'You see,' Anderson explained gently, 'it didn't quite stack up.'

She was about to protest, but before she could get a word out the woman sergeant pushed closer to her and said softly, 'You've been lying to us, Elaine. Haven't you?'

'I –' The words stuck in her throat. She looked helplessly across at Anderson, as if he would save her. He smiled at her kindly, but shook his head.

'Do you know that it's an offence to make false statements?' Fielding demanded. Elaine stared down at her, petrified. The woman looked as fierce as a wildcat. 'A criminal offence?'

'I didn't!' Elaine said wildly. 'Who says I did? Who says?'

'Your statement,' said the policewoman, 'is a load of bollocks.'

'It's not.'

'You went to the movies, did you? And you saw a film with Alec Baldwin? Which, by the way, didn't start or finish at the times you said. What happened in the film, Elaine? Have you had a chance to go and see it yet, to make a better story?'

Hadn't she seen on TV that the police weren't allowed to bully people? 'You can't do this to me. You can't just say that. I did what you wanted.' She appealed desperately to Anderson. 'I said what I was doing.'

'Who is your boyfriend, Elaine?' demanded Fielding. 'Who are you protecting?'

'Protecting?' Elaine was shocked almost speechless. Christ, oh Christ, they wanted to make it look as though Alan killed Eddie! If they knew what had really happened on Saturday – 'Nobody,' she insisted. 'No one. I haven't got a boyfriend.'

'Who passed us on the doorstep, then?' demanded the sergeant scornfully.

'I don't know. I don't know. The guy from downstairs.'

121

'Why did we hear him coming down the stairs, then? Why are there two mugs there?' The terrible little policewoman stuck out her hand, pointing at the remnants of their undrunk tea on the kitchen counter.

Elaine felt herself going scarlet. She couldn't help it. She tried to think of some other explanation, something, anything. But what exactly had she said before? If she said one thing, then another wouldn't work – Words whizzed round and round in her mind, leading nowhere. The sergeant was glaring at her furiously. It was like a nightmare. She tried a couple of times to say something, but in the end she hid her face in her hands and burst into tears.

After a moment she felt Anderson's hands on her shoulders, holding her. He was stronger than he looked. 'It's all right,' he said.

'It's not!' she wailed.

'Look.' His voice was very kind and reasonable. 'Elaine, I don't believe you had anything to do with Eddie's death.' She looked up at that. Did he mean it? 'Why don't you just tell me what you were really doing on Saturday? Then we can forget about all this.'

He was so calm and soothing. She sniffed violently, then gulped, 'Do you really believe it wasn't me?'

'Really. But you have to tell us the truth.'

She nodded and swallowed hard. Anderson kept his arm round her shoulders and led her across the room to the sofa. 'Now, sit down. Tell me what really happened.'

The sergeant had folded her arms and was watching her with an expression of undisguised scorn. Elaine was afraid of her. She couldn't speak.

'Well?' Anderson's voice, gentle and insistent.

'Oh.' What could she say? How much was it safe to tell him? 'All right. I do have a boyfriend. That's him you saw just now, Alan. Alan Banks.'

'Nice piece of rough,' commented Sergeant Fielding.

'Sergeant, please,' said Anderson. Fielding snorted and subsided.

'I didn't want to say about him,' she ran on, in a hurry now to get things out while they were straight in her head, 'because of Eddie, I mean, if Eddie's accountant knew, then I wouldn't stand any chance of getting any money from Eddie's will, would I?'

'You don't stand any chance anyway,' said the sergeant.

Bitch! The last thing Elaine wanted was to be reminded of what that accountant woman had told her. She thought a little, wondering how much was safe, then ventured uncertainly, 'I was with Alan on Saturday.'

She looked up into Anderson's eyes. He nodded slowly, gazing at her intently, like a cat watching a mouse. She was going to have to be careful. 'We went out to the pub about eight,' she said, 'just for a quick one, but there was nobody there we knew, so we left about nine and went to the video shop and got a video out to watch.'

'With Alec Baldwin?' asked the sergeant caustically.

'No.' She could feel herself flushing, but what was the point in hiding it? They would go to the shop and check up on her. 'It was *Electric Blue*.'

The woman laughed, but Anderson's face didn't change. 'What time was that?'

'I suppose we left about 9.30. Maybe a bit later. And then we went to the Indian takeaway down the road, the Curry Mahal, and we ordered a meal and we had to sit and wait till it came.' Careful now. She didn't need to lie, just stretch the truth a bit. And make sure that nobody could say any different.

'How long did you wait for the meal?'

She shrugged. 'Not sure. It gets really busy in there on Saturdays.' All true! It was always really busy in the Curry Mahal, and Anderson didn't know that she and Alan always ordered the quickest things on the menu to cut down their waiting time. 'I didn't notice. We were – busy.'

'Busy doing what?' demanded Sergeant Fielding.

Now the blush was helpful. 'Snogging.'

Fielding's face showed what she thought of someone whose idea of a hot Saturday night out was snogging in an Indian takeaway. Elaine dreaded another scathing remark, but none appeared. Anderson said, 'So when did you get home?'

'Not sure, really. About half past eleven, I suppose.' There! All done. And she was sure they hadn't noticed.

'Is the video shop a club?' Anderson asked her.

'Yes.' She jumped to her feet and found the club card so that they had her membership number. Yes, she thought the shop used a computer, it would show that she took the video out. Yes, they knew them at the Curry Mahal, a bit, anyway.

When she ground to a halt Anderson stood in front of her and looked into her face. His eyes were almost level with hers, but somehow he felt bigger. 'Elaine,' he said, 'are you sure that you're telling us the truth this time?'

'Yes,' she said faintly. Don't blush now, she begged her cheeks. Don't blush.

'Now,' Anderson said, 'what about that key, Elaine?'

She bit her lip. 'I've still got it. Here, on my key ring.'

She found her handbag and dived in it for the key ring. The sergeant said sharply, 'Wait! Don't touch it,' and brought a plastic bag out of the pocket of her trousers. 'Which key is it?' she asked.

'This one,' Elaine said faintly. She noticed, for the first time in ages, that the key ring was one Alan had given her as a joke, in the shape of two skeletons bonking. The sergeant handled it as if it smelt. Elaine was agonised with embarrassment. She watched apprehensively as Fielding detached the key, using the bag as a makeshift glove.

'Have you had the key all the time?' Anderson asked her.

'Yes. Ever since I left.'

'You haven't given it to anyone else?'

She could look him in the eyes now. 'No. Honest. Nobody. It's been on my key ring the whole time.' That, at least, was true.

And that seemed to be all. The sergeant lectured her on making false statements and Anderson looked at her very quietly and then they left. When the door closed behind them she didn't know whether to be pleased that she'd managed to put them off the scent or frightened that they would find her out. In the end she got on to her exercise bike and pedalled a fast five miles, to give her heart an excuse for racing.

'Very convincing,' Anderson said to Fielding as they climbed

124

back into the BMW. 'I expected you to beat her up at any moment.'

Fielding laughed. 'A lot of it wasn't an act, to be honest, sir. I can't bear these great big strong women who behave as if they're made out of cotton wool. Look at her, for Christ's sake. She's twice my size, and she falls into your arms as if you'll pat her on the head and tell her not to be a bad girl.'

'What did you think of her story this time?' he asked. He wondered whether Fielding's acting had affected her judgement.

'Most of it was true, sir, I'd say, but she's not being entirely straight with us. Did you see her face?'

'Yes, I saw it.'

'She was honest about the key, I think, but not about her evening. I'll check up on it. And I'll check up on Banks, too. I got a good look at him. I'll ask if any of the lads know him. He looked like a brickie to me.'

'Good. Get the details of her evening pinned down as closely as you can. If she still had that key, maybe it was as you suggested. You could try and track down Banks, too, and see if he corroborates her story.'

Fielding grinned at him. 'I tell you what, sir. You leave me here, and I'll wait until Banks reappears and then get his side of the story.'

He raised an eyebrow. 'What makes you so eager to interview the formidable Mr Banks?'

'Like I told Elaine,' said Fielding, still grinning. 'He looks like a nice bit of rough.' She opened the car door, ready to get out. 'What about you, sir? What will you do now?'

That had been occupying his mind, too. 'I still don't think Elaine did it,' he said. 'She hasn't got the nerve, and she's not bright enough. Someone very organised murdered Eddie Drax. I keep thinking about the key man insurance policy.'

'Julia Bond,' nodded Fielding.

'That's right.'

'I think it's Sealey,' said Fielding, after a pause.

He smiled. 'Time will tell. Anyway, this afternoon I'm going back to Drax & Bond. Enjoy yourself with Banks, Pat.'

'Trust me,' Fielding said, and slammed the door.

SEVEN
Wednesday Afternoon

Anderson was hungry. He had gone home to shave and change after leaving Catherine, but he had not had time for his usual breakfast. He drove from Elaine's house into the middle of the town and visited a smart sandwich bar for a mozzarella, tomato and basil ciabatta and a large espresso. As he ate he thought about Catherine. She had left the house in a tearing hurry, and she had been angry with him, so they hadn't made any arrangement for the evening. But he thought that she would respond favourably if he called her. She had gone to work wearing a form-fitting body under her business suit.

He decided in the end not to call her straight away. A little waiting never did anyone any harm, and he felt a desire to have completed his business with Julia Bond before making contact with Catherine again. It was as if Julia's smouldering, arrogant sexuality might contaminate whatever he and Catherine arranged. Better to leave it until later.

The sandwich was delicious. He ate it slowly, enjoying the combination of flavours. They were using a different sort of olive oil, and it was a distinct improvement. When it was finished he wiped his hands very carefully on the paper napkin, swallowed the last of his coffee, and set off for Drax & Bond.

Julia knew that Chief Inspector Anderson was waiting in reception, but she didn't rush her meeting. She was with an important client, one of Eddie's old clients, and it was taking all her skill to reassure him that his account would be just as safe in her hands. Anderson would have to wait. She had no desire to be helpful to him, and in any case, her business came first.

At 3.45 she finished the meeting and let Denise show the client out. 'You can bring back Chief Inspector Anderson,' she said, 'if he's still there.'

Then she went back to her desk and called the receptionist. 'Bev, it's Julia. Has Denise picked up that policeman?'

'Yes, he's just gone.'

'Was he angry at being kept waiting?'

'Didn't seem to be,' Bev replied cautiously.

That was aggravating. But then Anderson was super cool, he didn't show much. She smoothed her hair and checked that her clothes were perfect. They were, of course. She smiled. Her last encounter with Anderson had been very – stimulating. How far would she be able to push him this time?

'Chief Inspector Anderson,' said Denise at the door.

He looked as she remembered, groomed and sleek. Today the suit was single-breasted, in a pale olive shade that must be the devil to keep clean. He didn't look hot or annoyed, although he had been waiting more than an hour.

'Good afternoon, Baron Scarpia,' she said as Denise closed the door.

'Miss Bond. Thank you for rearranging your diary to suit me.'

The nickname irritated him, as she had intended. He didn't show it overtly, but the barbed comment revealed it. She was having an effect. 'I have a business to run,' she said coldly. She sat down in her chair, pushed it away from the desk and crossed her ankles. Her short skirt rode dutifully up her thighs, revealing a decent length of glossy leg.

'I'm sure,' he said, 'that business will be made a good deal easier by a cash injection of £5m.'

She took a long breath and leant back in her chair. The position showed off her breasts, and the flicker of his eyes registered the movement. 'Well,' she said slowly. 'Who told you about the key man?'

'Your finance director.'

His eyes were fastened on her face. He hadn't sat down, although a visitor's chair was right beside him. His presence was very commanding. He seemed to own the space in which he stood. She could imagine him knowing exactly what he wanted in bed. So did she and he wasn't it, but he wasn't to know that. She licked her lips sensuously. 'So,' she said, 'does that mean that you think I killed Eddie?'

'I'm not accusing you. I'm not cautioning you. This is just a preliminary interview.'

'But you want to accuse me.' All his attention was focused on her. It was actually rather flattering. If only she could manage it so that he made a pass at her. She would have him up on a disciplinary charge before he knew where he was. That would keep him off her back.

'Did you think that Eddie would obstruct the Dacre deal?' he asked her.

She could lie to him, of course, just to confuse him and muddy the waters even further. It would be fun to lie to him. He was so bloody cool, he deserved to be shaken. But lies weren't necessary. It would be more challenging to go along with him, to answer his questions truthfully and still to put him off. She said slowly, 'Yes, I did. He was such an awkward sod sometimes. And he'd got it into his head that he didn't like the Dacre directors.'

'What were you doing about it?'

'I was talking to him.' He was still standing up. She sprawled in her chair, literally looking up at him. He thought he was so cold and powerful. He didn't realise that she was the one calling the shots. She knew what he wanted, and that put her in a very strong position to make sure he didn't get it.

'What do you mean, you were talking to him?'

'I knew Eddie. I was talking to him, trying to persuade him. It was possible, if you knew what you were doing. In fact,' she said, 'that's what I was talking to him about on Saturday night.' This was skating on very thin ice, but she wanted to see his face brighten as she drew him nearer to the crux.

She was right. His eyes glittered and his chin lifted very

slightly, as if he had caught a scent. 'You were talking to him about the Dacre deal?'

'I was shouting at him.'

'Is that the sort of persuasion you favour?'

You don't know that I'm persuading you at this very minute, Baron Scarpia. 'I was angry. He was being so bloody stubborn.'

'You were angry with him.'

'That's what I said. He'd been drinking, he was being bloody minded just for the hell of it. So I was angry. This was our business he was mucking about with.'

'So what did you do?'

'I left.'

'You just left.'

'I just left. What do you expect me to say, that I let him drink himself under the table and then stuffed him in his Porsche? Is that what you think?'

Anderson was silent. She could almost have laughed. His face was as keen as a hawk's. He wasn't going to accuse her to her face, not now, but that's what he believed. She tilted her head back and licked her lips again. 'Perhaps if you beat me up a little I might confess,' she suggested, with arch humour.

'I doubt that will be necessary.'

His voice was absolutely even. Why was she not having the desired effect? Frustrated, she uncrossed her legs and leant forward, planting her elbows on the desk and looking up into his face. Something a little stronger, perhaps. 'If this is going to be a proper interrogation scene, like *Basic Instinct,* then I think I ought to take my knickers off and spread my legs.'

That got to him all right. His nostrils flared and his head went back. 'I told you, this is a preliminary interview. You're not under caution. If you think my behaviour is oppressive, you'd better call your solicitor.'

'I don't think that will be necessary,' she purred. 'It's not easy to oppress me. I can handle you all on my own.' Was that suggestive enough? She let her face look as if she would really like to handle him, to pull his trousers open and grab his cock and feel its heat and hardness. Her eyes rested significantly on his fly for a moment, then returned to his.

He was watching her, there was no doubt of it. She gave his crotch one last, long, lingering stare. 'So, what's the next question?'

'What happened before you left Eddie's house?'

'I told you, I shouted at him. I said that the Dacre deal was our chance to make a fortune. He said he didn't want to work for a poxy bunch of corporate financiers. I told him he was a stupid prick and he said I had no artistic integrity. I said there was no artistic integrity in graphic design and he was in it for the money just like me. Then he started laughing. So I left.'

'What state was he in when you left?'

'Pissed as a rat. He could hardly stand up. He'd drunk the best part of half a bottle of whisky. He turned the telly on just as I was leaving.'

'What time was that?'

She laughed. 'God, Baron Scarpia, do you really think you're going to catch me out? As I said days ago, I left his house about 7.45 and drove straight home.'

'As I recall,' he said coldly, 'when I first spoke to you you said that Eddie was extremely cheerful when you left him. Now you tell me that you had been arguing.'

'I told you he was laughing when I left. If that's not happy, what is?'

For a moment he stared at her, eyes narrowed as if he was thinking. Then he leant forward and rested his hands on the desk, bringing his face close to hers. 'How do I know you didn't go back there later?'

His breath was warm and smelled of basil, a hot sexy smell. What would he do if she leant forward and kissed him? But that would be no good. He had to be the one making the move. She would go on teasing him. What was the risk? If he had any evidence, he would already have arrested her. He thought he was playing with her, but he had it back to front. 'You don't,' she said. 'You've only got my word for it, haven't you?'

'Tell me what you were doing.'

'I was watching *Tosca* on the television,' she said softly. Her eyes were fastened on his pale mouth. His lips were slightly parted, just revealing his teeth and his tongue. Hooked! Time to turn up the heat. 'I was sitting in my chair watching the television. During the first act I drank a gin and tonic and ate half of a packet of Pringles. During the second act,' she moistened her lips with her tongue, 'I masturbated.'

He did not move, but the pupils of his eyes dilated. 'You masturbated.'

'I told you, it's a sexy opera. The man singing Baron Scarpia was gorgeous. He looked like you. I had one hand on my breast and the other hand between my legs and when he pinned Tosca to the table and kissed her I,' a little pause, just to increase the effect, 'I had an orgasm.'

He did not respond. 'And when you had achieved your orgasm,' he said in an icy voice, 'what did you do?'

'I watched the rest of the opera and went to bed.'

'You could have driven back to Eddie's house.'

'I could. But I didn't.' She parted her lips more in a snarl than a smile. 'If you believe that I did, Baron Scarpia, why don't you just prove it?'

He pushed himself away from the desk, his mouth setting into an angry line. 'You can't, can you?' she mocked him. 'You haven't got any evidence. You know I was at the house with him, but you can't prove I killed him, can you? Or you'd have arrested me.' She lay back again in her chair, arms spread wide, legs parted, a parody of helplessness. 'Oh, do arrest me, Baron Scarpia. Please.'

His face was rigid. 'I don't intend to arrest you. Not now.'

'Oh, please do. I'd love it.'

He gave her a sudden wolfish smile. 'That, Miss Bond, is the main reason why I do not intend to do it.'

Before she could think of a reply he turned and walked to the door of the office, opened it and left. The door closed behind him. She scowled and bit at her lower lip and thumped the arms of her chair with her fists. He had more control than she had expected. That was a bloody nuisance.

But still, it had been a most satisfying interview. Next time he would make a move, she was certain of it. And then she would have him just where she wanted him.

★

Anderson stood outside the closed door for a few moments, recovering his composure. On the surface his mind was calm, but he knew that beneath the surface he was seething.

He had expected to enjoy the interview. He had expected to find Julia as alluring as she had appeared two days ago. But he had been wrong. She had licked her lips and flaunted her body at him without subtlety, talking about masturbation and orgasms as if it would arouse him rather than disgust him.

She had been taunting him too, leaving him waiting in reception like a supplicant and then challenging him to prove her guilty. Did she think this was the perfect crime? Did she think he couldn't prove it? For a moment he was viscerally certain that Julia had killed Eddie. She had the motive, she admitted she had been there, she was cool enough not to let a man's life stand between her and a small fortune. And she was obviously determined to make the investigation as difficult for him as possible.

But this was irrational. The obvious suspect was Tony Sealey. One piece of clear forensic evidence and he would have Sealey arrested. Why was he suddenly so determined that Julia was the culprit? Just because he had found her initially attractive but had now revised his opinion?

His mind was whirling. With grim determination he set the thoughts and emotions aside and concentrated on the case. There were other angles to it, not just Eddie's murder. While he was at Drax & Bond he might as well follow them up.

It had taken no more than a few seconds for him to think things through. When Julia's secretary put down the telephone and asked politely, 'Can I show you out?' he replied as if he had planned to all along, 'I'd like to drop by the accounts department first.'

'Oh,' said Denise uncertainly. 'There've been so many policemen here, it's taken up so much time. I should ask Julia – but she doesn't want to be disturbed. If you don't mind waiting a few minutes –'

'Actually,' he said through his teeth, 'I would mind. I've waited long enough this afternoon. I know the way, thank you.'

She didn't object. He stalked down the corridor towards David Thompson's office, still wrestling with the irrationality of his feelings about Julia.

Samantha Smith was sitting at her desk in the open area of the accounts department. She saw him approaching, gave him a single malevolent look, got up, picked up her bag and moved unhurriedly away.

He watched her go, then presented himself at Lisa Cresswell's desk. She stared at him, startled. 'Ooh, Mr Anderson. Hello.'

'Good afternoon. I'd like to speak to David Thompson, if that's possible.'

Lisa shook her pretty head. 'I'm sorry, Mr Anderson, he's already gone home. He's going out tonight. He's got a big dinner with some people up in London.'

He was put out. For a moment he thought that Thompson had purposefully planned his meeting to be irritating. Then he recognised that the feeling was absurd. He was oversensitive because Julia had rattled him. 'Never mind,' he made himself say. 'Is he in tomorrow?'

'Not first thing, he's got a meeting at the bank. But after that he is. Shall I pencil you in to his diary?'

The phrase made him sound like a graffito. 'Not yet,' he said. 'I'll call you tomorrow.' The results on the comparison of Sealey's fingerprints with those found at Drax's house were due back at any time. If they matched, he might be too busy to concern himself with a potential fraud, no matter how appetising the perpetrator.

'All right, then,' Lisa said. She glanced over at Sam's empty desk and dropped her voice. 'Did you go to see Sam, then?'

He nodded. Lisa's eyes brightened. 'Did you see the boyfriend?'

'No,' he said with private irony, 'I didn't.'

Lisa looked discontented. 'Damn. I really wanted to know who he was.'

He leant on Lisa's desk. 'Lisa, you seem to have a good grasp of what goes on at Drax & Bond. Have you worked here long?'

'About a year,' Lisa said. She looked flattered, which was

his intention. 'It's my first proper job, actually. I was straight out of college. And I'm working for the finance director! It looks brilliant on my CV. My next job I'm going to try to work up in London as a PA to a director. Some of them have secretaries working for them, you know, so they don't have to do any typing.'

'You don't like typing.'

'Oh, I prefer organising stuff. You know, meetings and travel and things. And if I worked for a director who travelled a lot, I might get to go abroad with him. Club class.'

He wasn't interested in Lisa's career fantasies. 'I wondered,' he said carefully, 'what sort of a relationship you thought that David and Samantha have.'

Her pretty face became very still. 'What d'you mean?'

'Not sure,' he said easily. 'Anything. What are they like?'

'I don't know what you're getting at,' Lisa said. She was suddenly defensive and closed. Her arms crept together and wrapped in front of her as if they were going to protect her from some sort of assault. He remained silent, looking down at her with his eyebrows raised. 'There's nothing. I mean, Sam works for David. That's all.'

He was about to ask her something else, but she pulled a piece of paper towards her and set it up on her typing stand. 'I'm busy,' she said. 'I can't talk now. I'll tell David you wanted to see him.'

What was she hiding? What was going on in the accounts department? If Sam and David were engaged in some sort of fraud, it wasn't impossible that Lisa was involved as well. But in that case, why should she have been so stupid as to call his attention to Sam's expensive lifestyle?

He waited for a few moments, but there was no sign of Sam. He walked to the window and looked out at the car park. The red sports car was no longer in its slot.

This was discouraging. There seemed to be no point in remaining at Drax & Bond. His investigation team had spent several man days questioning the staff in all departments. There would be little if anything that he could add. He left the building, hurried across the steamy humidity of the car park, reached the BMW and turned on the air conditioning. Then he contacted Fielding, hoping for a piece of good news to cheer him up. 'It's Anderson here. Anything on Sealey's prints?'

'No, sir, I'm sorry.' Fielding sounded tired, too. 'There was some sort of a delay with the comparison. They're not expecting anything until tomorrow morning.'

'All right. How did you get on with the redoubtable Mr Banks?'

'I didn't.' She sounded as if she wanted to swear and was restraining herself. 'He never came back to the house. He hasn't got a record that I've found yet. I'm asking around, but I think if I want to interview him I'll have to go back to Elaine and find out where he lives when he's not with her. Sorry, sir.'

'I'm sorry for you. You seemed to be looking forward to it.' He paused for a moment, running over what he might achieve if he returned to his desk. Relatively little. 'In that case, I think I'll call it a day. See you in the morning, Pat.'

'OK. 'Bye, sir.'

He hung up and sat for a few minutes in thought. This feeling of aimlessness was a familiar feature of the mid-point of a case, when a great many things had been uncovered and too few of them had yet been tied together. He could tell that Fielding felt it too. She wanted Tony Sealey to be guilty. She must be very irritated by the delay in the fingerprint comparison.

Well, there was one course of action open to him which would compensate for the disappointment of finding that Julia Bond was cheap. He dialled Catherine's number.

After one ring her soft voice answered. 'Catherine Marshall.'

'Catherine, hello.'

There was silence. Then she said, rather unsteadily he thought, 'John. Hello. Just a minute.' The phone crackled and he heard her saying, very faintly, 'I'll come back to you in a minute. I need to take this call.' Then, the correct volume again, 'Sorry about that.'

'I'm disturbing you.'

'It's all right, it's a member of staff, not a client. They can come back.'

'How are you?' he asked quietly.

Another long pause. Then she said in a husky voice, 'I'm –
I'm fine.'

'I'd like to see you tonight, if you're free.'

'Tonight?' She sounded almost shocked.

'Since I've seen your house I thought you might like to
see mine. I'd like to make you dinner.'

He listened for a moment to her breathing. Then she said,
'All right. I mean, yes please. That would be lovely.'

'Great. Can you make it around eight? Will that give you
enough time?'

'Where do you live?'

He gave her instructions. 'It's easy to find, there's nothing
near it. It's the top floor flat.'

'Eight o'clock, then.' She sounded brighter now, as if she
was looking forward to it. 'What shall I bring?'

'Yourself,' he said with a smile, 'and a change of clothes for
tomorrow.'

She was silent. Then she said in a coldly reproachful voice,
'I meant something to eat, or a bottle of wine.'

'Absolutely not. I'll do everything. See you at eight,
Catherine.' He hung up and smiled. When he seemed to be
taking her for granted it shocked her. But she had still agreed
to come, and he was more or less certain that she would
bring a change of clothes with her.

The evening was looking up. He started the BMW and
pointed it in the direction of Waitrose.

Elaine was working out on her step when the phone rang.
Alan, at last! She ran across the room and grabbed it.
'Hello?'

'Elaine? Hi, it's Gary.'

'Gary! Do you know where Alan is?'

'Yeah, yeah, he's here at the flat. He asked me to ring you.
He said he didn't want to come back to your place while that
lady copper was hanging around.'

'Oh, right.' Alan was pretty sensible, even if she did wish
that he had come home. That awful Sergeant Fielding had
waited just outside the house for more than two hours, looking
about her as sharply as a rat. So Elaine had been alone all

afternoon, miserable and worrying. 'Is he coming round now?' she asked plaintively.

Gary sounded shifty. 'No, no, I don't think he is.'

'You're going down the pub, aren't you?' she accused him.

'I dunno. Look, Elaine, take care, won't you,' said Gary, and put the phone down.

She looked at the receiver, feeling tears welling up. She had told the police another lie and she didn't even have Alan to cuddle her and tell her it was all right. She couldn't forget Sergeant Fielding telling her about the penalties for making false statements. They had forgiven her once, but what would happen if they found out about the second time? What would they do to her? She didn't think that Chief Inspector Anderson would save her, even though he seemed nice.

Her breath was coming faster and faster and her heart was pounding. She felt as if she was going to faint. She had to ask someone for help.

Out of the blue a thought came to her. She ran for her diary and flipped frantically through the address pages, found what she was looking for, seized the phone and punched the buttons.

A male voice answered. 'Hello.'

'David?' she wailed.

'Yes,' said the voice, suddenly cautious. 'Who's this?'

'David, it's me. It's Elaine.'

'Elaine! What on earth is the matter? You sound awful.'

'Oh, David.' Tears were coming now. David was always so competent and organised. He would know what to do. 'David, you've got to help me.'

'What's the matter?'

'It's about Eddie.'

There was a silence. Then David said, 'What about Eddie?'

'The police have been here. They've been here twice. And there's something I haven't told them, and I'm so scared, and I've told them a lie and I don't know what to do. I know you'll know. Please, David, help me.'

'Hush,' said David's calm voice. 'Elaine, look, of course I'll help. I can't come around tonight, that's all. I'm going out in a minute. Are you in tomorrow?'

'Yes. Yes, of course.'

'All right. Look, I'm going to the bank first thing. You're not much out of my way. I'll come and see you then, first thing in the morning. Probably about nine, depending on the traffic. All right?'

'Yes,' Elaine nodded, gulping frantically. 'Oh David, thanks ever so much. I know you'll know what to do. You've always been really nice to me.'

'I'll see you tomorrow, then.'

He hung up. Elaine clutched the phone to her chest for a moment, swallowing sobs. But it would be all right now. She trusted David. He had always been kind to her when she worked at Drax & Bond, and he had sympathised when Eddie dumped her. He would know what to do.

Catherine walked into the lift and pressed the button for the top floor. She looked at herself in the smoked glass mirrors covering the walls. What was she supposed to wear when it was so hot? The dress looked pretty and feminine and it was cool, but she didn't know whether John would like it. He'd liked the sleek, tailored look of her body and skirt.

Good God, what was she worrying about? It was one of her favourite dresses. If he didn't like it he would have to lump it. She jerked up her head as the doors opened.

He was standing in the door of his apartment, dressed in pale trousers and a chambray shirt, a bright tie as always; and he had a clean tea towel draped over one shoulder. On him it looked like the latest sort of fashion accessory. He could have been photographed for GQ. He walked towards her and reached out to take her hands. For a moment he looked down into her eyes and she felt a spasm of unbearable, wonderful tension. Then he stooped his head and kissed her on the mouth.

His lips were so soft, so tender. She was shocked by the intensity of her reaction. Her throat felt tight and cold and dry, her nipples hardened, she couldn't breathe. Then he drew back and she realised that he'd taken her overnight bag from her hand. 'It's good to see you,' he said. 'Come in.'

She followed him to the door. He held it open for her,

stood back and extended his hand, gesturing in. She walked through and gasped. 'Oh, John, what a beautiful flat.' It was, too. Big, light, with a sense of coolness despite the appalling humidity of the evening. Her eyes swept around it, taking in the wooden floor, the fireplace faced with old bricks, the giant windows open on to the balcony, the view over the river and trees, a huge bookshelf filled with books. A small, expensive sound system was playing harpsichord music, Scarlatti's sonatas. At her feet was a Bokhara carpet, not large, but intricate. It looked like silk. 'It's lovely,' she said again, weakly.

He put her bag down beside the door. 'Can I get you a drink?' he asked. 'I'm having a kir.'

'A kir would be lovely.' She followed him through to the kitchen. The whole place was extremely neat, as she would have expected. He was in the middle of preparing dinner, but the kitchen looked as though it was about to be used for a TV cookery show. He had a glass ready on the side and reached into the fridge for a bottle of Bourgogne Aligoté. All his movements were very deft, assured. 'The kitchen is amazing too,' she said. 'Can I help at all with the dinner?'

'No, no.' He put the glass into her hand. 'It's nearly ready. Have a seat, why don't you.'

He guided her over to one of the big sofas and held her drink while she sat down, then waited until she had sipped it and nodded in appreciation of the sweet, refreshing coolness. 'Two minutes,' he said, and returned to the kitchen.

'How are you?' he asked, resuming his preparations.

She hardly heard him. She was examining the cushions on the sofa. They were all different, in varying shades of antiqued fabric, and their textures were irresistible: velvet, tapestry, canvas, linen, plush. 'John,' she said, 'where on earth did you find all these cushions?'

'Here and there.' He was arranging something on plates. 'All over, really. I pick them up when I see something I like. Some of them were made for me out of bits of fabric from other things.'

She picked up one in a mixture of blues and golds. The colours were faded and subtle. Almost without meaning to she scratched her fingers across it, enjoying its roughness. 'This one, for example. Where's this from?'

He looked up and smiled. 'That's from Lyons. It's a bit of old Aubusson tapestry. The rest wasn't worth saving.'

'You like France?'

'Very much.'

She was delighted to have the opportunity to find something out about him. She got up from the sofa and began to stroll around the huge room, inspecting things. For a moment he watched her, then smiled and returned to the dinner. She felt that he had given her permission to study his life.

Her feet took her first to the window. She stood enjoying the faint breeze, drinking in the view. It was easy to imagine that you were in the depths of the countryside, rather than fifteen minutes' drive from the middle of Guildford. The river ran right beneath the balcony, green with rushes. There was a table on the balcony, set for two with a white tablecloth and white china and a cast-iron candelabrum. She smiled and returned to looking around the flat.

The pictures interested her. They were all representational, pictures of things, and a number of them were old, Victorian watercolours of landscapes and buildings. But there were some modern ones too, very well executed. Mostly they were still-life watercolours, flowers and such, but there was one nude, a pencil drawing of a woman with her back turned to the artist and her hands clasped behind her. The sinuous curve of her spine was charged with eroticism.

There was a huge mirror over the fireplace. Catherine looked into it and saw John behind her in the kitchen, meeting her eyes with a smile, as if he was conspiratorially sharing her investigation of his home.

The enormous bookcase held a bewildering collection of books. A number of them were professional police works, everything from the familiar Butterworth's to the Sheehy report, and then there was a good collection of factual books about art and architecture and history, especially military history. But there was also a fair range of novels, many of them in French. She felt a twinge of inferiority. 'Oh, good grief,' she said aloud. 'You actually speak French.'

'*Bien sûr*,' he said.

'That always makes me feel so inferior. I don't speak any foreign languages, not properly. I mean, I speak enough French to get by.' She returned to the sofa and sat down. There was another carpet on the floor in front of her, a beautiful thing, patterned with a tree full of animals and birds. 'Do you go to France a lot?'

'When I can find someone to go with me. I like having company when I'm enjoying the good life.'

'What is the good life?' she asked him.

For a moment she was afraid that he would interpret the question in some deep meaningful way, but he didn't. 'In France,' he said, 'the good life is a quiet little hotel in Burgundy where the food is excellent and the wine is better and the countryside is glorious. Or possibly a week in Paris.'

'Paris,' she said faintly.

'There's a lovely hotel near the Place des Vosges, an old chateau. Beautiful. The most romantic place I know.'

For a moment she thought that he was going to suggest that they go there together. She had just time to realise that if he had suggested it she would have said yes; then he smiled and said, 'The first course is ready, madame, if you'd care to sit down.'

He came across to the table, held her chair for her and spread her napkin. In many men she would have found this attentiveness overrehearsed, false, even demeaning, but he did everything with so little fuss that it felt quite natural. He walked quickly back to the kitchen and brought through a bottle of wine in an ice bucket, then made another trip for their plates. 'Angels on horseback,' he announced.

The angels on horseback – scallops wrapped in bacon – were delicious. She complimented him on his ability to cook, though in fact she wasn't remotely surprised. John struck her as the sort of person who would be very competent at anything he chose to do. He watched her eating for a moment, as if he wanted to assure himself that she was content. Then he began on his own food.

She wanted to ask him a lot of questions. For a start, she

wanted to ask him how much a Detective Chief Inspector earned. She was an accountant, and she knew that beautiful things like the things that filled John's flat did not come cheaply. Did he have family money? But it was very rude just to ask. She frowned and took another mouthful.

'Go ahead,' he said with a smile. 'Ask it.'

Had her face given her away so easily? She felt herself blushing. Then, because he had already guessed, she said, 'Well, I was just comparing you to other divorced men I know. Most of them are strapped for cash, to put it mildly. And you don't seem to be.'

He raised his eyebrows and finished his scallops. She thought with a curl of horror that she had offended him. But then he said slowly, 'Well, it wasn't quite the ordinary state of things. My ex-wife, Sarah, was well off. A wealthy family. And she earned a lot, too. More than me at one point, in fact.'

His face was wry, as if his last mouthful had been bitter. Catherine nodded. Many men found it hard to accept that their wife's market value was higher than their own. And this did explain why divorce hadn't crippled him. 'You didn't have any children, then,' she ventured timidly.

A sour smile touched his lips and faded. 'No. By the time we split up that was about the only thing we agreed on.'

'Do you see her at all?' Now why had she asked that? It had come out in a rush, as if she had been waiting to ask it all evening. Jealous, she thought, already?

'Never,' he said, smiling more easily now. 'She's in the USA.'

'The USA?'

'Working. She's a commercial lawyer.' He took a deep breath and met Catherine's eyes. 'What about you? Do you see your ex-husband?'

She felt warned off, as if she had strayed further than he was prepared to allow. 'No,' she said. 'No, I never do. I –' She hesitated and twisted her hands together. 'I moved away. I came to Guildford five years ago. We lived north of London before.'

He nodded slowly, then got up and cleared the plates. Catherine was as exhausted as if she had run a marathon. Mutual confessions certainly took it out of her. It was time

142

for a less difficult subject. 'So,' she called through the open window, 'when you're not going to France with somebody else, where do you go on holiday?'

He returned with two more plates. '*Salade de chèvre,* madame. Not too goaty, they assured me at the cheese counter.'

'I like it even when it is goaty.' That was true, too. She tucked greedily into the salad. It was excellent.

'I inherited a little place in Scotland a couple of years ago,' he said, returning to her previous question. 'From my aunt. It's a croft, you'd call it. It needed a lot of work doing to it, but I've got it the way I like it now. I spend a fair bit of time there when I can. It's in the Western Highlands, near the sea, isolated. I read and do a spot of hill climbing and walk along the beaches. I like it.'

'You like being on your own, then,' she said. She looked into his dark bright eyes with a feeling of envy. In five years of solitude she had never really got to like being on her own, and she had never shed her feeling of failure.

'If I can't be with a beautiful woman,' he said, 'I like being on my own.' His smile was self-deprecating.

'I'll drink to that,' she said with a laugh.

Then she told him about what she did in the holidays, and they finished the salad and ate a bowl of strawberries with *crème fraîche* and she began to feel very relaxed and happy. John never took his eyes off her. She knew that he wanted to make love to her, and knowing it made her confident and cheerful.

The sun appeared at last from beneath the banks of cloud where it had loured all day. She gestured at it with her glass and said, 'The earth is flat.'

'What?' He sounded startled.

'The earth is flat. Haven't you ever noticed how even when the sun has been hidden behind the clouds all day, it comes out in the evening, when it gets low? That's because the clouds are flat, you see, over the flat earth, and when the sun sinks it pops out from underneath them.'

He was shaking his head at her, laughing. 'You're off your head.'

'Too much wine,' she said, and giggled.

He smiled at her as he got up from the table. 'It's too hot to go inside,' he said. He went into the living room, rolled up the carpet from in front of the sofa, brought it out on to the balcony and unrolled it. '*Voilà*.'

'Is it a magic carpet?' she asked, still giggling.

'Come and find out,' he said. His voice was suddenly husky and caressing and goose bumps lifted up along her arms. The way he looked at her filled her with a sense of danger, of risk. She wasn't used to taking risks. But she got up, all the same, and walked towards him.

'I like your dress,' he said, when she stood in front of him. She smiled with pleasure, ridiculously happy to have his approval. 'I like the fact,' he went on slowly, 'that it buttons down the front.' He extended one finger and touched the top button, then moved his finger down, lightly touching one button after another.

Her stomach felt hollow. She didn't know what he meant to do. Half of her was afraid, and the other half was deliciously excited. She swallowed hard and looked up into his face. It was good to know that she didn't need to say anything.

'Undo the buttons,' he said softly.

'What?' Now it was her turn to sound startled. She could have understood it if he'd unfastened them himself, but to ask her to do it! Was he lazy or what?

'Unfasten them,' he said again. 'I want to watch you unbutton the dress.'

He stepped back and leant against the balcony, legs negligently crossed, arms folded, expectant. She stood still for a moment, breathing fast. Then she said uncertainly, 'John, I think we ought to go inside.'

'No.' He shook his head. 'No, I like it out here.'

He didn't intend to move. He lifted his chin, signalling with his eyes that she should obey him. She hesitated, feeling like an exhibitionist. 'Someone will see.'

'Nobody will see. Undo the buttons, Catherine.'

Her lips were cold and dry. She looked down, feeling a hot blush rising to her cheeks, and put her fingers to the top button.

Slowly she unfastened the dress, all the way down. It hung

open, half revealing her body naked except for the prettiest underwear she could find. He stood still and looked at her. She felt his eyes like a touch.

'Take it off,' he said softly.

She was breathing fast, quick shallow breaths that made her breasts lift. Her heart was pounding. She should be ashamed. She couldn't understand why it should arouse her, to receive these cool, simple instructions and act upon them. But it did arouse her. Between her legs she felt hot and silky. She pushed the dress from her shoulders and hung it neatly over a chair.

Now she stood before him in her bra and panties and high-heeled sandals, acutely aware of the cooling rays of the evening sun striking her pale skin. He was still caressing her with his hot eyes. Her lips ached for him to kiss her, her body yearned for him to hold her. What more did she have to do to deserve it?

'Take off your bra and panties,' he said, smiling gently. 'I want to see you naked.'

'No,' she whispered, shaking her head helplessly. 'John, please.'

'Then I will,' he said. He straightened and came towards her. She thought that he would kiss her, but he just reached around behind her and unfastened her bra and drew it gently away. She crossed her arms instinctively over her bare breasts. He hung the bra over the chair and put his hands to her panties.

'Don't,' she said again, trying to hold him back. 'Don't.'

He pushed her hands away and tugged the panties down, down her thighs, down to her ankles. She couldn't stand there in a pool of them, and she reluctantly lifted one foot after the other to free them. Then she covered her breasts with her arm and shielded her triangle with her hand as if she could restore her modesty.

'Don't cover yourself,' he said. 'You're lovely, Catherine. Let me look at you.'

And then he knelt down in front of her and set his lips to her belly. The touch of his mouth seemed to go straight through her, like electricity, like ice. She gave a little cry and her head fell back. She felt that in a moment she would fall, and she was relieved when his strong hands grasped her hips and held her tightly, keeping her on her feet. She forgot her fears, forgot her modesty, forgot everything. His hands crept up her body, found her breasts and clasped them, and his lips moved steadily downwards.

Oh God, he was going to kiss her there. She gasped with eagerness and let him pull her hips towards his face. He nuzzled at her pubic hair, brushing his nose against the tight brown curls, and then his tongue slipped between her closed thighs and flickered against her clitoris and it was as if she had been struck by lightning. She dug her hands into his hair, feeling its combination of softness and harshness, resting her weight on him to hold herself up. He stroked his long wet tongue against her again and again, drawing out her swelling clitoris into a red-hot bead of delight. She couldn't believe the intensity of the sensation. And then she seemed to see herself as a watcher would see her, naked, exposed to the open air, writhing and crying out as a man licked her between her legs and squeezed her swollen nipples, and the vision of her own wantonness was so arousing that she convulsed and shuddered and pushed herself against John's mouth as she came.

He let her slip down to her knees beside him and smiled at her. His mouth glistened. 'You taste wonderful,' he told her.

She shook her head. Her whole body was still pulsing with the aftershock. She had to say something. 'You do that so well,' she managed to gasp.

'I like to please you,' he said simply.

Her confidence was returning. She smiled at him and said accusingly, 'And you owed me one, after this morning!'

He didn't look the least bit repentant. 'You were in a hurry.'

She dug her fingers into his hair and leant forward to kiss him on the mouth. He tasted of her, and she felt a frisson of delicious dirtiness. Her fingers found the knot of his tie and began to tug at it. She wanted to feel his body next to hers.

'What will your neighbours think?' she said in a whisper as she finally undid the tie and pulled it free.

146

'Why worry?' He let her unfasten his shirt. She slipped her hands inside it, running her palms eagerly over the flat smooth muscle of his belly. He had a little harsh hair around each nipple and a narrow line of it running down the centre of his chest to his navel. She pressed her face to his neck, drawing in the wonderful smell of him. She liked his aftershave.

'Take your shirt off,' she whispered, pushing at it. 'Please.'

Smiling, he obliged her. She crawled into his lap, wanting to be close to him. He wrapped his arms around her and pressed his mouth to her lips, to her jaw, and then, when her head fell back, to her throat. She felt his teeth and let out a little cry of protest. Then she thought of the neighbours, sitting underneath them, listening as they made love. It made her shiver. John's teeth and tongue lashed her skin and she pulled away, fighting him off the flats of her hands. 'Christ, John,' she hissed, 'don't give me a love bite, what would I say to the clients?'

'That you have a beautiful neck,' he said, biting her again. She shuddered and let him do it, because it felt so wonderful. His hands were on her breasts, trickling over her nipples so delicately that she quivered with pleasure.

'Undo my trousers,' he said softly. She stared at him, then ran her hands down his chest to the buckle of his belt. Beneath the fabric of the trousers his penis was stiff and ready. God, how she wanted to feel him inside her.

Her fingers fumbled with the button and the fly and at last managed to unfasten them. She pushed aside his underpants and touched his cock, biting her lip with excitement as she felt how hot and smooth it was. She had been thinking about this all morning, all afternoon. He had left her in a fine state, with her mouth feeling as if it had been stung by bees and her sex wet and ready. Until lunchtime she had hated him, and then she had just wanted him.

He was ready. He pushed her down his lap and spread her thighs so that she was kneeling over him. Her sex was poised just over the head of his cock, and the anticipation was killing her. 'Please,' she whispered, still thinking of the neighbours. 'Please, please.'

Slowly he lifted his hips. The head of his cock nudged between her labia, opening her very slightly. 'Please what?'

'Please do it.' She knew her voice sounded desperate, but she couldn't help it. She arched her back and pressed her breasts against him. 'Do it to me.' She tried to lower herself on to him, but he was holding her securely, his hands gripping firmly at the white swell of her haunches, in control. 'Please,' she whimpered again.

His eyes swept over her face, over her naked body. She looked back at him, trembling with wanting him.

And then, slowly, he smiled. 'Now,' he said, and very gently he lowered her on to his erection. She cried out helplessly as she felt him penetrate her. He seemed to go on for ever. Then she was sitting on his lap, full of him, his tense balls pressing against her bottom, and his arms were enfolded about her and he began to move, very slowly, very tenderly.

'John,' she moaned, 'John.' She clutched him and reached with her thirsty lips for his mouth and he kissed her and stroked her breasts and all the time he was moving inside her, steady, determined, rocking her on his deeply-buried cock so that her body rubbed and rubbed against his and she was reaching for another orgasm, reaching, reaching. The tension was unbearable, she was afraid, she thought she would lose it, she would have to fake it. Her breath sobbed as the sensations began to seep away, leaving her lonely and unfulfilled.

But he seemed to sense her fear and he held her close to him and lifted her and laid her down on her back on the silky carpet and kissed her properly, his face over hers, his body pressing her down. She arched her back, offering her loins to him, and he began to shaft her, hard, deliberate strokes, drawing his cock almost entirely out of her and then ramming it back into her so strongly that she gasped. His body slapped against hers and he grunted as he thrust. Oh Christ, the neighbours would hear, they would know that he was screwing her. She writhed with shame. But what could she do? She shut her eyes tightly and panted with agony and delight. He was on top of her and his hands were on her breasts and she couldn't have escaped even if she had wanted to, she was helpless, and he was doing it to her so wonderfully that the second orgasm started in her toes and blazed through her spine to her sex and her breasts. She was coming, and even as she cried out in delirious ecstasy, no longer caring about the neighbours, she heard him cry and knew that he was there too.

Afterwards she clung to him and pressed her body against his, hiding her face in his shoulder so that he wouldn't see how moved she was. And he kissed her hair and said softly, 'My neighbours are on holiday.'

EIGHT
Thursday Morning

David Thompson closed the door behind Penny and went to the front room, as he always did, to stand and wave while she put the children into the car and drove them off. He liked to be a good, reliable father. The kids were very important to him; more important than Penny, to be honest. At bottom he thought that she probably felt the same about him.

But the school fees were crippling. He walked through to the big family kitchen with his pleasant face set in a worried frown. The house was a handsome, spacious property, six years old, with hand-painted tiles in the bathroom and desirable features, but it had cost a fortune. It was also worth significantly less than he had paid for it. He was deep in negative equity. The investment of the 1980s turns to dust and ashes. Penny didn't understand, he couldn't make her understand without making it look as if he'd failed as a husband and a businessman, and so he kept on shelling out, shelling out, as if there would always be more money coming in than they could possibly spend. Thomas was eleven next month and in the autumn he would go to big school and that meant even more money. There was no end to it.

And now Elaine was in trouble. Or was she? He didn't trust the women at Drax & Bond. He'd believed Julia once, to his cost, and his accounts assistant was forcing him to collude in a poxy little fraud from which he was not benefiting to the tune of a single penny, and now Elaine was asking him for help. Was help what she wanted, or did she have some plan for screwing money out of him, too? Oh, she was stupid, a dim tacky bird whose only asset was her splendid body. But even stupid people had good ideas sometimes.

He should have eaten breakfast, but somehow he couldn't. The thought of what might be in store for him made him feel sick. He tried to convince himself that it was nothing, but things had been so bad over the last few days that he couldn't believe that this would turn out all right. He stood by the food preparation area, pulled one of Penny's Sabatier knives from its block and examined the blade thoughtfully. With a little frown of concentration he touched the point to his palm, then jumped. It was really sharp, and it cut him. His face twisted in revulsion as the blood welled up. He put the knife back in the block, sucked at the cut and ran it under the tap, then went to look for some Savlon.

Anderson arrived at the station early, but Fielding was there before him. She met him as he walked towards his desk, her face alight with excitement. 'The palmar, sir,' she said, holding out a report. 'Sealey's palm print matches it.'

Was this the answer, then? A simple case of *crime passionnel,* the cuckolded husband revenging himself on the adulterer? He felt vaguely disappointed, as if he had been cheated of something. There had been so many interesting angles to the case. He took the report from Fielding and perused it swiftly. There wasn't the remotest chance of error. All sixteen points of reference matched.

There was one relevant bit of untidiness left. 'What about the print on the drawer, Pat?'

Fielding looked startled. 'Not his, sir. But it could be old, it could be anybody's.'

No, it couldn't. It was the one remaining print on a drawer front which had been carefully wiped clean. It was the print of a careful, orderly person. Tony Sealey was not careful and orderly. The palmar was the print of an angry person banging on a door, and that fitted him. It didn't make sense. But the palmar proved that Sealey had been at Devonshire Avenue, and that meant that he had lied, and if he had lied about one thing then he might have lied about everything else.

Fielding was watching him like a dog about to be taken for a walk. It would have been too much to expect her to conceal her enthusiasm. At least she wasn't saying 'I told you so'. Rather than make her ask, he handed back the report and said, 'Another visit to Mr Sealey, Pat?'

'We have his whereabouts for the week. He's in the office first thing this morning. Shall we go straight away, sir?'

Elaine woke up late again. It was almost 8.30. David would arrive any minute. She fed Frosty and opened the kitchen window so that he could go out on the prowl, then put the kettle on. The moment the woman downstairs let herself out and went to work she ran down to the door in the baggy T-shirt she had slept in. She opened the door and twisted the Yale lock so that it was on the snib, ran up the stairs and did the same with the upper door. She might be in the bathroom when he arrived. He could find his own way up.

She looked out of the window, hoping to see his car parking. There was a space just outside the house. It was still empty and she felt a stab of disappointment. Then, to her surprise, she saw him walking down the street towards her. Why hadn't he parked outside? Perhaps he had forgotten exactly which house it was.

'David,' she called from the window. He looked up and waved. 'Come on up. The door's open.'

She ran to a mirror and fluffed her damp hair, then tugged down the T-shirt over her thong. The mirror looked back at her nervously. She looked terrified. That was no good! If he saw her looking scared he would suspect her, just like the police did, and then he wouldn't want to help her. She rubbed her fingers over her nose and mouth and took a deep breath.

David pushed his head through the open door of the flat. 'Elaine, are you there?'

She was so pleased to see him. 'David, hello!' He came into the flat, Mr Average in a blue pin stripe suit. She ran towards him, meaning to put her arms around him. But he stepped away from her with a look of shock and she pulled herself up short. 'I'm so glad you could come. Thank you.'

'It's no problem,' he said. 'But I'm in a hurry, Elaine, I have to get to the bank. So tell me what the matter is and I'll help if I can.'

'Do you want some tea?'

'No, I can't.' He was standing in the middle of the floor, looking around him at the disarray of the flat. He seemed uncomfortable, not his usual relaxed self. Why? They hadn't seen each other since that awful meeting in the golf club car park. Maybe that was it. She took a deep breath and hesitated while she got her thoughts straight.

'You said it was about Eddie,' David prompted. 'What's the matter?'

She looked at him anxiously. 'Well,' she said, hardly knowing how to start. 'Did you know – did you know they seem to think I might have done it?'

He nodded evenly. In a burst of spite she exclaimed, 'Julia told you I did it, didn't she? She told the police about –' And then she stopped herself. David and Julia were friends, colleagues. There was no point in bad-mouthing Julia, even if it did make her feel better.

'What happened with the police?' David insisted.

He seemed very uneasy, and there was something odd about the way he was standing in one place, not moving around, not sitting down. 'David, what's the matter?'

'Nothing. I'm just in a hurry to get away. Come on, Elaine, spit it out.'

'All right.' She took a deep breath and walked over to the window. Looking out at the ordinariness of the street outside somehow made it easier. 'David, it's like this. I've – lied to the police. Twice.'

'Twice!' He sounded shocked, as if once would have been bad enough.

'The first time I was stupid, I just made things up, and they found out. But the second time I said mostly stuff that was true but not everything. I didn't tell them about going round to Eddie's.'

'You went round to Eddie's? On Saturday?'

She hung her head. 'Yeah. I still had the key, you see. I

meant to nick some stuff from his house if he was out. Just CDs and stuff, you know. He'd bought them for me anyway. And he'd been such a bastard.' She looked up with eyes full of tears. 'You know how horrible he was, David.'

'Is that what you haven't told the police?'

She nodded fervently. 'I didn't dare. I mean, either they'd know that I went round to steal stuff from him, or they'd think I killed him.' Or, worse, she thought, they would think that Alan killed him for being horrible to me.

'What happened when you got to Devonshire Avenue?' David asked. 'Did you steal anything?'

'No.' She wrung her hands and turned to look out of the window. 'You see, when I got round to his house there was a car in the drive. Not his car. I mean, he had visitors. So I didn't go in.'

David's face had gone oddly pale. He frowned at her for a moment, as if he hadn't understood. Then he went over to the storage heater and lifted a drying tea towel from it. She said anxiously, 'David?'

'I'm thinking.' He wandered over to the exercise bike. Her dumbbells were next to it, half a pound and one pound for aerobics, five-pounds for toning. He picked up one of the five pound weights and hefted it, then turned to stare at her. 'What sort of a car was it?' he asked.

What a stupid question. Why did it matter what sort of a car it was? But he looked as if it might be important. 'I don't know. One of those big four-wheel drive jobs.'

David nodded, as if he had understood everything now. He walked towards her, then he said, 'Elaine, look!' and pointed out of the window.

She turned to look, and in a split second she realised that there was nothing there and that David was right behind her. Then he hit her, and she moaned with the pain and put her hands to her head, and he hit her again and she was falling.

Anderson and Fielding parked outside Sealey's office and got out of the car. The air pressed down on them like a smothering blanket, heavy with thunder. Anderson glanced up at the sky. It was grey, the colour of his car, leaden and threatening. He was wearing his lightest jacket, but underneath it his shirt was already sticking to his back between his shoulder blades.

'Sir,' said Fielding in a quick eager voice, 'there he is. Walking out to his car.' She didn't wait for him, but hurried across the car park towards the tall figure of Tony Sealey. 'Sealey!' she yelled, surprisingly loudly for a small woman.

Sealey stopped in his tracks, staring. For a moment Anderson thought that he was going to make a run for it across the car park, but then Sealey stood still and folded his arms and waited for them to come up to him.

This was Fielding's big moment. 'Going somewhere, Mr Sealey?'

He glared sullenly at her. 'Home. My boss suggested I might like to go home sick. They weren't too taken with your visit.' He glanced at Anderson as if he wasn't sure who was in charge this time. 'What's going on? Smudged the prints, did you?'

Anderson's brows contracted in surprise. That was a very stupid thing for Sealey to say if he was guilty. Fielding shook her head, not seeming to notice how Sealey's remark jarred. 'Mr Sealey,' she said, 'we want to talk to you about the death of Eddie Drax.'

She was being careful. She knew that this interview might lead to an arrest, and she didn't want anyone saying that she had misled Sealey. Anderson approved.

'I told you about him,' Sealey said. 'Listen, you want to talk to me, find another time. I'm not going to stand in a car park talking to you. This is a free country.'

'Mr Sealey.' Fielding's voice was very firm. 'This is a formal interview.' She cautioned him, and as he listened to her the blustering confidence left his face. 'Do you want to go to the station to continue the interview?'

Sealey frowned and shook his head. Fielding nodded, then went straight on. 'When we spoke to you before you told us that you were at your friends' house in Burpham the whole of Saturday evening.'

'That's right.' But now his expression was shifty and uncertain.

'In that case, can you explain why a palm print matching yours was found on the front door of 14 Devonshire Avenue?'

Sealey moved suddenly, as if he was stifling the urge to retreat. A muscle clenched in his jaw. He was getting ready to lie. 'It's wasn't me,' Sealey blurted, folding his arms tightly. 'I wasn't there.'

'The print matches yours exactly,' said Fielding. 'You know about fingerprints, Mr Sealey? No two are the same.'

Suddenly Sealey was furious, shouting. 'I know! I've been here before, remember? Six months banged up for something I hadn't done, thanks to one of you making up bloody lies about me!'

His anger sounded genuine. For a moment Anderson wondered if he had really been convicted when innocent, but after all it didn't matter. Fielding was telling the truth. It was Sealey's print on the door.

'Mr Sealey,' said Fielding, with imperturbable patience, 'how do you explain the presence of your print on the front door of 14 Devonshire Avenue?'

Sealey stood still for a moment. Slowly his arms unfolded and hung by his sides. His fists were clenching and unclenching and his face was working. The skin of his face grew pale as the blood left it, then slowly darkened. Anderson recognised the symptoms of rage and set his teeth. Damn it, violence was all they needed. It was bloody hot and he was wearing his most fragile suit. He came up on the balls of his feet, ready for trouble.

Lightning ripped across the sky, making them all wince, and almost immediately thunder roared overhead. Tony glanced up at the angry clouds, then without warning he ducked away from Fielding and Anderson and darted between two parked cars, heading for his Celica. Fielding was closest to him and she didn't hesitate, but flung herself in pursuit. She was small and slight and it was easier for her to manoeuvre between the cars than either of the men. Within thirty yards she had caught up with Sealey. She shouted, 'Stop!' but her voice was drowned by another ferocious thunderclap. 'Stop!' she shrieked again, then grabbed Sealey by the shirt and with the impetus of her run swung him against a car.

Anderson vaulted lightly over the bonnet of a Mercedes and put on all his speed. Fielding could look after herself, but she still looked horribly small beside big angry Sealey.

As he reached them the rain came down. It was torrential, huge drops battering downwards with the strength of hailstones, so thick that it was hard to breathe. Sealey pushed Fielding aside and broke away again. This time Anderson was ready. Sealey roared and rushed at him, fist lifted. He lunged and Anderson swayed out of the way of the blow and then Fielding was behind Sealey. She grabbed his right arm in a wrestler's hold and forced it hard up between his shoulder blades. Sealey howled with pain and bent forward, trying to throw Fielding over his head, but she hung on grimly, like a terrier holding a bull by the nose. Anderson stood back, blinking the rain out of his eyes and admiring Fielding's technique. He was ready to help, but she didn't look as if she needed it. Sealey staggered forward a couple of steps, then wailed, 'You're breaking my arm!' and dropped to his knees on the wet tarmac.

Fielding was panting, but she was laughing too. She had the right attitude. 'You're in trouble now, Sealey,' she said, still twisting Sealey's arm. 'Assaulting two police officers.'

'I didn't assault him,' Sealey protested. 'I didn't touch him.'

'All right, fair enough. Assaulting one officer and threatening behaviour towards the other. Like I said, you're in trouble, Sealey.'

Anderson came a little closer. 'All right, Sergeant. Let him up.'

Fielding glanced up at him. She was flushed and soaked. Her dark hair had worked itself loose from its plait and clung to her cheeks, flat wet strands down either side of her excited face. She looked reluctant, but when he signalled with his eyes she let go of Sealey's arm and stepped back, dusting off her hands.

'Perhaps I should have warned you that Detective Sergeant Fielding is a tutor on our self-defence courses,' he said ironically to Sealey.

Tony hung his head, panting. 'I didn't kill Eddie Bastard Drax,' he said to the ground.

'Were you at the house?'

Fielding seemed to have knocked the stuffing out of Sealey.

He didn't make any move to get up, just knelt there on the tarmac with the rain bouncing all around him. 'All right. Yes, I was. I went there Saturday night to tell him what a bastard he was. I wanted to beat him up, all right?' His head jerked up. 'And I knew if I told you bloody pigs that I had been there you'd try to pin the murder on me, and now that's exactly what you're going to do, isn't it.'

Anderson closed his eyes for a moment. His suit was already soaked. The thin fabric was like a wrung-out crumpled flannel, and there was every chance that the colour would run and ruin one of his favourite shirts. 'Get up,' he said coldly.

Tony got slowly to his feet, nursing his twisted arm. Anderson said, 'What happened when you went round to the house?'

'I want a solicitor,' said Sealey.

'You're not under arrest. Not yet. I'm just asking you what happened when you went round to the house.'

'I banged on the door and Eddie looked out through the window and saw me and didn't let me in.' Sealey gave him a look of mixed fear and defiance. He looked trapped and ready to fight at the slightest provocation. 'That's all, all right? That's all!' Fielding shook her head and Sealey whirled to stare at her. 'What are you getting at? Listen, you won't find any evidence in the house because I was never inside, all right?'

Fielding met Anderson's eyes. He nodded, giving her permission. She smiled and said with relish, 'Tony Sealey, I am arresting you...'

Anderson brushed disconsolately at his suit. It was wrecked. He felt a surge of anger. Sealey had better be bloody guilty, after this.

David looked down at Elaine's still body, panting. He resisted the urge to giggle hysterically. It had been just like a cartoon. He had said, 'Look!' and she had turned obediently away from him to look at nothingness. So stupid. So easy.

He stooped down and inspected her more closely, but without touching her. Touching meant fibres and hairs and forensic pathologists. He'd read enough fiction on holiday to know the form.

She was unconscious, not dead. Her baggy sleepshirt had ridden up as she fell, exposing her long legs and firm muscular hips and the scanty black thong that hardly covered her pubic hair. He was unmoved. She was not his type. She was breathing heavily through her open mouth. He'd hit her on the back of the head and he couldn't see any blood.

That was convenient. He examined the dumbbell, still wrapped in the tea towel and clutched in his hand. It was covered in soft foam rubber. A few of her long dark hairs were clinging to it, and he shook them off. Then he put the dumbbell back with its companions and replaced the tea towel on the radiator where he had found it.

What now? He clenched his hands. His pulse thumped inside his fists. She had seen his car outside Eddie's house, and she was too much of a coward not to tell the police in the end. He had to make sure that didn't happen. They were busy with Tony Sealey and Julia Bond, without what Elaine knew they'd never get around to him.

He moved cautiously towards the window, made sure the street was empty and looked out. One measly floor, not a far enough fall to kill anyone. Moving very carefully, to make sure that he didn't touch anything, he sidled through to the kitchen and crouched in front of the oven. It was electric. For a moment he thought wildly of causing an explosion, but then he looked for the boiler and there wasn't one. Storage heaters, damn it.

Perhaps he could use one of the kitchen knives? No, that was stupid. Apart from the blood and mess, it wouldn't stand a chance of looking like suicide unless he cut her throat, and he didn't have the bottle to do that. He had to make it seem that she had killed herself. It would be easy to believe. Look at the squalor she lived in now, after the glitz of Eddie's house on Devonshire Avenue. Poor girl, she just couldn't take it.

Yes, it had to look like suicide. No gas and the ceilings weren't high enough for a tall girl like Elaine to hang herself, even if he could find something strong enough to hold her up. He thought hard. Well, electricity could do it. Put her in the bath and chuck a fan heater in after her. He wrapped a tea towel around his hand and opened the cupboard under the sink, looking for a pair of rubber gloves.

There weren't any. He cursed. Well, he would have to drag her through to the bathroom and then just use the tea towel or something to pick up the fan heater. If there was a bloody fan heater. Would a kettle do the trick?

For a moment he stopped, looking down at his incongruous business suit. More than half of him couldn't believe that this was happening. But a very cool, logical part of him believed it implicitly and was working very hard to make sure that he came out of it all right. The alternative was just too appalling.

He walked out of the kitchen and over to Elaine. She hadn't moved. He didn't want to touch her, and for a moment he hung over her, hesitating. How would he avoid leaving traces, if he carried her across the flat to the bathroom? He'd have to clear up afterwards, really carefully.

He leant down to pick her up, and she moved.

At once he recoiled, heart thumping, breath coming fast. Lightning flashed outside, making him blink, and almost immediately a clap of thunder sounded, loud enough to rattle the windows. Elaine moaned and stirred on the floor. Her eyelids fluttered.

Panic gripped him. If she woke up she would scream. Christ, she would scream! For a moment he clenched his hands helplessly on empty air. Then he lunged for the sofa and pulled a cushion off it. He dropped to his knees beside Elaine and covered her nose and mouth with the cushion and held it down.

Elaine's eyes opened and her hands came up. She began to struggle and heave. Little choking sounds squeezed out from under the cushion. He gasped and pressed it down harder and harder. Her big body started to writhe, her feet threshing as she fought to breathe. Outside the rain rushed down, and another splintering crack of thunder made him want to howl like a beast. Now her heels were hammering on the floor and her hands were clutching frantically at nothing. It seemed to go on for ever. He crammed the cushion down over her face, leaning on it with all his weight and staring into her white-ringed eyes as if he could make her die just by wanting it.

She began to weaken. The frantic beating of her hands

and feet became spasmodic and jerky. How could she survive for so long? He made a small agonised noise and shut his eyes. The cushion scratched at his damp hands. Sweat trickled down his cheeks and fell from his face to land on Elaine's forehead.

At last there was no more movement. He opened his eyes and looked down, and Elaine looked up at him. Her gaze was fixed. He swallowed hard, fighting down a surge of vomit, then slowly withdrew the cushion.

There were no marks that he could see, but her lips were blue and swollen and her tongue showed dark red behind her teeth. It made him want to throw up, and it didn't look like suicide. He'd have to think of something else. He knelt next to Elaine for a few minutes, panting. Then he got up, carefully dusted off the cushion and put it back on the sofa.

Another flash of lightning made him blink and flinch, expecting the thunder. As the rumble died away a little sound behind him brought up the hairs on his neck. He turned slowly and saw that she was moving again, her hands twitching, her mouth closing slightly, the cords on her neck fluttering. He barely restrained a shriek of horror and rage. He leapt across the room and brought down his foot on her throat, stamping the life out of her, grinding down the leather sole of his heavy city shoe as if he were putting out a spark.

Her whole body tensed, arcing upwards from the floor. David gave a wordless shriek and drove his whole weight down on to his strangling foot. Slowly Elaine's mouth opened and her tongue emerged between her teeth, swollen and discoloured. Her body gave a convulsive shiver, then sagged.

At last he lifted his foot and stepped back, gagging. He stood with his eyes closed and his head bowed, breathing fast.

In a few moments he was calmer, and he knew what he was going to do. He went to the kitchen and dampened the tea towel in the washing-up water. He would have to make everything tidy before he made it untidy.

NINE
Thursday Afternoon

By 3 p.m. Anderson couldn't stay at the office for one more minute.

Fielding had an unshakeable grip on Sealey's case. Things were looking good for her. The lab analysis on the blue fibres had proved that they were indeed American cotton, probably from a sweater, and she was busily organising the searches of the Toomeys' house and Sealey's own house to look for the hypothetical garment. She was dealing competently with Superintendent Parrish, who was unhappy about the evidence against Sealey, and she had even written the text of an unhelpful statement for the local paper, which was planning a major article about the Drax murder in tomorrow's edition. She was determined to prove that Tony Sealey was guilty.

Anderson wished her luck, but he didn't believe it. For a start, he had spent more than two hours in an interview room, sitting next to Sealey's solicitor and watching while Fielding asked Sealey question after question, trying to get him to change his story. She had done a good job, he wouldn't have approached it in any significantly different way himself, but Sealey had stayed as steady as a rock. Fielding believed that Tony was a practised villain, relying on the protection of his solicitor and used to lying to the police. Anderson believed that he was telling the truth.

Besides, if Sealey was guilty too many things remained

unexplained. The smudged thumbprint was just one of them. Another was the way that Samantha Smith avoided him. Another was Julia Bond. She had as good a motive as Sealey, she had no alibi, and he believed she was capable of murder.

However, frustration at Fielding's sheepdog-like worrying of the case was not what drove him away from work. He could not take one more arch, sarcastic or downright offensive remark about the state of his clothes. Parrish had let out an amazed, 'Bloody hell, John, what happened to you?', a Francophone member of CID had muttered darkly about *vers moi le déluge,* and the desk sergeant had been heard repeating an old nursery rhyme to any colleague who would listen, the one about Dr Foster who went to Gloucester in a shower of rain and stepped in a puddle right up to his middle. It wasn't often that his colleagues had the opportunity to make jokes at his expense, and they were enjoying every minute of it.

At last he said, 'I'll leave you to it. There's some things I want to follow up.'

Pat didn't look remotely displeased. Parrish was right, she was gunning for her promotion. He added as an afterthought, 'You're doing a good job.' He wanted it to look as if he was leaving her alone on purpose.

'Where are you headed, sir?' she asked, though her offhand tone revealed that she didn't think it really mattered now that the criminal was in custody.

'I'm going to go and see if Samantha Smith's girlfriend Emma is at home,' he said. 'And after that I'll come back here and see how you're getting on with Sealey.'

But first he went home. He took off his suit, mourned over it, and hung it at the end of the cupboard reserved for dry cleaning. Rita would take it away tomorrow, when she came to clean the flat. As he had feared, colour from the suit had run on to his shirt. He filled the sink with soaking solution and dunked the shirt in it in case it was capable of rescue, then went to shower away six hours of discomfiture.

When he emerged from the shower he walked naked to the telephone, scrubbing his hair dry with a towel, and called

163

Catherine. He knew her number already by heart.

'Catherine Marshall,' said her calm, competent voice.

'Hello,' he said.

'John!' Her voice changed from the cool professional to her own voice, her real voice. She sounded pleased to hear from him and afraid that he might realise. He smiled, amused and affectionate, although she couldn't see him. 'I'm so glad you called. I've been thinking about you.' There was nobody in her office this time. 'I don't like to call you at work. How are you?'

'I'm fine,' he said, and now he meant it. 'Listen, things are calming down here. What would you like to do tonight?'

'I can't. I'm really sorry. I have an Institute dinner I can't miss. It's going to be hideously boring, and I have to go.'

'Tomorrow then,' he suggested.

'Tomorrow would be wonderful. What would you like to do? Shall we just see how we feel?'

'Would you like to go to the theatre?'

'Well –' She was diffident. 'Truly, John, I can't say today. I might feel different tomorrow. Can we decide later?'

He didn't understand why she was reluctant to make a decision now, but he was happy to do whatever she would like. 'Sure, if you prefer.'

Her voice changed. 'I'm sorry, but I have some people just arriving. I'll speak to you tomorrow, then.' Stiff formality overrode her warmth. ''Bye, John. Thanks for calling.'

The phone clicked and buzzed. He smiled ruefully. He could appreciate how difficult it was to make a call of such a personal nature from an office. He stood quietly for a moment, reflecting on his disappointment that Catherine was not free that night. Had he hoped to see her, to compensate for his other disappointment over the Drax case by making love to her again? She was very rewarding to make love to; she received everything that he bestowed upon her with such amazement, such delight. And she had a streak of modesty, of unwillingness, that made it all the more exciting to subject her to unusual demands, to make her blush and then cry out in the middle of the blushing. How much more satisfying to give slow leisurely pleasure to a woman like Catherine than to carouse in the rank enseamed bed of Julia Bond.

So, he asked himself as he went through the careful process of dressing, what sort of a grudge was he nursing against Julia? Had her apparent attempt to seduce him – not realising, of course, that he was not the sort of man who could be seduced – left him sufficiently predisposed against her to manipulate the evidence, to overemphasise, to adjust?

He didn't think so. But the possibility made him uncomfortable.

It was after 4.15 when he left the flat, but he wasn't worried about the time. He was free for the evening, and he might as well continue his involvement with the case.

And before he went back to the station, he would drop around to Samantha Smith's apartment and find out if the pretty, amenable Emma was at home.

The traffic was thickening, but he knew the back routes. He arrived at Sam's flat at 4.40. If Emma was at home, he would have some undisturbed time with her before Sam returned from work.

Emma's breathy little voice was almost inaudible on the entryphone. 'Hello?'

'Emma, it's DCI Anderson here. May I talk to you?'

There was a long silence. For a moment he thought that Emma was going to say no. Then the little voice said, 'All right. Come up.'

When the lift let him out on the penthouse landing, eight floors up, the door to the apartment was closed. He frowned and knocked on it, a quick double rap. He heard nothing for a few moments, then a scurry of feet. The door opened and Emma stood there, big eyes even wider than usual. 'Sorry.'

What had she been doing? Her cheeks were flushed, as if she knew that she was guilty of something. Or perhaps she just liked to feel as if she was guilty all the time. She looked, if possible, even younger than the last time he had seen her. She was wearing a short, thin slip dress, white with little pink flowers, and her arms and legs and feet were bare. 'Sorry,' she said again. Her blush deepened. She dropped her head and stirred her toe against the carpet like a child found stealing from the larder. 'I was on the phone.'

On the phone to whom? Probably Samantha. She could be apprehensive about giving audience to a policeman alone and unchaperoned. He might not have as long as he had expected. 'Thank you for seeing me, Emma,' he said gently. She already looked afraid of him, there was no need to make it worse. 'Shall we go and sit down?'

'All right.' Her big eyes flickered up to his, then away again. She wrapped her arms around herself defensively. The action cradled her small breasts, lifting them towards his eyes. She wore no bra, and her nipples were erect. The darkness and slight swell of her areolae just showed through the thin white dress. She went before him through the door into the living room and sat down on one of the big sofas, tugging the dress down around her thighs as she arranged herself. It was an oddly unnecessary, modest movement. It drew his attention.

'What do you want?' Emma asked him uncertainly.

He sat down opposite her and leant forward, his hands folded loosely in front of him, a relaxed, unthreatening posture. 'I was just wondering, Emma, how long you and Sam have known each other.'

She frowned as if she was surprised. 'Ages. We were at school together. I mean, she was in the sixth form when I was new, but I knew her. She was sort of famous.'

He could believe that. 'What was she famous for?'

'Oh,' Emma smiled, 'being bad, mostly. You know, flaunting rules. Smoking. Boys. All that.'

'Boys?' His tone was gentle, but probing.

'She did used to go out with boys.' Emma lowered her eyes as if the thought appalled her.

'What about you, Emma?' When he used her name she looked up at him. She looked so small and defenceless. How conscious was she of the effect she had? How much of it did she do on purpose? 'Did you ever go out with boys?'

The huge eyes narrowed slightly. 'Once,' she admitted.

Her face showed that she was becoming suspicious of the way he was taking the conversation. Time for a change. He leant back in the chair and looked around the flat. 'This is a really nice place,' he remarked. 'How long have you been living here?'

'Just a few months,' Emma said. She looked as if her disquiet had been soothed. 'It is great, isn't it?'

'Do you mean to stay here long?'

She gave him another frightened glance. 'I'm on my year off,' she said. 'I'm going to go to university next year. I've got a place and everything.'

He would have liked to have known what Emma's parents thought of the way that she was spending her year off, but he hadn't come to rescue her. She was grown up enough to make her own choices. 'That's great,' he said, and watched her smile at his approval.

There was a little pause. Then he asked, 'What do you and Sam do when she's not at work?'

Emma shifted on the sofa as if the thought excited her. Her dress rode up her thighs and she caught at it quickly and pulled it down again. Why did she keep doing that? She didn't behave like a flirt in other ways, so why go to such lengths to show off her naked legs? 'We have a good time,' she said. 'We go out a lot. To clubs and stuff. It's fun.' Her big eyes sparkled. 'Sam's so brave. Nothing scares her. She does whatever she wants, and she looks after me.'

'How did she get to be so brave?'

Emma's elfin face lit with a smile. 'She says it's because she's named after a beer. She got so teased at school she had to get really bolshy to cope with it.'

A beer? Of course, Sam Smith. Anderson chuckled. He and Emma exchanged looks of shared amusement. Then he shook his head with a puzzled air and said, 'I still don't understand how she manages to afford this flat. Is there money in her family?'

'Sam's family? No!' Emma laughed again. There was an odd quality in the laugh, one almost of pity, and he knew as if she had told him that there was plenty of money in Emma's family, but none to speak of in Sam's. Pretty little Emma wasn't just living with a girl, she was socially slumming it.

'So where's all this come from?' he asked, waving a hand to encompass the big room, the pale carpet, the velvet sofa.

'Oh,' Emma said, 'I —' And then she stopped speaking and lifted her head. The turn of her neck as she stared at the door was heart-stoppingly graceful. She listened for a moment, then jumped to her feet, calling out, 'Sam!'

Damn. It had been going so well. He watched Emma run past him to the door. Her dress fluttered and lifted and his breath caught in his throat. He was sure that he had seen a flash of pale skin, a brief glimpse of a tuft of fiery fur between her thighs. Christ, was she naked under that dress?

'What are you doing here?' demanded Samantha. She stood in the doorway with her briefcase in one hand and her other arm wrapped protectively around Emma's waist.

'Emma and I were talking.' He didn't get up. Samantha would be only too pleased if he pushed back against her aggression. There was no need. He could deal with her perfectly well from where he sat.

'What the hell were you talking about?'

'This and that.'

'Nothing, Sam,' Emma said earnestly. 'I promise. Nothing. I was just saying that I'm going to go up to university next year. That's all.'

'Emma, sit down,' Sam snapped. Emma hung her head and walked back to the sofa where she had sat before. She resumed her place, tugging her skirt down around her thighs. Anderson found himself looking at her, trying to see whether he had really glimpsed her nakedness. He couldn't tell.

'Mr Anderson,' Sam snarled. She really didn't like him examining her little pet. He lifted his head with a lazy smile and met her eyes. Challenging this tough young lesbian was the most fun he'd had all day. 'I can't believe that you will learn anything from Emma that's relevant to Eddie Drax. She never met him. We've wasted quite enough time talking to you and I want you to leave now.'

He rested his chin on his hand. 'What makes you think I'm here on the Drax investigation?'

Sam's vivid eyes widened briefly. The rest of her remained suspiciously still. 'What are you investigating, then? I'd hardly believe that this was a social call.'

She was quick and clever. She knew how to answer a

question with a question, a technique that he often used himself. 'Miss Smith, I came to talk to Emma, not to you.' He looked over at Emma. She was watching Sam with a face of rapt adoration. It nettled him. 'Emma,' he said, and when he had spoken he realised that he just wanted her to look at him. She turned her huge eyes to him slowly, as if Sam was much more interesting. 'Emma, I don't know your surname.'

Emma glanced quickly at Sam as if asking permission to speak. 'Hetherington,' she said at last, her voice barely audible.

'Emma doesn't want to talk to you any more,' Sam said. She came across and stood between him and Emma, blocking his view with her body. 'This is my flat and I want you to leave now.'

He got to his feet. He moved closer to Sam, threatening her with his height and presence. When they were so close that their bodies were almost touching he stopped and looked down at her. She jerked up her chin and stared him out. He was sure that she had plenty to hide, but he had to admire her. What she lacked in subtlety she made up for in raw courage.

'Don't smile at me,' Sam said. 'You condescending bloody voyeur. You only came here because the thought of two women tickles your fancy.'

Was she right? No. He was intrigued by the thought of Sam and Emma together, but not because he wanted to watch them. What fascinated him was Sam's control over Emma, her possessiveness, her ownership. Now that was appealing.

'Sam,' he said in a dangerous soft voice, 'what do you know about the fraud at Drax & Bond?'

Her body didn't move, but she couldn't conceal the sudden dilation of her pupils. For a moment her eyes looked almost black. When she said scornfully, 'What fraud?' he already had his answer.

'Thank you for your hospitality,' he said with gentle irony. 'I look forward to seeing you again soon, Sam. On a matter closer to your heart than Eddie Drax.'

Sam closed the door behind Anderson with a definitive shove, then turned back into the flat. She was angry, and she let it show. 'Emma!'

Emma was there, quivering. 'Sam, I'm sorry. I couldn't send him away, could I? Wouldn't that have looked worse? And I didn't tell him anything. And he was nice to me.'

'Nice to you? I bet he was! He'd like to fuck you, wouldn't he?'

Emma stared at Sam in real horror, then spun away from her and lowered her head, gazing at the floor. She looked so lovely, so fragile. Sam controlled her anger. After all, it was Anderson the intruder she was angry with, not Emma the victim. And it was highly arousing to imagine Emma with Anderson, naked and defenceless beneath her thin dress. She put her hand gently on Emma's bare arm and slid it up towards her shoulder. Emma trembled and Sam smiled. She was so delicate, like a flower. The cloud of her auburn hair floated down her back, softer than a skein of silk. 'Emma.'

Slowly, reluctantly, Emma turned around. She didn't look up. Sam ran both hands through the mass of her hair, lifting her face. 'You were a good girl to call me. I came home straight away.'

Brightness touched Emma's face, like a ray of weak sunshine breaking through cloud. 'I'm glad you came so soon.'

'Detective Chief Inspector Anderson!' Sam whispered conspiratorially. 'Who's afraid of him? Did you see him staring at you?'

Emma bit her lip. 'I think he realised that – that there was nothing under the dress.' She leant her cheek against Sam's stroking hand. 'I was just ready for you to come home.'

'He must have thought you were a very dirty girl,' Sam said softly. Emma closed her eyes and drew in a long shuddering breath. 'A real little madam, in this little thin dress with nothing on underneath it. Look, Emma, he could see your nipples through it.'

Her hands left Emma's hair and ran down the front of her dress to find her small pointed breasts. She trapped the erect nipples between her fingers, testing their hardness. 'Mmm, Emma, feel this. Did you like him looking?'

Emma shook her head and didn't speak. Sam stood for a

few moments caressing the younger girl's breasts, teasing them with her fingernails until they swelled beneath her hands. Then she stepped back and began to unfasten the buttons on her jacket. She stripped herself slowly, removing jacket, blouse and skirt. Emma's eyes were on her the whole time. At last she was naked except for her bra and her lacy panties and her high heels. As always, she felt stronger and more powerful undressed than dressed.

'Emma,' she said, 'take off your dress.'

Emma licked her lips. Then she put her hands to the hem of the dress and lifted it off over her head, all in one movement. Her body was as white as the inside of a shell, starred with bright colour; her nipples, the red smudge of her triangle.

'I know you didn't mean to attract Mr Policeman Plod,' Sam said softly, 'but you did, Emma, didn't you? You saw the way he looked at you?'

'But I didn't mean to,' Emma said, her eyes shining.

'All the same, you were bad.' Sam sat down on the sofa, lifted her arms above her head and spread her legs. The harsh velvet of the cushions caressed her back and thighs with prickly fingers. 'Now, Emma, I want you to make me come. And then we'll think about how to punish you.'

With a little sob of eagerness Emma dropped to her knees between Sam's open thighs. She pressed her face against Sam's vulva and drew in a long, ecstatic breath. Sam closed her eyes and leant back her head, sighing with pleasure. Emma was so wonderfully obedient.

Wouldn't you like to inspect this, Detective Chief Inspector, she thought as Emma humbly pulled aside her panties. Wouldn't you like to see her kneeling here and licking me. Look, look, Mr Detective, look what she's doing to me.

She could see him so clearly, his narrow intent face and his dark blue glittering eyes, the way he leant forward with taut controlled eagerness. They were two of a kind, both hunters, knowing what they wanted and out to get it. But the difference was that she, Samantha, had got it. She had Emma, Emma whose little clever tongue was circling her clitoris, whose small deft fingers were stroking her labia and dipping oh so gently into the wet tunnel of her sex, Emma who was quivering and moaning with the bliss of serving her.

She imagined him watching, but separated from them by a sheet of glass. His hands were pressed against the glass as if he wanted to burst through it, his face was desperate, the outline of his swollen erect cock strained against his elegant trousers. He wanted to come and take Emma away, and he couldn't, because Emma was hers. Emma licked faster and faster and Sam moaned with pleasure. As her orgasm approached her image of Anderson began to shout and beat on the glass between them, but he couldn't make her hear him. The expression of frustration and anger on his face stirred her with a delirious consciousness of her own power. She put her hands in Emma's hair and lifted her hips, rubbing herself against the busy tongue and lips.

With a whimper of delighted submission Emma fluttered her small clever tongue against Sam's clitoris and drove two fingers deep into her. Sam opened her mouth wide and cried out as the spasms seized her, and as he watched her coming Anderson sank to his knees, defeated and despairing.

Another thunder shower broke as Anderson walked out to his car. He leapt in, slammed the door and brushed angrily at the drops of rain on the second suit of the day.

It was good that there was still work to be done at Drax & Bond, but not surprising. Crime was rarely tidy, that was why it was fascinating. The world was a disorderly place, full of chaos and confusion. He did not like disorder, and he drew daily satisfaction from knowing that the rigorous exercise of his intelligence and logic either imposed order or punished the disorderly.

The radio beeped. It was Fielding, at the station. She sounded tired and depressed. 'What's going on, Pat? Any luck with Sealey?'

'No, sir. He won't budge. The old man is getting edgy about it.'

That wasn't surprising. Parrish wanted results, and fast. He would have liked tomorrow's paper to have carried respectful adulation of the police for their quick action, not groundless speculation. The Drax case was just the sort of juicy material journalists liked.

'How about the searches?'

'Nothing, sir. I mean, no blue sweater in either house. We've got the experts there looking for fibres, but it doesn't look likely. Amanda Sealey denies that Tony ever had such a sweater.'

'Bad news,' he said evenly. Fielding already knew his reservations, he didn't want to crow. But if there was no physical evidence linking Sealey to the inside of 14 Devonshire Avenue any half-competent defence barrister would have the case thrown out of court. The Crown Prosecution Service wouldn't even bother with it. Sealey's story explained away his palm print, and his chequered past could excuse him for making a run for it.

'One thing did come in, sir.' Fielding sounded as if she was trying to cheer herself up. 'It's probably not relevant, but I thought you ought to know. Gerry talked to the people at the takeaway where Elaine and Alan Banks went on Saturday night.'

'Elaine and Alan left before they said they did.' It was the only explanation. Otherwise why should Fielding bother to tell him?

There was a little silence, then Fielding said, 'Yes, sir.' Her voice was wary and respectful. 'About 10.30, more than half an hour before they should have done to get home at half past eleven. They were driving, their car was parked just outside. The manager at the Curry Mahal remembered them very well.'

'I'm not surprised, two six-footers engaging in foreplay in the middle of a restaurant.'

'Snogging, sir,' said Fielding, with some hesitation.

'That's what I said. Well, I'm already in my car, Pat. I'll pay another visit to Elaine. Perhaps I might also have the pleasure of meeting Mr Banks.'

'That's typical, isn't it,' said Fielding wearily. 'I'm stuck in the office with Tony Sealey and you get to interview the big blond hunk.'

He drove slowly through the pelting rain, headlights on and wipers going double time. The rush-hour traffic was exacerbated by the weather. By the time he turned into Elaine's street it was almost 6 p.m.

As he found a parking space the rain stopped and a weak sun emerged from behind the towering thunder clouds. Steam began to rise from the shining pavements. When he got out of the car the damp heat struck him like a blow in the face with a wet towel. He hitched his jacket up and down a couple of times to allow some movement of air and glanced up at the sky, wondering whether some more rain might clear the atmosphere of its sticky humidity. But the clouds were lifting. There would be no more rain today.

The pavement was in bad condition, seamed with tarmac from cable-laying. He watched where he trod, avoiding puddles. Then he glanced up at Elaine's house, looking for signs of occupation.

The front door was slightly open. He waited for a moment in case someone was about to emerge, but nobody did. One of the windows of Elaine's flat was open too, and the net curtains were protruding from it, stuck to the glass by the rain.

He walked slowly up the path, eyes flickering as he sought for signs of who had been here before him. There were none, of course, the rain had washed everything away. At the door he did not use the doorbell, but pulled forward his sleeve to cover his hand and pushed the door open with it.

The Yale lock had been fastened back. Rain had formed a broad dark patch of dampness on the tatty patterned hall carpet. Two free newspapers lay in the wet, slowly corrugating. He felt a flare of anger at whoever had delivered the papers and hadn't had the curiosity even to call out.

The door of the downstairs flat was shut. He knocked on it, but there was no reply. He went to the bottom of the stairs and looked up. The door at the top was open too, still and reproachful.

'Elaine,' he called. 'Elaine, it's DCI Anderson.'

Silence. He took a long breath and climbed the stairs. He did not touch the handrail and he walked a little to the side, not wanting to disturb anything. There were no such things as premonitions. It was probably just a common burglary.

That's what it looked like when he reached the top of the stairs. The flat was a mess, furniture upended, clothes pulled out of drawers. He stepped delicately into the confusion, like a cat on wet grass. Then he turned his head and saw Elaine, sprawled by the window, eyes open. Her cat was sniffing at her hair.

He was beside her instantly, on his knees on the wet carpet, feeling for her pulse. But there wasn't any point in trying to revive her. Her flesh was cool beneath his hand and her eyelids wouldn't close. Dead several hours.

Slowly, carefully, he got to his feet. The cat had vanished, tail fluffed up like a milk bottle. He radioed Control for scene-of-crime assistance, replaced the radio on his belt and stood looking down at the corpse.

Elaine looked as if she had just got out of bed when she was killed. Her sleep shirt had ridden up around her waist, revealing her lower torso. She was wearing a black thong which drew attention to her pubic area rather than hiding it. Above her waist the T-shirt was wet with rain from the window. It stuck translucently to her skin, revealing erect nipples. He caught his lower lip in his teeth. He hadn't liked Elaine. The combination of her stupidity and her hopelessness was anathema. But he had admired her splendid physique, as he might admire a classical statue. Soon she would be as cold as marble. What a waste.

Footsteps on the path. His head came up. A man's voice in the hall called, 'Elaine? Are you there, love?'

It must be Banks. Anderson abandoned the body and darted to the door. His first priority was to keep the scene intact, all clues preserved for the forensic team.

'Elaine?' The voice sounded puzzled and slightly anxious. Whenever a murder was committed the most obvious suspect was the dead person's lover, if they had one, but it didn't sound as if Banks knew anything about Elaine's death.

Banks was standing at the bottom of the stairs, one hand on the baluster. He was a big young man, dressed in a singlet and shorts, with the muscular physique of a manual labourer. His long blond hair was tied back in a ponytail. 'Here,' he said, 'who the hell are you? What are you doing here?'

He sounded as if he thought that Elaine had a lover. Anderson came down the stairs towards him and said, 'Alan Banks?'

'Who wants him?'

'I'm DCI John Anderson, Surrey Police.' He said nothing more. He wanted to watch Banks's face.

Banks's expression changed, becoming anxious and wary. 'You were here yesterday, weren't you?'

'What are you doing here, Mr Banks?'

Alan glanced up the stairs and swallowed hard. 'I've come to see Elaine. What are you doing here? What's going on?' He craned his neck to try to see past Anderson and his lower lip began to tremble like a child's. 'Oh shit, what's happening?'

'I'm going to have to ask you to come outside,' Anderson said. 'You mustn't stand here. There may be evidence.'

'Evidence of what?' Banks wailed. He knotted his fists together helplessly.

There was never a good way to do this. 'Mr Banks, I'm afraid that Elaine is dead. I just found her body upstairs.'

If Alan had known, then he was a consummate actor. For a long moment he stared at Anderson, his jaw trembling, nostrils flared and white. He started to shake his head and his eyebrows contracted, tense bars over his wide eyes. For a moment it looked as if he was going to try to burst upstairs, but he seemed to change his mind. He staggered back down to the hall and let Anderson put one hand on his shoulder and guide him through the door.

'What happened?' Alan whispered. He was staring up at the open window. The net curtains had dried in the evening sun and were beginning to flutter slightly, incongruously cheerful.

'She was murdered,' Anderson said. Banks looked at him once, then at the ground. His big body was quivering slightly. He was in shock, but this was a good time to ask questions. If Elaine had programmed him with any lies, he'd probably have forgotten them. 'Alan, listen to me. I came here today to ask Elaine what you did last Saturday evening, after you picked up your takeaway. Can you remember?'

Slowly Alan lifted his head. There was no blood in his

cheeks, his tan looked sallow. 'After we got the curry?'

'Yes. What did you do?'

Banks swallowed hard. 'We went home.'

'I mean before you went home. You got into the car after you left the restaurant and you went somewhere else. Where was it?'

'We didn't do anything,' Alan blurted suddenly. 'We just drove past, that was all.'

'Drove past where?' Anderson asked, calm and patient.

'Eddie Drax's house. If he was out Elaine wanted to go in and take some stuff, just some CDs and stuff, you know? But he was in and there was someone with him, so we didn't stop.'

'Who was with him? How did you know?' Anderson kept his voice steady, but he felt a thump of excitement. At last! This could be the connection that they needed.

'I dunno. Elaine was in the passenger seat. The road was full of cars —' Banks broke off and made a sudden movement as if he wanted to run into the flat. Anderson caught his arm. It was like holding a tree, but Alan didn't fight him. 'Let me go up!' he wailed. 'I want to see her!'

Anderson shook his head. 'I don't think you do, Alan.'

'What's happened to her? How was she killed?'

'Finish telling me how you know Eddie Drax had company,' he said implacably.

Alan buried his head in his hands. 'Elaine said there was a car in the drive. Not Eddie's Porsche. So we drove straight on.'

'What sort of a car?' This was the motive for Elaine's death. It must be. A murderous burglary would have been much too much of a coincidence.

'I don't know, I didn't see.'

Damn! Was it so near, and yet so far? 'Alan, this is important. Whoever drove that car may have killed Elaine to prevent her from describing it. Are you sure you didn't see it?'

'I was driving,' Alan moaned. 'The road was busy, all right? I didn't see.'

Which car had it been? Julia Bond's yellow Fiat or Tony Sealey's red Celica? Both bright cars, vivid, noticeable. It was much more likely to be the Fiat. Elaine's body was still tepid, she must have died that day. Sealey couldn't have killed her after 8.30 in the morning, not if he was going to get to his office in time to be arrested in the car park at 9.15. And how would Sealey have known that Elaine had been at Devonshire Avenue? It had to be Julia. She had disliked Elaine, and the feeling had been mutual. 'What about the colour?' he asked Alan. 'What colour was the car?'

'I didn't see. I only glanced at it. Maybe it was some sort of dark colour.'

Dark? That didn't fit. But there were pink street lamps in Devonshire Avenue, it could be a case of a red car looking black by artificial light. The same might apply to a yellow one, under certain conditions, though it was unlikely. He frowned into Alan's face. There were too many questions. 'Dark? What sort of dark?

'I don't know. Black or dark grey or whatever.' Alan looked as though he was about to burst into tears. 'I glanced at it, that's all. I hardly saw it. I didn't notice. I'm sorry.'

The scream of a siren announced the arrival of some of the support team. DS Fielding jumped from the first car and ran up the path. 'Sir.'

Anderson said, 'Alan, this is Detective Sergeant Fielding. Pat, Mr Banks is being very helpful.' Fielding gave a brief nod, accepting that Banks was not a suspect. 'Get Hart or someone to talk to him about when he last saw Elaine and where he has been since. You come up to the flat with me.'

Fielding nodded and ran back to give quick orders to another member of the team. Then she returned to join him, moving more slowly. Her lips were folded together into a tight line. 'Sir, is Sealey off the hook?'

'He might be, Pat. I'll tell you what Banks told me, and you'll see what I mean.' For a moment Fielding was silent. Her face twisted in disappointment, then straightened as she made a visible effort to calm herself. She let out a short sigh, then said heavily, 'Oh, *fuck*.'

'Smothered,' said Fred, 'to start with at least. Then choked. From the bruising I'd say that whoever killed her leant on her, with his elbow, maybe. We'll know more at the PM.'

'What was she smothered with?'

Fred fished in Elaine's nostrils and open mouth with a pair of tweezers.'Pale threads,'he said, dropping them into a sealable bag.

Anderson and Fielding both looked down at the sofa. Fielding stretched out her gloved hand and slowly lifted up the crooked cushion from the end nearest to the corpse. She turned it over and they saw the marks on it, stains of saliva, pulled threads where the fabric had caught against teeth. Fielding let out a little satisfied snort and called for a big plastic bag.

'Wait,' said Anderson, when she was about to put the cushion into the bag.'Look.'

On the upper edge of the cushion was a little dark stain. 'That looks like blood,' Fielding said.

He took the cushion from her and held it as the murderer might have done, by the edges, ready to cover the nose and mouth of his victim. His gloved palm was directly over the bloodstain.'We may not get any prints off the fabric,' he said. 'But perhaps our murderer has left a mark this time.'

Fielding frowned. 'You think it's the same person, sir?'

He noticed with approval that careful use of the word 'person'. 'I think it's connected. Elaine might have known who was at Eddie's house on Saturday.' He told her about Banks and the sighting of the car. 'Plus, Pat, do you really think this looks like an interrupted burglary?'

Fielding looked steadily around the flat.'No,'she admitted. 'It's a mess, but nothing seems to have been moved that a burglar would have been after. The CD is still where it was.'

'And look at the floor,' said Anderson.

Obediently Fielding looked down. The floor was covered with debris and scattered CDs from the fallen bookshelf. Fielding examined it for some time, then shook her head. 'I'm sorry, sir,' she said, in a tight voice. 'I don't know what you want me to look at.'

'The floor has been Hoovered,' said Anderson softly. He ran his foot along one of the shadowy lines left in the carpet when the vacuum cleaner changed direction. 'Someone

Hoovered the flat before it got into this state. And this cushion, too. Elaine had a cat, the sofa was covered in white cat hairs when I came here before. Now there aren't any. Do you think that could have been Elaine? I don't think cat hairs bothered her.'

'The same person,' Fielding whispered. She shook her head. Then she looked up, eyes bright. 'It could still be Sealey, sir, depending on the time of death.'

'Don't ask me about time of death,' snapped Fred from the floor. 'Bloody hell, it's always the same, you CID blokes think I can work miracles. What am I supposed to make of a room temperature of 23 degrees and cold rain pouring through the window? It could be anything between early morning, 6 or 7 a.m., and lunchtime.'

'Thanks, Fred,' said Anderson ironically.

'If it was early morning, sir, Sealey is still possible.'

She was very eager to nail Sealey. How much of this was lingering resentment at having been addressed by Sealey as a WPC? 'Pat, how did Sealey know that Elaine had seen a car at Devonshire Avenue?'

'I don't know, sir. We'll have to ask him. And we can ask Banks who else knew what he and Elaine had been up to on Saturday night. Besides, how could Julia Bond have done this? This is a violent murder, and Elaine was a big woman.'

'Someone hit her first,' offered Fred. 'There's a swelling on the back of her head. No blood, but she would have been stunned.'

'There won't be any prints,' Anderson said. He crouched down beside the fallen bookcase and pointed to a smear in the dust on its surface. 'Whoever it was wrapped fabric around his or her hand before touching anything. That's probably why the doors were still open; closing the locks could have meant leaving a fingerprint. A careful, thorough person.'

Fielding closed her eyes against the flare of the photographer's flashgun. 'Sir,' she said, 'when we've finished here, do you fancy a drink?'

He looked up in surprise. He wasn't the sort of chief who offered to buy his team a round, and he couldn't remember the last time that one of his people had unilaterally suggested a trip to the pub. The proposal had a pleasant novelty. 'Good idea,' he said. Fielding smiled at him, but she didn't look happy.

By the time they left the office it was almost closing time. Pat looked at Anderson sidelong, wondering if he would still be prepared to go to the pub. It was late. They were both tired, and she, for one, was distinctly pissed off. But she wanted to go. It had taken a lot of nerve to ask him.

He saw her look, of course. 'Well,' he said, in a warmer voice than usual, 'what about that drink?'

'The wine bar down the road has a late licence,' she said, absurdly pleased. 'One spritzer won't make me incapable of driving home.'

The wine bar was self-consciously smart. The moment they walked in she wished she had suggested somewhere else. Anderson, of course, looked quite at home; his steel-grey suit and clotted-cream shirt could have stepped out of a colour supplement. But unlike her jammy chief Pat had not had the opportunity to go home and change. Her trousers were crumpled and her blouse was sticking to her in places where it shouldn't. She felt conspicuous.

'Dry wine?' asked Anderson.

'Yes, please.' She had thought of making some sort of statement by insisting that she buy the drinks, but in the end she did not even try. There was something about him, some natural assumption of superiority, which she was too tired to fight. She let him go to the bar and instead found a table far from the other patrons, in a dark, quiet corner. One of the staff came over and lit the candle. People would think they had come for a romantic drink. She laughed internally at the very idea.

Anderson appeared, carrying two spritzers. That was typical too. Most coppers were too macho to order anything softer than bottled designer beer, no matter how upmarket the watering hole. He drank a spritzer and made it look as if the others were posturing.

'Thanks.' She took a long pull at the drink. Its icy cold, refreshing sharpness cut through the furry nastiness of too much station-issue coffee. 'God, that's good.'

'Cheers,' said Anderson. He sipped at his drink and watched her over the top of it. Suddenly she wondered why he had agreed to come out. What was his agenda? He was too bloody clever to do anything except for a reason. He wouldn't have come for a drink because he just fancied one.

It was all too complicated. She gulped half of the remaining spritzer and began to unfasten her plait. She always untied it as soon as she was off duty. It was a small but necessary ritual. She dug her fingers into her hair close to her scalp and began to lift and separate the heavy dark locks. It was thick hair, dead straight by nature, but today it had been soaked and then tied up in a plait all day and it loosened into a mass of shining dark waves, as if it had been expensively finger-dried.

Anderson was watching her with silent interest. Christ, he probably thought she was trying to make herself attractive to him. She said defensively, 'I always let my hair down as soon as I'm off duty.'

'You're lucky to be able to do it in such a convenient way,' he said, smiling.

She was glad he was feeling humorous, but she couldn't respond. She put her elbows on the table and rested her chin in her hands. 'It can't be Sealey,' she muttered.

'I thought you were off duty,' he said gently.

She looked up into his face. In the candlelight his eyes looked almost black. Pat had never seen navy-blue eyes before she met Anderson. Looking at him now, she noticed that he also had long, thick eyelashes. That must be one of the things that made his eyes sparkle so much. Women would kill for eyes like that.

Now what was she doing? She had not asked him out for a drink so that she could contemplate his physical attractions. Sympathy, that's what she wanted. And if that meant talking about work off duty, well, she would bloody well do it. 'He insists he didn't even know Elaine. And he couldn't have got to her house and then to work, if he's telling us the truth about when he left Burpham.'

Anderson nodded. 'He says both the Toomeys can vouch for him. There's no case there, Pat.'

She ran her hand again and again through her hair, fluffing up each lock. 'Then maybe he killed Eddie Drax and Elaine's death is just what it seems. Just a burglary gone wrong.'

She knew that she sounded desperate. She half-expected an impatient slap down from Anderson, who was not normally tolerant. When he said, 'We already agreed that was unlikely. And I don't think you're going to find Sealey easy to break,' the gentleness in his voice was so unexpected that she found herself undermined. She had been expecting to have to fight, and he was being nice to her! All of a sudden her eyes filled with tears. She turned away at once, horror-struck. A detective sergeant passed for DI, crying in front of a senior officer! It was because she was tired, overwrought, it had been a long day. The suspect she had pinned her hopes on was going to be released without charge, and there had been a dead body, too. She had seen dead bodies that were much worse to look at than Elaine, but there had been something horribly undignified, something pathetic about Elaine's corpse, the way she had sprawled half-naked, legs spread, pubis offered upwards, flaunting her body in death as she had flaunted it when she was alive.

Pat squeezed her eyes shut, fighting the hot pulsing behind her eyelids. If he said anything, if he was sympathetic, she wouldn't be able to cope.

After a few moments she had herself more or less under control, though a gentle word would start her off again. She swallowed hard and lifted her head.

'If it wasn't Sealey,' Anderson said, 'who else could it have been?'

She could answer a direct question. It was good of him to ask, to give her something to do. 'You think it's Julia Bond, sir. But there's less evidence that she was at Devonshire Avenue than Sealey.'

'Maybe she's got a blue sweater,' he suggested.

They looked at each other for a moment in silence. His face was hard to read. He kept his thoughts to himself, shielded behind that smooth skin, those hooded eyes. He wouldn't tell her anything. Even if he'd got it all sussed out, he wouldn't share it with her. Exhaustion made her shoulders slump.

Anderson finished his spritzer and smiled. 'There's another possibility, of course. We might have been looking at the wrong people; all the wrong people. I wonder if we're both personally attached to our pet solutions. You've had it in for Sealey since you met him, haven't you? And I have to admit, I feel much the same about Julia Bond.'

Pat was utterly taken aback. Without thinking she blurted out, 'I thought you fancied her.'

'No,' he said silkily. 'I don't. But she makes it very clear that she is interested in me.' He examined the empty glass. 'I should interview her again. Find out where she says that she was yesterday morning, for example. Would you like to come along and be my chaperone?'

Pat stifled a giggle. Chaperone! The word conjured up an image of Anderson quivering in a corner, trying to protect his modesty, while the voracious Julia Bond advanced upon him, shedding her clothes step by step. 'I'd love to,' she said. 'It sounds a damn sight more interesting than letting Sealey out of the nick.'

'Good. First thing, then.' Anderson smiled at her.

He was all right. He wasn't as cold as people said. He was actually being kind to her. The knowledge made her shy and uncomfortable. She looked quickly down into the remains of her drink.

'And after we've spoken to Julia,' said Anderson, 'it's time we spread the net a bit wider.'

'Wider.' Pat shook her head. 'Sounds as if we're starting again from scratch. What are we looking for, someone else with a motive?'

'That's always a good place to start.'

Pat felt a sudden swimming of alcohol. One spritzer, and she was almost pissed! She hadn't eaten, that was the problem. She desperately wanted another drink. In fact, she wanted to get pissed. But she knew she couldn't, and she resented it. Sometimes being a police officer was bloody tough. 'Motive,' she muttered into the empty glass. 'Half Guildford seems to have had a motive to kill Eddie Drax. Love, loathing, lucre and lust: that's the old mnemonic, isn't it?'

She glanced up and saw that Anderson's face was sombre.

'That's it. But there's not much love around in this case, from what I've seen.'

It was true. The people involved were sad and sordid. 'So that leaves loathing, lucre and lust,' she said sorrowfully.

'Well,' Anderson said, and she could hear that he was making a conscious effort to lift the tone, 'we've got somewhere to start, anyway. You talk to Banks, Pat. Find out who knew that he and Elaine had been to Devonshire Avenue on Saturday night.'

'All right.' There would be no fun in talking to Alan when he was grieving, but Anderson was right. 'What about you?' She wasn't calling him 'sir'. Why was that?

'I'm going to go back to square one, back to where I started,' Anderson said. He pushed back his chair and got up. 'Good night, Pat. Go home, you're tired.'

'Thanks for the drink,' she said, suddenly bereft.

'It was a pleasure.' He turned away and walked out without a backward glance.

She watched him go, then buried her face in her hands. It was nearly 11.30, and she didn't want to be alone. That was easy, she'd go over to Charlie's. He was used to her turning up at peculiar hours. He was probably already asleep. But she could wake him.

TEN
Friday Morning

Waking Charlie up was all very well, but it nearly made Pat late. She pulled into the car park at the nick in a screech of tyres and got out just as Anderson emerged from the lobby, looking at his watch.

She ran up to the BMW to wait for him. An apology was on her lips, but she decided she didn't need to apologise. She wasn't late, she was just, well, very on time.

'How do you want to play this one, sir?' she asked as Anderson swooped the car into the traffic. It was blissfully cool inside the BMW. Her own car, an elderly Ford, did not benefit from air conditioning.

'Straight,' he said. 'I ask the questions, you take notes. And watch her. She plays up to me so much I wonder if I may be missing something.'

That was pretty unlikely, but it was interesting that Anderson should admit the possibility. He seemed more human every day. She watched him drive, lean hands firm and competent on the wheel, eyes constantly shifting. 'Are we going to concentrate on Elaine's death, sir? Or shall we take it back to Drax, too?'

'Let's see how she behaves,' said Anderson. He glanced across at her. His eyes were opaque this morning, not sparkling. Suddenly she realised that he was not looking forward to this interview. Why should that be? He couldn't be frightened of

Julia Bond, she was sure he wasn't frightened of anything. So why the tension in his face?

'You did some of the interviews at Drax & Bond, didn't you,' he said.

'Yes, sir. With the designers, mostly. An interesting bunch.' A weird bunch, women with black clothes and black hair, men with ponytails and collarless shirts. She was sure she had smelt pot in the smoking room. 'Several of them hated Eddie's guts, but they all had verifiable alibis for Saturday evening.'

'What did you think of the company?'

The question surprised her. She thought carefully before replying. 'The employees like the company, sir. They seem to be most interested in whether they get work that's fun for them, and they all said that Eddie and Julia do a good job in getting clients. Apparently their client list is formidable.'

'That will be why Dacre & Co. are interested in a takeover,' he commented.

'Only one or two of the employees seem to know about that, sir. I'm not sure how the rest of them would take it. Most of them said they liked the small-firm atmosphere. A few of them who've been around for a long time say that it's not the same now as it was when it started, but people always say that.' She hesitated. 'Is this relevant, sir?'

'It could be. Go on.'

'They say things have changed since Eddie and Julia started putting more emphasis on the financial side of things. I get the impression that nobody used to take much notice of where money went. But David Thompson's been there six years now and he's got things well under control. They don't like him. The senior designer, the one who knows about the possibility of the Dacre deal, said that the one good thing that would come from a takeover would be that they would replace the finance director. They don't like his assistant, either.'

'Samantha Smith.'

'That's right. They call her David's bloodhound.'

Anderson laughed. 'If you ask me, Pat, David's bloodhound is biting him when nobody's looking.'

She knew about Anderson's visit to Sam and Emma. 'Yes,

sir. I don't know if I'm looking forward to that particular investigation.'

He laughed at her. 'Don't tell me you're worried about taking on Samantha Smith!'

'Perhaps I feel the same way about her as you do about Julia Bond.'

Now what in God's name had made her say that? They stopped at a set of traffic lights and Anderson turned his head to stare at her, a long cold stare that made her cheeks hot. She thought for one awful moment that he was going to rebuke her. But he didn't say anything, and then the lights changed.

He was back! He couldn't keep away. Now was that because her plan to ensnare him was working, or was it because he thought she was guilty? Either way it was a bloody nuisance. Julia had better things to do with her time than talk to Anderson. Why didn't he leave her alone? What more did she have to do to get rid of him?

But since he was here, she needed to act consistently. Time to play the vamp again. It was a risky thing to do. If she went on pretending that she wanted him, she might end up wanting him for real, and that would be disastrously embarrassing. She would have to watch herself.

She spread her arms wide, stretching as if she embraced the air, then looked down at herself. Short skirt, tight blouse, high heels; fine. Should she unbutton the top of the blouse? If she did, her Wonderbraed cleavage would be splendidly on show. Was Chief Inspector Anderson a tit man?

On reflection she decided to leave the button fastened. According to Bev there were two policemen this time, and one of them was the small, dark female Detective Sergeant who had spent some time at Drax & Bond earlier in the week. There was no need to look obvious with another woman there to see.

The door opened. Julia swung her big chair around and got up. 'Chief Inspector,' she said, smiling broadly. 'How very nice to see you again.' She walked towards him, stretching out her hand. She hadn't managed to touch him yet, and this was a perfect opportunity.

He looked not startled, but suspicious. Perhaps people didn't usually shake hands with detectives. Well, she wasn't going to take no for an answer, and she stood with her hand extended, waiting.

At last he clasped her hand. He didn't smile. His grasp was warm and strong. She pressed her fingers against his palm, making her clasp as sensual as she could. His lips tightened and she barely restrained a smile of satisfaction. He was working hard to control himself. 'Ms Bond. Have you met Detective Sergeant Fielding?'

'Yes,' Julia did not attempt to hide her dislike. She nodded to Fielding and returned to her chair. With another woman present she might find it more difficult to succeed in her plan to put Anderson off the scent. Also, Fielding was altogether too slender and too pretty. 'Now,' she said, ignoring Fielding and focusing her gaze on Anderson, 'do sit down. How can I help you today?'

'I want to ask you about Elaine Williams,' Anderson said.

'Elaine!' So did he suspect Elaine at last? Well, that had been her intention from the start. She lifted her phone and pressed the button for her secretary. 'Denise, would you bring us in some coffee, please? Milk and sugar?' she asked Anderson.

'Black,' he said.

'Black, Denise,' said Julia.

'I take milk,' said Detective Sergeant Fielding.

Julia put the phone down and leant back in her chair. Anderson was watching her stony-faced. It suited him. He looked authoritative and powerful and as tense as a compressed spring. How far would she have to push him before he would break? And once he broke, what would he be like? What would happen when all that energy burst out? He'd probably be a real demon. Perhaps he would be violent. It would be interesting to see him violent.

'Well,' she said, 'Elaine. I'm glad you're taking her seriously at last. You know I always thought she did it.'

'How well do you know her?' Anderson asked.

She sniffed. 'As little as I could get away with, but I used to socialise with Eddie and she lived with him for nearly a year, so I didn't have a lot of choice. Appalling vulgar girl. She

189

only ever wanted Eddie's money. Do you know that she had another boyfriend all the time they were living together? She used to sleep with him.'

'How do you know?'

'Eddie's cleaning lady Elsie told me that he came round one day. Eddie knew about it later. He was none too pleased.'

'Do you know where Elaine is now?'

'My God, haven't you tracked her down yet? I think she's moved to some squalid little flat the other side of town. And serve her right.'

Denise came in with a tray of coffee. She had brought milk. Julia poured coffee for Anderson and gave it to him, but he handed it to Detective Sergeant Fielding. They exchanged what she could only have described as an intimate glance. She simmered with anger. Gloves off! As Denise went out and shut the door Julia caught Anderson's eyes and deliberately unfastened the top button on her blouse.

His eyes flickered once to her bosom, drawn by the movement of her fingers. Then he returned his gaze to her face. He could have outstared a cat, but she was determined not to give in. If she let him gain control now, she would never recover the advantage. She licked her lips and smiled very slightly.

'Ms Bond,' said Anderson, 'I found Elaine Williams dead in her flat yesterday evening.'

Christ! But she kept herself steady to meet his steady eyes. 'What's that got to do with me?' she asked him, matching chill for chill. 'What happened, did she kill herself?'

'She was murdered,' Anderson said. He leant forward a little, his narrow face bright and sharp. Being the focus of his attention made her shiver with satisfaction. The smell of his aftershave floated to her nostrils. 'Ms Bond, I would like an account of your movements yesterday.'

He suspected her now of two murders. She would never get the police out of her hair. What a waste of bloody time! Anger made her ignore his question. At least needling him relieved her frustration. 'Presumably,' she said, 'you have as little evidence about this murder as about Eddie's. Otherwise I imagine that you would already have arrested me.'

'Where were you yesterday morning, Ms Bond?' he repeated.

She leant forward and rested her chin on her folded hands. Her face was only a yard from his. His skin was very smooth, supple-looking. It looked younger than his age, in the same way that his greying hair looked older. She stroked her fingers over her lips and said, 'Well, to start with, Baron Scarpia, I was in bed.'

A derisive snort made her sit up, startled. She glared at Fielding. The woman turned the snort into a cough and patted her fingers against her thorax. 'Sorry,' she said, 'bit of a frog in my throat. Do carry on, Ms Bond.' And she poised her pen over her notebook, cocking her head on one side, the parody of a bright attentive secretary.

Julia let her face stiffen into an expression of rigid dislike, but Fielding didn't seem to notice. 'Where was I?' Julia said, hoping to prompt a response from Anderson.

'In bed,' said Fielding, reading from her notes, 'with some Baron or other, is that right?'

Sarcastic little bitch. Humour undermined sensuality, it would wreck everything. Julia wished Sergeant Fielding dead. She turned her shoulder to her and looked again at Anderson. 'Then I got up. I was a bit late yesterday, I think. I got in to the office about 9.30. Denise will tell you.'

'Did anyone see you during your morning, Ms Bond?'

She parted her lips in a feral smile. 'You always seem to ask the same thing, Baron Scarpia. As you know, I live alone and my house is isolated. I drive to work in my car along with thousands of other people. There is no reason why anyone should be able to confirm what I did or didn't do yesterday morning.'

'Did you stop for petrol? To buy a newspaper?'

'I didn't need petrol, and my newspaper is delivered to the office. I'm afraid you'll just have to take my word for it.' She leant back, folding her hands and smiling silkily.

'Which route did you take to work?'

'The most direct one. You've been to my house, haven't you? You know the way I would go. I went that way.'

'You didn't go round to Elaine's flat?'

'No,' said Julia coldly. 'Good God, Chief Inspector, are you really suggesting that I killed Elaine? She was six inches taller than me, the Amazon. I'd stand a better chance of killing Eddie than her. They'd laugh you out of court. Besides, what makes you think that the deaths are connected?'

He smiled slightly. 'I believe that Elaine was killed because she knew who was at Eddie's house on Saturday,' he said.

That sleek self-satisfied look made her cautious. What was he hiding? 'If she's dead, how do you know that?' she asked warily.

Anderson didn't reply. He finished his coffee and said, 'Thank you again for your time, Ms Bond.'

She was losing the initiative. Time to ingratiate herself again, that always seemed to make him uncomfortable. 'Oh, you know that you're welcome any time, Chief Inspector.' She made her voice into a husky purr. 'Any time. Day or night.'

His dark eyebrows lifted. It could have been enthusiasm, but she felt a sudden stab of fear. Was he laughing at her? 'Thank you,' was all he said. 'I'll remember that.'

Pat managed to keep a straight face until she got out to the car. Then she began to laugh. 'My God!' she exclaimed. 'Awful woman! Who does she think she is, Lauren Bacall? I practically expected her to say, "Any time you need me, just whistle." '

Anderson looked at her sidelong. 'Thank you for your protection,' he said ironically.

'And what's this "Baron Scarpia" business?' The idea of anyone, let alone a suspect, having a nickname for Anderson was irresistible.

'Baron Scarpia is the chief of the Roman police in a Puccini opera,' said Anderson. Something about his tone of voice made her stop laughing. Perhaps the nickname was an insult. She'd have to ask Charlie, he was crazy about opera, he had all the guides. Anderson glanced at her again. 'What do you think?' he asked.

She sobered up and consulted her notes as Anderson started the drive back to the station. 'Well,' she said after a few minutes, 'she could have done it, sir. She denies it, but there's nobody to say that she was anywhere else when Elaine was killed.'

'That's what I thought,' said Anderson, his eyes on the road.

'So if she didn't do it,' Pat mused aloud, 'what on earth is up with her? She seems almost to want to be arrested. Was she like this about Eddie Drax's death? I mean, determined not to justify herself, proud of the fact that she's got no alibi. And throwing herself at you.'

'Yes,' said Anderson. 'That's quite consistent.'

'It's odd, though, isn't it? I mean, I don't believe she really fancies you. It's as if she's almost teasing you. Us.'

'Me,' he said slowly. 'She's teasing me.'

Catherine was reviewing a complex tax return when the phone rang. She thought for a moment of ignoring it, but her concentration was already broken, and it could be an important client. 'Catherine Marshall,' she said, still staring at the page of numbers.

'Catherine, hello.'

'John!' She dropped her pen and smiled with relief. When she'd put him off yesterday she'd been afraid that he would take it as a brush-off. That would have been a disaster. 'Thanks for calling. How are you?'

'I'm fine. Catherine, may I come to your office today? I need to ask you some more questions about Eddie Drax.'

So it was business, not pleasure. His voice sounded different, cool and distant, its velvety warmth converted into a sort of prickly roughness. She was disappointed and suddenly apprehensive. 'Yes, all right. But I've got meetings all afternoon. Can you come now?'

'I'll be there in twenty minutes,' he said.

The phone went dead. She looked at the receiver before replacing it. He had been brusque. She wasn't imagining it.

Was this already the beginning of the end? Two evenings of bliss, and now he was bored with her? It wouldn't surprise her. It would be par for the course.

But his lovemaking had been so intense, so passionate, she could hardly believe that he wasn't serious. Perhaps it was something else. Perhaps the case was going badly. Anyone could be abrupt when things were bad at work.

Feeling a little better, she got up and began to clear her

desk, then called through to Sue for the file on Eddie Drax.

He arrived a little sooner than he had said, at just before 11 a.m. She had coffee ready on her desk. When Sue showed him in she got up and stood watching him, uncomfortable, conscious of the formality of the situation. He looked tired. She wanted to kiss him, but she didn't dare even touch him. Shaking his hand would be worse than not touching him at all. 'Please,' she said, hearing the quiver in her own voice and angry with herself because of it, 'sit down.'

'I'm sorry that I have to come back to you,' he said. 'I hoped I had got all I needed on my first interview, but –'

He broke off. She sat down and poured the coffee. She had told Sue to make it extra strong, the way she knew he liked it. 'Are things not going well?' she asked. 'I'm sorry.'

He didn't respond. Was sympathy misplaced, then? She bit her lip. She had no idea how to handle the situation. She didn't think she could guide it, so in the end she said, 'How can I help?'

He met her eyes and she shivered. When they made love his face had a quiet, concentrated intensity that moved her deeply. Now she saw the same intensity in every feature, but it was focused differently – not on her, but on what she knew. She felt like an insect pinned to a board, scrutinised through the scientist's microscope.

'You explained to me about Eddie's will,' he said. 'But there are some other things I'd like to know more about. For example, I understand that the directors of the company had key man insurance.'

It was going to be business, then. She set her personal feelings aside, or tried to. 'Yes,' she said. 'I only found out about it this week. David Thompson sent me through the details.'

'Why did he send it to you?'

'There are tax complexities with key man policies. Would you like me to explain them to you?'

The ghost of a smile touched his face. 'Not for the moment. We'll come back to it if it seems relevant. Do you know why Thompson sent them to you this week?'

She shook her head. 'No. The policies had been in place

for a few months. He'd probably only just got around to it.'

There was a short silence. John sipped his coffee. She found herself watching his mouth, those pale firm lips that had made her cry out. She tore her eyes away. Was she obsessed with him or what? She wasn't a schoolgirl in the throes of a crush, she was an adult and she'd only been out with him twice.

'What do you think of David Thompson?' he asked.

Surely he couldn't suspect David! 'He's a very nice man,' she said defensively, and the words sounded prim and mealy-mouthed even to her. 'He's got a lovely wife, Penny, and two kids, Thomas and Louise. They're a sweet family. He's asked me over to their house once or twice. Not all clients are as pleasant and helpful as him.'

'How much does he know about the company? I mean, the directors' affairs?'

'Everything, I should say. He's been there six years and he's conscientious. Eddie and Julia both trust him. I mean, Eddie trusted him. They got on all right. I never heard that he argued with Eddie.'

John nodded as if accepting the information. Then he said, 'I admit that when I first spoke to you I forgot a question I should have asked. You wrote Eddie's will, you would know. What will happen to Eddie's shares?'

'You mean, as opposed to his personal wealth?'

'Exactly.' He looked at her, quiet and expectant. There seemed to be a machine behind his eyes, a computer, silent and efficient. It was unnerving to watch him thinking.

'The shares are governed by the articles,' she explained. Normally she enjoyed making technical things accessible to laymen, but now she felt as if she was being put through a sieve. 'Eddie couldn't have left them through his will. You could have asked David, he knows all about this.'

'Does he?'

'Yes. In fact, we had a meeting about it a month or so ago.' She could hear her voice getting less controlled, faster, as she tried to pour out more and more information. Why did she feel so pressured? Why did she want him to smile, to approve of her? She felt stupid and incoherent. With an effort she closed her eyes and took a deep breath, ordering the facts in her mind. Then she said precisely, 'Many private companies have restrictions on the transfer of shares. It's quite usual. When there are only two directors, you can see that each of them would want to have some control about what happened to the shares in the event of the other's death.'

He nodded. His eyes were fixed on her, as they had been when he told her to unfasten her dress. She seemed to feel the balcony's warm air on her naked skin. Shivering, she went on, 'In the case of Drax & Bond the arrangement was that in the event of the death of a shareholder the directors have the opportunity to buy the shares at current market value.'

'The directors, not the other shareholders?'

'Yes.' He was listening with close attention, then. That was an important point. 'When the articles were drafted Eddie and Julia were the only directors. It should have been shareholders, really, but these slips in drafting happen. It didn't matter, of course, until they made David a director, and that was only two years ago. I noticed it a couple of months ago when I was doing some other work. I mentioned it to David and he knew straight away that it was a mistake. That's why I was talking to Eddie about changing it. The trouble is, Eddie and Julia had no patience for that sort of paperwork. I'd sent the new articles to David and he was trying to get Eddie and Julia to sign the minutes to change them, but no luck yet.'

John leant forward a little, his lips parted. 'So what exactly is the position at the moment?'

'At the moment, David and Julia both have the right to buy Eddie's shares at market value.'

His eyes narrowed. 'Would that be an attractive proposition? I mean, with the Dacre & Co. deal waiting to happen?'

'Oh, certainly. It's all to do with valuation.' He made a little gesture with his hand, encouraging her to continue. 'At the moment there's no offer from Dacre & Co., not even any firm interest. So as far as the Inland Revenue are concerned the company will be valued as just what it is, a smallish private company with no dividend record and rather erratic profits. I could probably argue for a very low valuation, just a few pounds a share. But then when Dacre & Co. buy, you see, they are buying the future potential of the company. The price per share would be much, much more. Ten, a hundred times more. I don't know, they haven't discussed the price, but I would guess that they would pay £15m over a current arguable share value of maybe £2m; maybe less, if I do a good job.'

'That's a £13m gain,' he said slowly.

'Absolutely. And of course Dacre & Co. would buy with paper, a share for share, so there wouldn't be any tax on it until the Dacre & Co. shares were sold.'

There was a long pause. John sat back in his chair, looking out of the window. She watched him in silence, then leant forward to refill his cup. She wanted to say something, but didn't want to interrupt him. And how odd it was, that all through the conversation they had not used each other's Christian name. Such a position of awkwardness they found themselves in.

At last he looked back at her. 'What do you imagine will happen?'

'Julia will buy the shares, I suppose.'

'Why Julia and not David?'

'Well –' She thought about it. 'The articles entitle the directors to buy the shares between them equally. So if David went by the articles, he could take half of Eddie's 50 per cent.' His eyes seemed to be boring into her. 'But he won't,' she added hastily. 'It's not the way it was supposed to happen.'

'Just suppose he did,' John asked softly, 'how would he get the money to buy the shares from Eddie's estate?'

'Any bank would lend him most of it. They understand valuation. What would they lend him, maybe £500,000? It's nothing, compared to the company value.'

'Would Julia have to borrow to buy the shares?'

Catherine hesitated. She knew a lot about Julia's personal affairs, but it would be most improper to release the information without permission. 'I'm sure you'll understand that I can't tell you that without talking to Julia.'

He leant forward again, his eyes on her. 'I just want an idea of whether she could easily have bought Eddie out.'

'I'm sorry.' She wanted to call him John, but the name

stuck on her tongue. 'I can't tell you that. You'll have to ask Julia.'

For a moment he stayed where he was. Then he sat back. 'All right. Just one more question, then.'

It sounded as if he was interrogating her! Suddenly she was angry. How could he come here and put her through this, and on top of everything ask her questions which he knew that as a professional person she shouldn't answer?

He said, 'What will happen to David Thompson if Dacre & Co. buy Drax & Bond?'

That was an interesting question. She considered it for some time. Then she said, 'Well, to be honest, I should think that Dacre & Co. will let him go.'

'Let him go? Sack him, do you mean?'

'Not sack him. You sack someone for incompetence. No, I mean, Dacre & Co. is a big organisation. They'd probably bring in Drax & Bond as a division, not a separate company. There are no tax losses or anything that would make them leave it as it is. So it would probably fall under an existing finance director. They just wouldn't need David. They'd make him redundant.'

'What would the terms be?'

'He's on a one-year contract. So a year's salary. About £85,000. Mostly taxable.'

Anderson watched her in silence. Then he said, 'How old is David?'

'God, I don't know. Forty-two, forty-three? About that, anyway.' She looked at his motionless face and felt suddenly afraid. 'Look,' she said, again stifling her desire to use his name, 'surely you don't think that David was involved in Eddie's death. I told you what a nice man he is.'

He got up suddenly and walked over to the window. It was wide open, in a vain attempt to let in cool air. Catherine was suddenly ashamed that she and her fellow partners were too mean to install air conditioning. At least the humidity made sure that the traffic fumes stayed down below. For a moment John looked at the traffic passing by, three floors down. Then he turned back to her and said, 'Did you know that Elaine Williams was murdered yesterday?'

Sickness struck like a blow at her stomach. She put her hand to her throat, fighting down a heave of bile. 'Oh, my God. No. No, I didn't know.'

'She was smothered and choked in her own house. Whoever did it tried to make it look like a burglary, but it wasn't very convincing.'

'Oh, God.' Catherine turned away, hiding her face. All the catty things she had said and thought about Elaine filled her mind with remorse. 'Oh, that poor girl.'

Something touched her shoulder. She jumped violently and looked up into John's face. He was standing above her, one hand resting gently on her upper arm. 'I'm sorry it had to be me that told you. But whoever I am dealing with is both ruthless and determined. I have to follow all the leads I can.' He released her shoulder. 'Are you all right?'

'Yes,' she lied.

'You'll forgive me, I have to go. Thank you for your help. It's been most illuminating.'

For a moment he looked into her eyes. He didn't smile, and before she was ready he turned away and walked out of the office. Catherine sat shivering in her big chair, her arms wrapped closely around herself. Absurdly, all that she could think about was that she had been wearing the white body under her suit, and he didn't even seem to have noticed.

ELEVEN
Friday Afternoon

'Fielding here, sir.'

'Pat, I've just been talking to Catherine Marshall. She's been explaining the share capital of Drax & Bond. It was extremely interesting. There's something I need you to do.'

'Yes, sir.'

Anderson paused while he guided the car over a mini roundabout. 'David Thompson told me a lie in our first interview. I don't know whether it was deliberate or not, but it's suspicious.'

'Thompson? The FD?'

'The FD. I want you to check the other facts. When I interviewed him the day after Drax died he told me that on Saturday evening he was up on Beacon Hill, taking a walk. I want you to see if there's any way of checking that out.'

'Yes, sir.' She sounded hesitant. 'I'll ask whoever it is who had that beat. Maybe they stopped by the car park some time that evening. What type of car does Thompson drive?'

'I don't know. Get records to check it out. Or call Drax & Bond, if it's a company car. If you do, you can tell them I'm going there now.'

'Back to Drax & Bond?'

'To speak to Thompson. Or to Julia Bond again, if he's not there.'

Fielding muttered something he couldn't catch. Then she said, 'OK, sir. Is there anything else?'

'Yes. Ask Banks how well Elaine knew David. They must have met. Thompson played golf at the same club as Drax, they used to meet there socially. Ask Banks what Elaine thought of him.'

'OK.'

He hung up and let himself flow into the sensation of driving, of pushing the big powerful car towards Drax & Bond just as fast as he could without breaking the law. He liked to drive. The concentrated pattern of action and reaction acted as a stimulus to the logical part of his brain.

He should have asked Catherine today's questions earlier. But there was no point in recriminations. All of the arguments supporting Julia as Eddie's murderer were still in place, and to add to them he knew that she had known and despised Elaine Williams. But now there was a new possibility in David Thompson.

He thought back to their initial interview. Thompson had struck him as an ordinary man, nothing special; like himself a fraction under six feet tall, rather thickset, with light brown hair and pale eyes; an unremarkable pinstripe suit. Fractious and irritable, hostile even, but that was hardly surprising under the circumstances. The police tended to be most apparent at times of trouble, and as a result people often blamed them. It need be no more than that.

But why had he lied about what would happen to Eddie's shares? Well, there might have been reasons. Perhaps he had simply forgotten.

Anderson pulled into the car park at Drax & Bond, stopped the car and for a moment leant back against the headrest and closed his eyes.

He was still certain that Julia was the culprit. However you looked at it, she stood to gain the most from Eddie's death – either 100 per cent of the company value or, if David took up the option of buying his share, 75 per cent. In either case it was a small fortune. And she had known Elaine, and hated her.

But he was rapidly growing to detest Julia Bond. He had

thought that Fielding might suppress the worst excesses of her behaviour, but he had been wrong. She had been just as bad as ever, licking her lips and opening the button of her blouse to proffer him her breasts. He couldn't believe that she really wanted him; she was just trying to infuriate him. Using that ridiculous nickname, with one of his team there to hear her! He had needed all his control to stay calm.

How could he be just to her, if he hated her? And if he tried to compensate for his hate, how would he know that he had not gone too far, and given her the benefit of the doubt when he should not have done?

There was no answer to it. He had to rely on himself, as he always did. He must separate thoughts from emotions and look at Julia with a disinterested eye.

He went straight to the accounts department. Sam was sitting at her desk, working at a computer terminal. She gave him one cold stare, then ignored him.

Lisa Cresswell was rummaging in the drawer of her desk for something. She did not hear him arrive. 'Lisa,' he said.

'Oh bloody hell!' Lisa jumped and fluttered her hand against her heart. 'God, you'll give me a heart attack!'

'Lisa, I'd like to speak to David Thompson again.'

'I'm sorry, Inspector,' said Lisa without a trace of apology. 'He's not in today. He called in sick.'

'I may have to speak to him at home. What's his home address?'

Lisa looked dubious. 'If he's not well, I don't think –' Then she registered his stare and her voice became small and timid. 'All right. Here you are.' She wrote an address on a post-it note and passed it to him.

He thanked her with a nod, then headed in the direction of Julia's office. He saw that Sam was looking at him and turned to meet her eyes. Had the fact that he wanted to talk to Thompson worried her? Or was that just sheer dislike that he saw in her face?

Denise, Julia's secretary, also looked startled. 'Mr Anderson! Back again?'

'So soon,' he said. 'Is Ms Bond in?'

'She's having lunch,' said Denise awkwardly.

He raised his eyebrows. Julia's yellow sports car had been parked next to the door, so wherever she was lunching it wasn't likely to be out. 'I'd like to talk to her,' he said imperturbably.

Denise looked at him uncertainly, then lifted the phone. 'Julia, it's Denise. It's Mr Anderson back again. He wants to talk to you.'

She replaced the receiver a moment later and managed a polite smile. 'Please go in.'

'Hello,' crooned Julia as he came through the door. She had her lunch spread out on her desk: sandwiches from Marks & Spencer, a plastic plate of crudités with a dip, a bag of crisps, some grapes. 'Couldn't you keep away?'

'There's something else I want to ask you about.' He sat down opposite her.

'Please. Want a sandwich?'

'No, thank you.' He was hungry, but the idea of sharing a meal with her was insupportable.

She dipped a stick of carrot into the dressing and put it to her lips. She didn't bite it, just sucked the dressing off it. He did not betray his ever-increasing distaste. 'Well,' she said, running her tongue around her lips to catch an errant blob of dressing, 'how may I be of assistance?'

If she was a murderer, she was an exceptionally cool one. But murderers came in all shapes and sizes, and a woman was as likely to be cool and unperturbed as the most ruthless male villain. Also, why shouldn't she be cool? There was no evidence to link her with either crime; unless the lab report showed up that the blood on the cushion wasn't Elaine's, or Alan's, or Frosty the cat's, God forbid. Then, maybe. Maybe.

'I want to talk about David Thompson.'

'Oh, the bean counter,' she said, and laughed. 'That was what Eddie called him. Just to annoy him, of course. Poor old David. It must be a bugger, looking after the money in a creative organisation like this. All the problems and none of the thanks.'

'So why do it?'

'We do pay him,' said Julia sarcastically. She dipped a celery stick, held it to her lips, bared her white teeth and bit firmly into it. 'Food,' she whispered. 'The ultimate oral gratification. Or is it?'

He would not reveal how much her behaviour disturbed him. 'Tell me what would happen to David if Dacre & Co. buy you out.'

She took another mouthful, chewed, swallowed, and smiled at him. 'I love the way you ask questions,' she said. 'You're so blunt. Masterful, you could say. "Tell me what would happen." Mmm. Are you the same in bed, Baron Scarpia?'

He wanted to order her to answer him, but that would just be grist to her mill. 'I'd be grateful if you would answer the question,' he said calmly.

'Does this mean that you suspect David now, as well as me?'

'I want to know more about him.' She seemed determined not to answer him. Perhaps he could get to the information he wanted some other way. 'Where does he stand as far as control of the company is concerned?'

'Control?' She sounded surprised. 'He doesn't have control.'

'Even after Eddie's death? He's a director, isn't he?'

'No, you don't understand at all. He is a director, but Eddie and I had the shares. And we had an agreement that when one of us dies the other one can buy their shares from the estate. So that's what I'll be doing, of course.'

He didn't intend to tell her about the articles yet. 'So David has no shares at all?'

'No. He was going to have, but it came to nothing, poor love.' She pushed a sandwich across the desk towards him. 'Look, Baron Scarpia, do eat something. I feel terrible sitting here stuffing my face and you sitting there all lean and hungry. Actually, that's rather a good description of you, isn't it. *Yon Cassius hath a lean and hungry look. He thinks too much; such men are dangerous.* Perhaps I ought to call you Cassius instead of Scarpia.'

She seemed completely indifferent to his icy disdain. She must be playing with him. For a moment he imagined actually succumbing to her, reacting to her taunting with some sort of violence, sexual or physical. Perhaps she would laugh at him. The thought was appalling. He couldn't bear to be mocked.

At least he knew that his face showed nothing of his anger and frustration. He asked, 'What do you mean, he was going to have?'

'Sure you don't want a sandwich? Oh, all right, be like that. Try a grape.' She arched her eyebrows at him, delighted to be maddening. When he didn't respond she pouted and ate a grape herself. 'God, you're so boring. I thought that detective and suspect were supposed to engage in a scintillating interplay of something or other.'

So she was playing with him. He knew it. 'I've got a job to do. I want answers.'

'Oh, all right. Let's see, what was the question? Oh, about David. Yes, well, when he joined we did talk about giving him share options. You know about share options?'

Anderson nodded curtly. He didn't want to speak if by doing so he would give her another excuse for going off at a tangent.

'Well, we started it out. Catherine Marshall was helping us design the scheme. But it was terribly complicated, it involved all sorts of new shares and God knows what, and it took years to get it sorted out. And then Eddie got shirty about it and wouldn't agree.'

'Wouldn't agree to what?'

'Well, any shares that we gave to David would end up diluting what we had, wouldn't they? And between the time he joined and the time that we had the details hammered out the company had done so well that it would have meant giving away really quite a lot. I wouldn't have minded, not much, because we did say that he could have them, but Eddie decided to dig his heels in.'

'And what happened?'

'Well, a little while ago the Inland Revenue changed the law, and then it wasn't worth giving David options anyway. So there wasn't anything we could do. Eddie said he felt better about it. You know, it wasn't his fault, then.'

Thompson might well have seen things quite differently. Anderson said only, 'How did David take it?'

'He was a sweetie. He's frightfully reasonable, you know. And we did pay him a big bonus once or twice. Which is more than we get; the creative directors don't take bonuses.'

She picked up a grape and began to peel it, easing the golden skin away from the translucent pullulating flesh. She slipped the grape between her lips, held it there and looked meaningfully at him, as if she expected him to lean forward over her desk and remove the grape from her teeth with his mouth.

'Catherine Marshall,' he said carefully, 'tells me that according to the articles, David may have the right to buy some of Eddie's shares at an advantageous price.'

She swallowed the grape rapidly and looked about to choke. 'Really?'

'Apparently.' Was her shock just surprise, or was it that she had expected to end up with every share in the company?

'Oh.' She sat back in her chair and began work on another grape. 'No, you're right. I remember David saying something about it. Something in the articles. I was leaving it to Eddie. I hate that sort of legal gibberish. I'm a marketing person and a client handler, not a bloody lawyer.'

'How do you feel about that?'

Her big blue eyes were very cool. 'Well, if he ends up with a stake in the company I suppose it would be only fair. He'd have to borrow the money, but that wouldn't present much of a problem. Though he'd have to pay through the nose on the interest, without any security.'

Anderson thought of the address in his pocket, one of the most desirable around Guildford. 'Couldn't he secure it on his house?'

She laughed. 'Baron Scarpia, darling, he bought that house six years ago. He must be deep into negative equity. Should be all right in a couple of years, but he probably owes the bank more than he's worth right now.'

'Thank you,' he said, not without irony. 'You've been very helpful.'

'Well, I'm sure I didn't intend to be. Are you going to arrest me today?'

'No.'

A creamy smile spread over her face. 'You don't need all the evidence to arrest someone, do you? You just need a reasonable suspicion. What about it?'

He shook his head. 'Not yet,' he said steadily.

'In that case –' She leant forward, her gaze suddenly dark with challenge. The top button of her blouse was still undone, and now her fingers unfastened the next button and the next. Her breasts were full and very white, rich orbs of soft flesh nestling in the cups of her bra. 'In that case, Detective Chief Inspector, perhaps we could think of something else to pass the time.'

Thank God he had finished his questions. He had to stay polite to her, and she knew it. She seemed determined to drive him beyond the point of no return. 'That's not possible,' he said, and got up.

'Why?' She pulled back the front of her blouse and trailed her fingers over the swell of her breasts. 'What's the problem? Are you not supposed to have relationships with suspects?'

Was this the right time to put her down? He decided against it. He wanted to do it, but for personal satisfaction only. If she was guilty, there would be plenty of time to disabuse her; and if she was not, she might still be useful to him. All he said was, 'Quite right. I'm not supposed to.'

'But you'd like to,' she whispered. 'Yes?'

He didn't reply. She smiled up at him, no doubt assuming that silence signified assent. 'In that case,' she said softly, 'another time.'

He felt hot, not with desire but with loathing. He turned away from her at once and walked towards the door.

The steam-bath humidity outside felt cool by comparison.

He was eager to talk to David Thompson, but he made himself stop for something to eat. Hunger was distracting, and Julia's lunch had looked appetising, at least when she wasn't playing with it. He ate his food carefully, not rushing. It was good to take a little while to himself and allow the conflicting emotions aroused by his interview with Julia to settle.

He arrived at Thompson's house at a few minutes after 3 p.m. The house was conveniently placed for the centre of

Guildford, for Drax & Bond and for the A3. It was just as he had expected, a big half-timbered modern executive mansion, large, imposing and soulless, without even the perverse contrast of the ordinary and the self-consciously modern which characterised Drax's house. It was easy to imagine the salesman's blurb, consisting largely of the words 'luxurious' and 'no expense spared'.

He pulled up on the drive and called Fielding. 'Pat, any news?'

'His car's a Land Cruiser, sir.' Unnecessary information: the BMW was parked next to it. It was dark grey. 'I've spoken to Alan Banks. He hasn't met Thompson personally, but he says Elaine liked him.'

'Any news on his alibi?'

'No, sir. It was PC Savory's beat. He's not in until tomorrow morning earlies.'

Should he tell Fielding to contact Savory at home? No, it would be premature. 'Thanks, Pat. I'm about to speak to Thompson now. I'll keep you posted.'

He rang the doorbell. It sounded faintly in the distance, proving the size of the house, in case proof were needed. After a few minutes the door was opened by a pretty woman. She was dressed in jeans and a sweatshirt, but the casual clothes did not conceal her trim figure. 'Yes?' she asked, frowning.

'Mrs Thompson?' He showed her his ID. 'DCI John Anderson, Surrey Police.'

He said nothing more. Did she have any idea why he might be visiting? She looked at him unwelcomingly and with apprehension, as people always did when the police arrived to disarrange the easy normality of their lives. Then she said, 'Is it about Eddie?'

'Yes,' he said. 'I'd like to speak to your husband, if it's possible.'

'He's not well,' she said, still holding the door in her hand.

A voice called down the stairs, 'Penny, who is it?'

Penny Thompson made a face and said, 'You'd better come in.'

She opened the door for him and brought him into the hall, then called up the stairs, 'It's the police, darling, about Eddie.' To Anderson she said, 'Would you like some tea?'

He would have liked a cup of tea, but Thompson was a suspect. So he said, 'No, thank you.'

'I'm coming down,' roared the voice from upstairs.

'I'm sorry your husband is not well,' Anderson said to Penny. 'What's the matter?'

'Oh,' she said, 'probably some sort of summer virus. He came down with it yesterday. He went in for a meeting first thing, at the bank, and then he went in to the office, but by lunchtime he felt so bad he had to come home.'

'What time did he leave the house?'

Penny frowned at him. 'His usual time, I suppose. About 8.30. Why do you ask?'

Footsteps on the stairs announced the arrival of David Thompson. He was dressed in dark blue jogging pants and sweatshirt, which did not conceal the fact that he was beginning to nurture a small paunch. His hair was standing on end as if he had just got out of bed, and he hadn't shaved. 'Oh,' he said, when he reached the bottom of the stairs. 'Yes, we've met before. Andrews, was it?'

'Anderson,' said Anderson calmly. 'I'm sorry to disturb you at home, Mr Thompson, especially as your wife tells me you're not well. I'd like to talk to you.'

David looked for a moment as if he would refuse. Then he said, 'Come in the study.'

'I'll make you some tea,' Penny offered. 'Then I'll have to leave you to it. It's time I picked the kids up.'

'Thanks, darling.' David opened one of the doors leading off the huge wooden-floored hall and led Anderson into a large, well-equipped study. One wall was lined with bookcases and there was a desk beneath the window laden with computer equipment, printer, fax and answering machine. A curl of shiny paper lay beneath the fax. David glanced at it and cursed. 'Bloody office. They can't leave me alone for half an hour, never mind a day.' He flung himself down in a large black leather armchair. 'Sit down, Mr Anderson. What's up?'

'I'd like to talk to you about Eddie Drax,' Anderson said.

'We talked about Eddie already.'

'There have been some developments. There are other questions I need to ask you.'

'What sort of questions?'

'Where were you on Saturday evening, Mr Thompson?'

David scruffed his hand angrily through his hair. 'We already went over all of that.'

'I want to make sure that I have the details exactly correct.'

There was a silence. David rubbed one finger hard down the side of his nose, then bit at his left thumbnail. There was a little scab on his palm. It looked fresh.

Anderson was about to ask him when he had cut himself when David said suddenly, 'I'm not happy with this. I want a solicitor.'

'A solicitor? Mr Thompson, this isn't a formal interview. If you don't want to talk to me, I can't make you.'

'No, I'll cooperate. But I want a solicitor with me.'

'You have to be cautioned before anything you say can be used in court.'

'I want a solicitor.' David's posture was half-defensive, half-aggressive, arms folded tightly, head thrown back. The mixed messages were not lost on Anderson. David got up, seized the phone and began to dial. The door opened and Penny Thompson came in with a tray of tea. 'Here you are,' she said. 'Sorry I can't stop, but the school run, you know.'

'Thank you,' Anderson said. If tea was going to be foisted upon him, he would enjoy it.

He occupied himself pouring the tea while David spoke to his solicitor. David was short with the firm. Behaving like a wealthy client. What had Julia said? A big expensive house, a pretty wife, two children at private school. It wouldn't be easy for David to find the money to order a solicitor around, too.

'Gardner is on his way,' David said, dropping the phone back on to the hook. 'He'll be here in fifteen minutes. You'll excuse me, Mr Anderson, if I leave you here while we wait for him to arrive.'

'In that case,' Anderson said evenly, 'I shall enjoy my tea.'

David gave him a sidelong, suspicious look and left the room. Anderson settled himself more comfortably in the chair and sipped the tea. It was Earl Grey, a little weak, but acceptable.

Reluctance to answer questions without having a solicitor present had to look suspicious. But it was not necessarily an indication that David was involved with either murder. He might be implicated in a fraud. If he was, he might well want to be protected from the possibility that the questions might lead on to something which could be disastrous for him. Did that suggest that Eddie had found out about whatever it was that Sam was doing, which David might be involved in?

Anderson finished his tea, scouted the shelves for a book and browsed half-heartedly through *The Competitive Advantage of Nations.* It was all economics, a subject for which he had little time. As far as he could tell, economists were paid to get things wrong.

It was half an hour before the solicitor arrived. At last David re-entered the room with Gardner in train. Peter Gardner was a well known local figure, a big florid man in his fifties with a cap of tightly curling grey hair. He was primarily a commercial lawyer, so David had probably trespassed on Drax & Bond's relationship with Gardner's firm when issuing his summons. Gardner knew Anderson, and hailed him cordially.

'Right,' David said, sitting down. 'Peter, I want to know what sort of rights the Chief Inspector has at this point.'

Anderson didn't wait for Gardner to reply. 'Every citizen has a civic duty to help the police in the course of their enquiries, Mr Thompson. Preliminary informal interviews are carried out on the basis that you are simply helping me to establish the facts of a case. I may make notes, but they are solely to supplement my memory of our discussions. If we want to follow this interview with a formal one on police premises, you'll be cautioned and your words will be written down or tape-recorded and may be used in court.'

'I don't have to say anything?'

'You don't. But I have the right to ask.'

Gardner looked puzzled in the extreme. What sort of briefing had he been given before he came in? He looked like a man who didn't know why he was there. 'Chief Inspector,' he said, 'is David Thompson a suspect at this point?'

'This is a preliminary interview,' Anderson repeated evenly. 'If that changes, of course, I will say so immediately.'

David looked sharply at Gardner, who shrugged. 'I don't

211

know why you want me here, David. I thought you had some officious constable in your drawing room. Chief Inspector Anderson can probably recite the Police and Criminal Evidence Act from memory. He doesn't have a history of browbeating and oppression of witnesses.'

'I'm not a witness,' David snapped.

This had gone on long enough. Anderson sat forward in his chair and held his notebook ready. If Thompson was going to stand on ceremony, then so would he. 'Mr Thompson, please tell me again where you were on Saturday evening.'

'I told you before.'

'For the record, please tell me again.'

David glanced at Gardner, who arched his eyebrows in an exasperated fashion. Sullenly David said, 'I met a business colleague at the Farnham Park Golf Club. Then I went to Beacon Hill to walk for a bit.'

'When did you arrive there?'

'About, I don't know, about 8.30. I didn't check.'

'And what did you do?'

'I walked on the hill. I was there quite a long time. There was a moon. It was a pleasant evening.'

'Where was your car?'

'In the car park,' David said pointedly.

'When did you leave the hill?'

'About 10.30, I suppose. I got home about eleven.'

'And did you notice anything particular, when you were walking?'

David looked at him narrowly. 'What do you mean?'

'Just what I asked. Did you notice anything particular?'

Gardner was interested now. David frowned, hesitated, and finally said, 'No.'

A low-risk answer. There might not have been anything to notice, and even if there was, he could always plead ignorance.

'And where were you yesterday morning, Mr Thompson?'

David said at once, 'I don't think that's relevant.'

'Why not?' asked Gardner.

'He's asking about Eddie's death. What's that got to do with yesterday?'

Anderson said steadily, 'There was another murder yesterday, Mr Thompson.'

'Good God,' Gardner said.

David put his head on one side. He had gone pale. 'Another murder? Who was killed?'

'Elaine Williams, Eddie Drax's ex-girlfriend.'

'Elaine,' David whispered. Was there something flat in his tone, something unconvincing, or was it just shock?

'How well did you know Elaine, Mr Thompson?'

David was shaking his head, looking at the floor. 'Elaine. That's terrible.' He looked up. 'I didn't know her that well. I remember her from Drax & Bond, of course. And once or twice since she left I saw her socially with Eddie.'

'When was the last time you saw her?'

He hesitated. 'Last week. The day Eddie and Tony Sealey argued at the golf club. She came to try to talk to Eddie and I convinced her to go away.'

'How did you manage to convince her?'

David opened his mouth to respond, then stopped. 'I can't see why this matters.'

'Why does it matter, Chief Inspector?' asked Gardner.

'It may be relevant,' Anderson said coolly. Gardner appeared more intrigued than concerned. He probably hadn't been pleased to have been dragged from his office in the middle of the afternoon. Under the circumstances his presence was hardly likely to be much restraint. Anderson said again, 'How did you manage to convince her?'

'She listened to me,' David replied at last. 'I suppose she trusted me. She used to say I was different from Eddie and Julia and the creative types. It was a nuisance, to be honest.'

Someone who was trusted might well be let in. 'Mr Thompson, where were you yesterday morning?'

'I was at home,' David said. 'Until about 8.30. Then I went to a meeting at the bank. Then I felt ill and came home again.'

Was there uncertainty in David's tone, or was the man genuinely ill? 'When did you cut your hand?' Anderson asked suddenly.

David stared, then slowly turned over his left hand and looked at his palm. 'Why?'

'Please just answer the question.'

'Chief Inspector,' Gardner put in with a slow smile, 'you know Mr Thompson doesn't have to answer any question if he doesn't want to. If he wants to understand why you're asking, that seems fair enough to me.'

'I can't disclose why,' said Anderson. 'It has a material bearing on the case. When did you cut your hand, Mr Thompson?'

David shook his head. 'I don't understand. I won't answer.'

There was a silence. Gardner looked at Anderson and raised his bushy, grizzled eyebrows. It was easy to read his mind. *Is that enough? Is he going to caution him now?*

It wasn't enough. Silence was hardly ever enough. Time for another tack. 'Mr Thompson, are you aware that your accounts assistant, Samantha Smith, appears to have a lifestyle far in excess of her income?'

'What's that got to do with me?' David flared. 'She might have private means, mightn't she? She might be on the game as far as I know.'

Gardner drew a quick shocked breath and Anderson smiled. The possibility had not occurred to him, but what amused him was that David was clearly discomfited. 'Mr Thompson, I asked you before if you have cause to believe that there might be fraudulent activity taking place at Drax & Bond.'

David's face was very still. 'And I told you', he said slowly and clearly, 'that if I had any reason to suppose a fraud, I would have called in the auditors and the police. So you already have my answer.'

'When we spoke before, Mr Thompson, you told me that you did not know what would become of Eddie Drax's shares in Drax & Bond.'

'That's right,' David said, but the rigidity of his features betrayed uncertainty.

'Is it true that you discussed certain changes to the company's articles with the company's tax advisor a couple of months ago?'

There was a bead of sweat between David's eyebrows. 'I may have done. I don't remember. I can't remember every poxy little thing. Why is this relevant?'

Anderson turned the knife further. 'How would you

describe your personal financial situation, Mr Thompson?'

Now there was hot colour in David's face. 'That's none of your bloody business.' He pushed himself to his feet. 'I've had enough. I've had enough of this. I won't answer anything more.'

Anderson got up and met David's wide angry eyes. 'Thank you for your help, Mr Thompson. I'd like to ask you to go to the police station as soon as convenient and make a formal statement of what you have told me.'

'Do I have to?'

Anderson and Gardner exchanged glances. Gardner said, 'He can insist, David. It would be better to cooperate.'

'And at the station I would be grateful if you would allow yourself to be fingerprinted.'

Suddenly David looked more confident. 'Fingerprinted? Why not?'

'And at some point,' Anderson added silkily, 'I would like you to give a sample of blood for analysis.'

At once there was another change. The flush receded from David's cheeks. He stammered after a moment, 'I don't want to.'

'Why not, Mr Thompson?'

'Why not? For God's sake!' David exploded. 'I can't stand needles, all right? Now look, I've had enough. I want you to leave.'

'When will you go to the station, Mr Thompson?'

David stood still, breathing fast. Then he said, 'I'll bloody go now, if it will keep you quiet. Come on, I'll show you out. I've had enough.'

Gardner's expression was mischievous. David showed his visitors through the front door in silence. He slammed the door, ostentatiously double-locked it, snapped an angry goodbye to Gardner, ignored Anderson, climbed into the Land Cruiser and roared away in a cloud of twin exhausts.

'Anderson,' said Gardner, 'you don't really suspect him, do you?'

Anderson replied with a stare. Gardner laughed aloud. 'From what I hear,' he said, 'you've got precious little evidence to prove anybody guilty. You were in a bit of a hurry to arrest Sealey, weren't you?'

No point in asking how he knew. The solicitors' grapevine worked in excess of the speed of light. Anderson said nothing, and Gardner went on, 'A few dabs and no witnesses, is what I heard. Not much evidence, eh? I hope you've got something more from this second murder, if you want to make anything stick. Well, goodbye, Chief Inspector.'

'Goodbye,' said Anderson.

'Going back to the station?'

'I'm going to wait here until Mrs Thompson returns and let her know where her husband has gone.'

'Going to ask her a few questions, too?' Gardner grinned. 'Well, good luck. I've got clients to see to.' He climbed into his glossy green Jaguar and drove off with a merry wave.

Anderson's face was set as he watched the Jaguar go. Gardner's gentle mockery had cut close to the bone. But perhaps something Penny Thompson said would not match with her husband's story. He leant against the bonnet of his car to wait for Penny to return, patient as a spider.

Catherine sat up straight as she saw John get out of the big BMW. He looked tired. She jumped out of her car and hurried across the Mill's car park towards him. 'John!'

He spun round. His face showed his surprise. 'Catherine, what's the matter?'

Was she showing so obviously that something was the matter? 'I'm sorry to waylay you like this. I wanted to talk to you.'

'Have you been waiting here long?'

'Not long. I didn't leave work till 7 p.m. Can you talk?'

'Yes.' Something was different about him. His face and body were as controlled as always, but she felt that he was suppressing a simmering excitement. 'Of course. Come up with me.'

He reached out to take her arm, but she pulled back. 'Don't,' she said sharply.

John turned at once to face her. His face was intent, focused on her, and again she felt exposed, scrutinised, as if there was nowhere to hide. 'What's wrong?' he asked in a low voice.

'I don't want you to distract me,' she said. She realised that she was holding up her hands as if to fend him off, and she made herself lower them. 'It's important.'

'All right. Come up.'

Did nothing worry him? Was he never apprehensive? He led her in, held the door for her and called the lift, seemingly as calm as ever. His gaze was fixed on her and she knew that she was avoiding the eye contact, looking anywhere but at him, as if she was the guilty one.

At the top he showed her into the flat and smiled at her. 'Drink?'

She couldn't bear these social niceties when she was burning to confront him. 'John,' she burst out, 'you've got to tell me what's going on. You asked me about David today and you went away with hardly a word and I can't stand it. What's happening? Do you think David killed Eddie?'

He took a long breath and met her eyes. 'Catherine, you know I can't tell you about the progress of an investigation. You wouldn't tell me about Julia's finances, would you? It's the same thing.'

'But you might use what I said against David!'

There was a pause, as if he was considering his reply. Then he said, 'Yes, that's possible. Whoever is guilty, you may be called as a witness for the prosecution.'

Panic grabbed at her. 'I won't do it. I can't.'

'Catherine,' now he was smiling, 'we met in court.'

'It's different!' she cried desperately. 'I was an expert witness. And for the defence!'

'Are you saying you don't want a murderer to be punished, just because you happen to know that person?'

She might have known that he would trap her with logic. 'No, no, of course not. But I don't know – I can't –' The words wouldn't come. She fought herself for a moment in silence, then clenched her fists and turned away.

His hands grasped her shoulders. 'Catherine,' said his velvety voice.

Was he the same as the man who had sat in her office, questioning her, raking her with chilly eyes? He sounded now as if he cared for her, but she didn't want to believe it. She couldn't reconcile the two men into one. 'Don't,' she said, hunching her shoulders to try and escape him.

'Catherine,' he said again. His breath was warm on her neck. His strong hands tensed on her arms and turned her to face him and she was looking into his eyes and she knew that he was going to kiss her. Her body stiffened with resistance. She wasn't going to let him talk her round in bed. He behaved as if he owned her, and she couldn't bear it.

Perhaps her face showed her feelings, because she thought she saw an answer in his eyes, a spark of acceptance to her challenge. He took her face in his hand and lowered his lips gently to hers. She tried to keep still, not to respond. Instinctively she knew that she could hurt him most by failing to be moved by him. She kept her eyes open and her mouth still. His tongue probed at her lips and she did nothing.

After a moment he drew back. His eyes were narrow and sparkling. He didn't ask her what the matter was, he didn't argue with her. His hands tightened on her shoulders and with a sudden jerk he pushed her back against the wall. She made a sound of protest and lifted her hands to try to free herself and then he was kissing her again. This time his mouth was so strong, so demanding, that her resistance collapsed. His lips crushed hers and his tongue thrust between her teeth and she cried out and felt herself acceding to him, beaten down and conquered by his determination.

His kiss touched her breasts and her belly with fire, but even as she moaned under his lips she was angry with him. He was using her, manipulating her with the promise of the pleasure he could give her. She caught at his shoulders with her hands and tried to push him away.

He did not lift his mouth from hers, but his hands caught her wrists and pinned her arms above her head. He trapped her against the wall with the weight of his body. Her breasts were crushed against his chest and his erection throbbed against her hip. She writhed in a desperate attempt to free herself, but her own helplessness struck her with a powerful lash of arousal. Instantly, viscerally, she wanted him.

I am not turned on, she told herself. What am I, his slave, his sex object? I just want to get away from him. But even as the words filled her mind she heard herself moaning beneath the onslaught of his kisses.

His left hand held her wrists above her head. His right hand moved down to her blouse, unhurriedly began to open it. She arched her back, half struggling, half begging his caresses. His hand slipped beneath the crisp cotton, found the swell of her breast, cupped it. His fingers drew back her bra, fastened upon her nipple and pinched it into agonised hardness. His thigh forced its way between her legs and even as she cried out into his open mouth she knew that she was rubbing her vulva against him, eager as a beast on heat.

In a moment she would fall, she would begin to return his kisses. She braced herself for one last attempt at resistance.

And then he stopped. His lips drew back from hers, his hands released her. She opened her eyes, dazed and giddy, and saw him smiling.

'I want to make love to you,' he said.

She couldn't believe it. He wanted to prove his mastery over her. He wanted her to admit that with a dozen kisses and the touch of his hand he had swayed her from obstinacy to eagerness. Tell him to sod off! she commanded her tongue and lips. Tell him you're not his toy.

But the words wouldn't come. He watched her closely and she shut her eyes and turned her head aside, searching for the strength to refuse him.

She had no strength. Stubbornness fought with desire and lost. When she looked at him again and whispered his name she knew that she was saying yes.

He led her to the bedroom and sat down on the bed. 'Take your clothes off,' he said.

She put her hand to her face. He was testing his own power now, issuing commands, certain that she would obey him. How could he be so sure? She could refuse, laugh at him, tell him to take his clothes off first, turn and walk out of the room.

She could do all those things, but she did none of them. Her breath heaved as if at any moment she would burst into tears, and slowly, reluctantly, she began to remove each garment.

John sprawled comfortably on the bed, hands folded behind his head, and watched her.

In moments she was naked except for her bra and panties. She hesitated, then realised that she was hoping that he would notice that she was hesitating and order her to take them off.

He did not disappoint her. 'Everything,' he said softly. 'I want you naked.'

As she unhooked the bra and dropped it to the floor her body shivered with conflict. She detested his assumption of power. But the knowledge that he wanted to see her body filled her with gratitude and a deep wave of arousal. She pushed off her panties and stood still, trembling with anticipation as she awaited the next command.

'Come here,' he said.

She climbed on to the bed and he took her arm and made her lie down, arms above her head, legs slightly parted. His hand brushed down the whole length of her body and she shivered and arched her back with pleasure. 'Beautiful,' he said.

His eyes glittered like a night sky full of stars. She looked up at him, hoping that he would kiss her again. Her lips ached for him. But she couldn't speak.

Again he ran his hands down her body, caressing the outer curve of her breasts, stroking the edges of his nails against her nipples, exploring the tiny forest of her pubic hair. She whimpered a little and let her legs part a little, inviting his touch. His face was quiet, competent, certain. His control was absolute. What would he order her to do now? What shameful, wonderful, delicious thing?

'Catherine,' he said softly, 'show me how you masturbate.'

She quivered with shock. This was too much. She shrank away from him as if she would hide in the sheets. 'No!'

He put her right hand gently on her pubis. 'Show me,' he repeated.

His voice was soft, not stern, but she could not disobey him. His eyes held hers like a hypnotist's. Slowly, reluctantly, she slipped her hand between her legs, feeling for the familiar spot. Her thumb slotted into the groove of her lifted thigh, her index finger seeking for the buried gem of her clitoris, her middle finger dipping into the juicy well of her vagina. With her other hand she cupped and squeezed her left breast. It was obscene to do this with John watching, and yet so easy. She was wet, and the moment she coated her quivering clitoris with a film of her own eagerness she trembled with pleasure. Her buttocks clenched, lifting her hips towards his intent gaze. Normally she would have sought refuge in fantasy to lift her to orgasm, but now she needed none. Rubbing herself before his eyes was as potent as any fantasy.

In less time than she could believe she was on the point of coming. She closed her eyes and cried out and worried her clitoris with urgent fingers and her orgasm hovered above her as bright as a meteor.

Then he caught hold of her hand and drew it away. 'No,' he said, 'I want to make you come,' and instead of her hand his hand was there, feeling for her centre. Two fingers slipped deep into her vagina and the ball of his thumb fondled her swollen clitoris and she opened her eyes and stared at him as her orgasm fell on her like a breaking wave.

While she still shivered and cried out he lay on her and slid his erect cock into her and began to fuck her. So soon after her climax she could hardly bear it. She was still on the plateau of pleasure, still spinning with bliss, and every stroke of his penis seemed to take her higher, climbing into clouds of ecstasy. It was unendurable, and she linked her hands behind his neck and hung all of her weight upon him and sobbed as he reached his own orgasm, buried deep and throbbing within her.

For what seemed like hours they lay together, her naked limbs twined with his clothed ones, his softening penis imbedded in her body. Gradually the tingling echoes of pleasure receded and Catherine came to herself.

She had done everything that she had promised herself she would not do. She had let him make love to her. Worse, she had let him give her orders as if she were a slave and he her master. God, she had touched herself to give him pleasure. She hated her own weakness, and she hated him for exposing it.

There was only one thing to do. She had come meaning to resist him, meaning just to talk to him, and it had been impossible. When she was with him she let him take control. So if she wanted to stay herself, she must not be with him.

Her body told her that she was mad, but she knew that she couldn't respect herself if she allowed herself to give in so completely to another person. She set her jaw, preparing herself for battle.

As if he sensed the tension in her body he lifted himself from her and let her go. 'Stay with me,' he said softly.

'No.' She got up and began quickly to dress, covering her treacherous body.

'Catherine.'

He was insistent, but she would not look at him. She fastened her blouse and tucked it in to her skirt. For a moment she stood with her eyes shut, looking for words. Then she said, 'John, I don't want to see you again.'

No protests? No pleading? He looked at her steadily, as if he was unmoved. Then he said, 'Why?'

She shook her head, struggling to articulate. 'You – scare me. It's too much too soon. It's as if you want to own me. I can't.'

He zipped up his trousers and got off the bed. She turned hastily away, knowing how the potency of his physical presence could undermine her. 'You're too cold,' she said, hurrying through into the living area. 'You manipulate me. I can't bear it, John. I can't bear it.'

'But you enjoy it,' he said, as if that was all that mattered.

'That's not the point!' She was working herself up now to be angry with him. 'That's not important. If I let myself be ruled like that, what's left? What am I?'

Another man would have promised to be different, would have apologised. John just looked at her very steadily, his face full of quiet regret. 'I am the way I am,' he said. 'I told you, you have to trust me.'

'I can't,' she whispered. She was on the point of tears. 'I can't. I have to go.'

He followed her to the door. Still there were no protests, no promises. She couldn't believe that he would let her go without a fight, without even trying, and in the doorway she hesitated, not liking to admit even to herself that she was waiting for him to beg her to stay.

As if he had read her mind, he said, 'I'm sorry you feel as you do. I'd like to see you again.'

Thank God! She shook her head vigorously. 'No.'

'If you change your mind, will you call me?'

'I won't change my mind,' she said.

But she had to fight to walk to her car. She looked over her shoulder, up at his balcony, and saw him there above her, looking down. She could still feel his eyes on her as she drove away.

TWELVE
Saturday

At 10.30 a.m. Fielding dashed into Anderson's office, her face alight with excitement. 'Sir, he's lying about his alibi.'

Anderson nodded, unsurprised. David had told several lies, and another one was not unexpected. 'Sit down, Pat. What did you find out?'

She perched on the edge of her chair, twitching with eagerness. 'Thompson told you he was in the car park from about 8.30 till after 10 p.m. He's lying. I spoke to PC Savory when he came off shift this morning. There was an incident in the Beacon Hill car park on Saturday evening. You know the youngsters use it for courting?' She oscillated her dark eyebrows, signalling that she was using the word as a euphemism for vigorous teenage copulation.

'I believe I had heard,' he said dryly.

'Well, a couple of lads had an argument there on Saturday night over a girl. It got violent and someone with a mobile called us. Savory went round to sort it out. He has a note of every car in the car park at between 9.30 and 9.50. There was no Land Cruiser there, no four wheel drive vehicles at all.'

So David lied about the alibi, lied about what he had known about Eddie's shares, and probably about Sam as well. Was it enough to arrest him on suspicion of murder? Which murder, Eddie's or Elaine's?

'Is it enough, sir?' asked Fielding.

'No.' He shook his head. Disappointment was naked in her face. 'Pat, you know it's not. It's all circumstantial. I believe he's involved in a fraud. He could be lying to cover up for something to do with that. We can't risk a charge without sufficient evidence. There has to be more. At the moment the only thing that points to Thompson instead of Bond is that he's lied to us.'

'And she just isn't bothering.'

'Exactly.' More than not bothering, she was positively asking to be arrested. If she was guilty, then she was the coolest killer he had met.

'You still think it's Julia Bond, sir.'

She sounded as if she was accusing him. He said, 'I don't know.'

'Don't give me that!' Fielding flung back her head, then added quickly, 'Sir. But I mean, you must have an opinion.'

He shook his head. 'Pat, I don't know. We have two suspects and either of them might have done both murders. Neither of us know which one it was and until we have some firm evidence either way I won't have an opinion, either.'

She stared at him, then dropped her head and ran her hand wearily over her face. 'If only Banks could remember what sort of a car he saw that night at Devonshire Avenue.'

'He said it was a dark colour, that's all.'

'There's the dab, sir,' she added, brightening.

He nodded. 'Yes, I know. They'll try to match it today. But that print was fragmentary and smudged. A good expert witness could pull it to pieces.'

'The blood on the cushion. The lab report should come through next week. I mean, not just blood groups, they can do DNA analysis.'

'He wouldn't give a blood sample, and we can't force him.'

'That's evidence in itself, isn't it, sir?'

'Not when you can afford the best solicitor in town, Pat, and you know it. We're in a cleft stick.' He looked at Fielding's tired, excited face and smiled. 'Look, you're exhausted. You've worked all week on this. Go home.'

She showed a flash of anger. 'I can't believe there's nothing

I can do now!' Her eyes challenged him. 'If there's nothing to do, sir, why are you here?'

'I'm going to visit Samantha Smith,' he said.

'Can I come?' Fielding asked at once.

'I think not.' Her face closed up. He explained with more patience than he felt, 'Pat, it's nothing to do with you personally. Samantha Smith is a difficult woman. I think I'm beginning to understand her. I don't want to introduce another person now.'

Fielding shook her head. She did not attempt to conceal her distaste. 'Why do you keep on going back to her?'

'If David is lying to us because there's a fraud going on, then he's less of a suspect for murder. I think Sam knows all about whatever is happening at Drax & Bond.'

'But why should she tell you?'

Why indeed? He thought of Sam's naked hostility and her resentment of his authority. When he pushed her she resisted. So he would surprise her by pulling, not pushing. 'Because,' he said, 'I'll ask her nicely.'

He hadn't told Fielding everything, of course. It was true that David might be cleared of the murders by being implicated in some other crime. But there was another option. It might be possible to use whatever he could find out against David as a lever, either to provoke a confession or to extract information that would convict someone else.

He hadn't been honest about why he was not at home, either. He wanted to work to keep his mind from Catherine.

Last night he had returned home like a cat on hot bricks, full of restless energy. Meeting her like that, unexpectedly, all he had wanted was to make love to her. He had taken what he wanted. He knew he gave her pleasure, and he had thought the pleasure would be enough to keep her with him, however uncertain she felt.

He had been wrong. He had gone too far, and Catherine had never seemed more desirable than when she walked away. He had never wanted her more. If he was at home he would be thinking of ways to make her change her mind. But he had to resist the temptation to interfere. His triumph would be all the greater if she came back to him on her own. So work was a good thing to do, and especially visiting Sam, who saw herself as his rival. She would keep his mind busy. He had dressed with particular care this morning, knowing that she appreciated it.

Samantha had been angry with him the last time he visited, so he didn't ring the entryphone. When someone came out of the door he walked with cool confidence up to them, said, 'Thanks very much,' and strolled in. So much for security.

Sam got out of the shower, dried herself and put on her thin dressing gown. She was just towelling her hair when someone knocked on the door. 'Emma, are you expecting anyone?'

They slept late on Saturdays. Emma, too, was wearing just her dressing gown. She looked up from Saturday's paper. They had only just had breakfast, and the remnants of bacon sandwiches were spread about on the coffee table. 'Don't know,' she said. 'Bill from the ground floor said he might come up with that CD he's lending me.'

'Bill!' said Sam. 'He's after you, Emma. Remember the rules.'

She walked to the door and looked through the peephole, expecting to see Bill's geekish countenance distorted by the little lens. What she saw was DCI Anderson, looking back into the peephole as if he knew she was there.

'Christ,' Sam hissed. What was he doing here again? Her heart began to thump. She set her jaw and said loudly, 'Go away!'

'Sam,' he said, 'I need to talk to you.'

'Go away!' Sam repeated. 'If you weren't a policeman I'd call the police and say you're harrassing me.'

'I need your help,' he said. 'I need to ask you about David Thompson.'

David Thompson? She hesitated, gazing sightlessly down at the carpet. Why did Anderson want to ask about David? Could it be – could it possibly be that he was a suspect for the murders?

She pulled the door open and stood there with her hand across the gap, barring the way in. Anderson didn't attempt to enter, just looked at her with his unreadable blue eyes.

Suddenly she was very conscious of her undress, of the damp silky fabric of the dressing gown clinging to her naked body, of her wet hair falling heavily about her shoulders. His gaze was dark. God almighty, did he find her attractive? Her mind fled from the very idea. She resisted the urge to tug her dressing gown shut. 'What about David Thompson?' she demanded.

'May I come in?' he asked. 'I don't want to ask this sort of question where I can be overheard.'

She couldn't resist the opportunity to get that bastard David into trouble. 'All right,' she said ungraciously, turning her back on Anderson and stalking through into the lounge.

'Who is it?' asked Emma.

'It's our favourite homophobic misogynist policeman,' Sam said. She sat down beside Emma on the sofa, ready to enjoy herself. She could taunt Anderson to within an inch of his life and fuck up David Thompson at the same time. 'Sit down,' she snapped, gesturing at the chair opposite her.

'Thank you,' he said, composing himself comfortably in the chair.

Sam gathered Emma into the crook of her arm and let her hand hang down the front of Emma's body, almost imperceptibly stroking her breast. Emma drew in a deep breath and bit her lip as her nipple tensed and hardened. She lowered her eyes and began to blush. Nothing looked so beautiful as Emma when she was embarrassed but determined to be obedient.

'Now,' Sam said, brushing her thumb against Emma's stiffening nipple, 'what do you want to know about David?'

She wanted to sound light, but she could hear the overtones of hatred in her voice. When Anderson said, 'You've worked for him six years, haven't you,' she had to turn her face away to try to hide the rictus of anger that seized it whenever she remembered those first few months of working for David.

'That's right,' was all she said.

'How do you feel about him?' Anderson asked.

Her feelings were not relevant. 'Nobody likes their boss,' she snapped. 'Just ask whatever it is you want.'

Emma looked anxiously up at her and pressed closer to her side. Sam allowed her hand to settle around the slight curve of that delicious, tender breast. Emma sighed and her breath was warm.

For a moment Anderson didn't say anything. Then he sat forward in the chair, his elbows on his knees, his hands open. 'Sam, I want you to help me. I think you know what I need.'

'What?' she said crossly. 'Get to the point, will you? Emma and I have got things to do.' And to illustrate the things she had in mind, she lifted Emma's chin and kissed her. Not a proper kiss, not all the way, but enough to shock.

Emma's gaze was dark with shame and desire. 'Sam,' she whispered, 'don't.' The words trembled with bliss.

'I want you to tell me something he doesn't want to be known,' Anderson said in an utterly steady voice. Sam lifted her head in surprise and stared at him. He was looking at her, not at Emma, and his eyes were harder than sapphires.

She could have said that there was nothing, but she was intrigued. 'Why?' she asked. 'Why do you want that?'

'I have two suspects for two murders,' he said. He was talking to her as he would talk to an equal, as he would talk to a man. 'David is one. I want to pin him down or rule him out. While he has several secrets I can't do that. And I think you know at least one of his secrets.'

She knew more than one. Her immediate impulse was to give Anderson what he wanted. But one of the secrets wasn't hers, it was Emma's. She looked down into Emma's face and said softly, 'Emma, darling. What do you think?'

Emma pushed closer to her and lifted her lips. Sam saw the yearning in her face and smiled, then kissed her again, properly this time, mouths open, tongues exchanging desire. Her hand closed instinctively over Emma's breast, squeezing it.

Then Emma drew back a little and said, 'It's all right to tell him, Sam. He was nice to me. I trust him.'

Sam's own breasts were tight and swelling with arousal. It was so sexy, to be caressing Emma, stimulating her, in front of this silent, powerful man. It emphasised her own power. She felt an urge to order Emma to strip, to show off her naked body. But that would be too much, it would not be subtle. Let him struggle, let his imagination run wild.

She smiled at Emma and kissed her again, then turned back to Anderson. He hadn't moved. His control was remarkable. 'Listen,' she said. 'What are you going to do with what I tell you?'

'Use it to threaten him,' he said.

Her gut told her that he was telling the truth. 'I thought the police weren't supposed to do that sort of thing.'

'We're not. I won't rely on it in court.'

'In court!' Her imagination showed her David in the dock, shuddering with shame, and herself and Emma in the gallery, laughing at him. 'All right,' she said quickly. 'All right. How about this. He likes girls.'

'Girls?'

'I don't mean women,' she said scornfully. 'Look at me, all right? I'm too old for him. He had me six years ago, when I first worked for him. But not for long. How long do you think Lisa will last? He gets through a secretary every six months. Recruits them, fucks them, gets bored with them.'

'What if they say no?'

'They don't stay, do they? Not longer than a month.'

'That's harrassment,' he said.

'Harrassment!' She almost burst with scorn. 'Tell an eighteen-year-old fresh out of college, proud of her first job, tell her it's harrassment when her boss buys her presents and asks her to go to the pub with him in the evening and says his wife doesn't understand him and he'll say he's working late. He fills her up with gin and then he puts her into his big car and says he wants to fuck her and mostly they say yes, don't they?' Her voice revealed her bitterness. 'I did.'

'So he's –' Anderson hesitated. 'He's having an affair with Lisa?'

'He bends her over his desk and fucks her,' she said brutally. 'Lisa likes it. She's got her eye on the main chance, that one.'

Anderson's face was very still. She could sense his brain whirling. At last he said, 'That's embarrassing, potentially. But I don't know if it will be enough.'

She showed her teeth. 'There's more.' She held Emma more tightly. 'Promise you'll screw him, Anderson, if I tell you. Promise.'

'I'll do everything I can,' he said.

It was absurd to trust a man, but she found she did trust him. She trusted his calm steady eyes and his still voice. All the same it was hard to begin. 'I think,' she said, 'I think I was the first he tried it with. He kept me going for a couple of years. That's why he made me accounts assistant, it was a promotion. Then –' The hurt was still there, still fresh. 'Then one evening when we were in the pub he saw Emma at the bar and he dumped me that same evening. He didn't know I knew her.'

Anderson frowned. 'When was this? Four years ago?'

'That's right.' He was smart. He would work it out for himself.

'Emma,' Anderson said softly, 'four years ago, you were only fourteen.'

Sam felt Emma trembling against her arm. She held her more firmly, comforting her. 'That's right. My respected family finance director picked up a fourteen-year-old in a pub, got her drunk, put her in his car and deflowered her.'

Anderson's lips parted, then closed into a white line. 'Did you tell anyone, Emma?'

'Don't make me laugh,' Sam said violently. 'He threatened her. He found out how old she was and then he got scared and said if she told anyone he'd say it was her fault, that she fooled him into it.'

'He'd still be culpable in law,' Anderson said.

'Do you think Emma knew that then? God help us, policemen! He's a bastard, do you understand me? He had her once and then he dumped her. Poor little Emma! At least she didn't get pregnant.'

Emma pressed her head against Sam's breasts and clung to her, trembling. That was enough. It had to be. Anything more would upset Emma too much. 'How's that?' Sam asked, lifting her head to challenge Anderson with her eyes.

'That's enough,' Anderson confirmed. Slowly he smiled. 'Thank you, Sam.'

'Don't charge him with it,' she said hastily. 'I don't want Emma to have to give evidence. She won't.'

'How much does he pay you, Sam?' Anderson asked.

His face still wore that lazy smile and his eyes were laughing. He looked as if they were fellow conspirators. She suddenly wanted to smile back at him, but she made herself stern. 'I don't know what you mean.'

'Oh, come on, Sam, don't play games. What is it? Straight blackmail, or are you putting it through Drax & Bond? What is it, false subcontractors' invoices?'

Her hands closed tightly on Emma's body, but she managed to keep her face straight. How in God's name had he guessed? He really was bright, brighter than she expected a policeman to be. 'However did you think of that?' she said, keeping her face the picture of innocence. 'It would never have occurred to me. You're very ingenious.'

'Almost as ingenious as you,' Anderson said. He got up and stood smiling down at her. 'Are you sure you want me to screw him, Sam? Are you sure it won't spoil your revenge?'

Suddenly Emma spoke. Her voice was tight and thin. 'I want you to screw him,' she said.

'If he's in jail, Sam, he can't pay out. How will you keep Emma in the style to which she's becoming accustomed?'

Sam gently detached Emma's hands and stood up too. She looked into Anderson's eyes. 'First,' she said, 'I still don't know what you mean. And second, whatever you mean, let me worry about it. I want you to put him away for what he did to Emma.'

There was a silence. Anderson looked into her eyes and she looked steadily back, this time without hostility. For once she was able to accept that a man might have power and control and still be an ally.

'So,' he said, 'do homophobic misogynist policemen have their uses?'

'On occasions,' she said. And she smiled.

Back in the BMW Anderson stretched in the driver's seat and considered what he had learnt.

He liked Sam. He liked her courage and her determination. He found her exceptionally attractive, and he felt good about the way that she seemed to have acknowledged him as an equal. Under other circumstances he might have thought of pursuing her; but Sam was clear about what she wanted out of life, and her plans did not include a male lover.

He was also satisfied that Sam had given him information which he could use against David Thompson to extract the truth from the many lies he had told. But she hadn't told him anything that made it more likely that Thompson was the murderer. In fact, it was less likely. She had revealed David as a liar and a, well, cad wouldn't be too strong a word. But that could in itself explain all his lies. David was probably covering his tracks on Saturday night because he had been in another car park in his Land Cruiser, screwing some hapless teenager.

So he was no closer. If the same person killed Eddie and Elaine, then the first motive, the important motive, was the one that led to the death of Eddie. And still, despite all David's lies, what he had gained was uncertain. It was Julia who had a clear benefit. Why should she not be the murderer?

He fired the engine and put the car into gear. He would go and talk to David again. Armed with this information he would get to the truth.

Penny stuck her head around the door of the study. 'We're off to the pool, David. Are you sure you don't want to come? It might make you feel better.'

He shook his head. Penny scowled and snapped, 'Look, whatever has got into you, will you just shake it off? You're really difficult to live with.'

Before he could swear at her she slammed the door. Moments later he heard the Fiesta trundling off.

He blinked hard and stared at the screen of his computer. His modem was connected to the Drax & Bond accounts department. The company's bank balance would be good as soon as the key man insurance came in: and the moment it did, he would start siphoning. A million should do it; less, if necessary. There would always be jobs in Rio for clever accountants. Maybe the kids could join him one day, when they'd finished school. He could still pay for school.

The telephone rang. He answered it almost without thinking. 'Hello?'

'David, it's Sam.'

The woman was like a bloody nemesis! 'What the hell do you want?' His voice was guttural with hate.

'Temper, temper.' He could hear Sam laughing. It drove him mad. 'It's time to put the price up again, David. I've had our favourite policeman back again. He seems to be very interested in you.'

'What do you want?' he repeated, shivering.

'One hundred thousand. Now. Cash.'

'A hundred thousand? You're mad! How can I get that?'

'You're the accountant. You figure it out. I want it by Monday, David. You've got my bank details, arrange a BACS transfer. Or I tell Detective Chief Inspector Anderson all about our little secret.'

He took two deep breaths, then said easily, 'All right. I'll come round. We need to discuss the transfer.'

This time she had gone too far. What did she think he had left to lose?

He went upstairs to pack a bag.

Anderson was about to turn in to the driveway of David's house when the Land Cruiser appeared in the gate, nosing outwards on to the road. David was in it, alone. At once Anderson turned off his indicator and steered back into the busy Saturday traffic, following the Land Cruiser.

The Land Cruiser headed towards the centre of town. He followed it, a few cars back. As they approached a retail development his radio beeped. 'Anderson.'

'Sir, it's Thompson.' Fielding's voice quivered with excitement. 'It has to be. I just took a call from the young son at number 16 Devonshire Avenue. He didn't know we were asking for information, his parents dealt with the house to house. He read the story in the paper and called us as soon as he could get to the phone without his parents knowing.'

He steered the car around a roundabout, his eyes fixed on the big grey 4X4. 'What did he see?'

'He was in his room all evening, surfing the Net, he said. He doesn't like parties. He said –' Fielding hesitated as she found the place in her notes. 'First there was a yellow car. After it left a man came in a red car and banged on the door, but nobody let him in. So much for Sealey.'

Another roundabout. Anderson went to follow the Land Cruiser around, but a car coming from the right sounded its horn and pulled across. It was followed by a stream of traffic.

'Damn!'

'Sir?'

'I've lost him. I was following Thompson.' The traffic was still coming on. 'What else did he see?'

'After the red car, sir, a big black 4X4. The man in it went into the house, Eddie let him in. The boy didn't see him come out, he says he went to sleep.'

'What time was that?'

'About 11 p.m., he thinks.'

At last the traffic flow ended. He drove across the roundabout at high speed, but he couldn't see the Land Cruiser anywhere. He cursed to himself and pulled over to the side of the road. 'Will this evidence stand in court, Pat?'

'Yes, sir. I think it will.'

Her voice brimmed with confidence. 'All right,' he said. 'Let's bring him in. I lost him a few moments ago by the retail park.' He gave the location. 'Get the cars looking for him. Keep me posted.'

'Yes, sir!'

He put down the radio and pulled back into the traffic. There was no point in driving aimlessly around. Where could David have been going?

And he knew. He had left Sam knowing that her source of secondary income was about to dry up. What more natural than that she should try for one last inflow before the drought?

He crossed a line of traffic, making horns blare, and turned right. The patrol cars would probably find David within a few minutes, and even if they didn't there was no reason why he shouldn't get to Sam's in time.

So why was his heart pounding?

David pulled the car into a space around the corner from Sam's apartment block. He wasn't too angry to be careful. He would need to get as far as the airport.

Sam answered the entryphone at once. 'Yes?'

'It's David.'

'Come up,' she said.

She met him at the door. 'Where's Emma?' he asked her.

'Out spending your money,' she said with a vicious grin.

He caught hold of her and tried to bang her head against the door. She struggled and bit his arm. He cursed and hit her in the face, then dived after her as she tried to run from him. He caught her arm and jerked her violently around. She opened her mouth to scream and he hit her again, stunning her into silence. She looked so shocked that he wanted to laugh. He grabbed her by the hair and clamped his hand over her mouth and then he did laugh, into her open panic-stricken eyes.

'All right, Sam?' he demanded fiercely. 'Is this quick enough for you?'

She struggled desperately, kicking and writhing, her nails reaching for his face. He jerked back out of the way and his hand slipped in her hair. She tried to pull free, but he grabbed her back. His fingers knotted in the dark waves and he tugged back her head so hard that her eyes bulged with pain over his smothering hand. Then he hit her head against the door frame. He had to do it three times before she slumped.

Anderson jumped out of the BMW and looked quickly around the car park. No Land Cruiser.

Damn! Had he been wrong? For a moment he was glad that he hadn't called Control. He hated to look stupid.

But he wanted to be certain. He went to the entryphone and pushed it.

There was no reply.

He looked again around the ranks of parked cars. Sam's little red sports car was there, slotted neatly into a space near the door.

He rang the entryphone again and again there was silence. He stood for a few seconds, breathing quickly. Then he ran back to his car and called Control for assistance.

There was no time to wait for help. He might have condemned Sam by pushing the entryphone button. He hurled himself back and rang the buttons from the bottom up, his lips moving silently as he waited for an answer.

On the third button someone answered. 'Hello?'

'Surrey Police,' he snapped. 'Open the door.'

'Go on,' chided the voice. 'Who is this?'

'This is Detective Chief Inspector Anderson, Surrey Police.' He kept the fear from his voice, it would achieve nothing. 'I have reason to believe there is an intruder in the building. Open the door!'

After a second the door clicked open. He gasped with relief and hurled himself into the lift.

The journey to the eighth floor was interminable. When the doors at last slid open he leapt to the door and pounded on it with both fists. 'Sam!'

Silence.

'Sam!' he bellowed again. 'Sam, Emma, it's John Anderson. Open the door!'

Then, beyond the door, he heard a heavy sound, the sound of something breaking. He glanced down at his suit. It was his summer favourite, pale slate blue linen. But he had no choice. He closed his eyes and sighed, then hurled his shoulder at the door.

It was strong and held against him. He reeled back, clutching his arm and gasping with pain. 'Police!' he shouted, and lunged again.

This time the door burst open a little way. The security chain was on. He took a step back then kicked the door, hard and accurately, just where the chain joined. Two kicks and the chain splintered away from the wood.

'Sam!' he shouted.

And David Thompson's voice replied, 'Stay where you are, you bastard!'

Anderson jumped through the open door and stood in the hall, panting. There was movement ahead of him. David, in the lounge, dragging the still body of Sam towards the glass door leading to the balcony. The sun poured through the open door, forming an incongruous halo in David's hair and glittering in the beads of sweat that trickled down his white contorted face. 'Stay there!' he shouted again.

Did he have a weapon? What was the risk? Anderson

hesitated, narrowing his eyes to see against the blinding sun. David was tugging Sam by her armpits. He must have dragged Eddie Drax in the same way.

Both his hands were visible and both of them were empty. Anderson lunged across the lounge as David reached the door to the balcony and pulled Sam out. Anderson got to the door and David heaved Sam's body up on to the edge of the balcony and shrieked, 'Don't come a step closer!'

Anderson stopped in the doorway and stood utterly still. His eyes were fixed on Sam. She was only ten feet from him on the other side of the balcony but he couldn't get to her. Her lax body was precariously balanced. One push from David's clutching hands and she would fall. How long would it take for Control to send a backup? How long before they realised what was happening and got someone below the balcony with a suicide blanket? People could survive a fall of eight storeys into a blanket. Sam's head hung back limply and her eyes were closed. There was blood running from her nose and mouth, but she was breathing. She was alive. He had to distract David until help came so that she stayed alive. 'David,' he said steadily, 'this won't help you.'

'It can't make it worse, can it?' demanded David. His eyes were ringed with white and his teeth were bared. He looked like a madman. 'And it'll make me feel better, won't it? The bitch – she's made my life a misery –'

The hand that gripped Sam's arm whitened as if he was about to push. Anderson's heart surged in his chest. He made himself stand still. 'Listen,' he said. 'I understand about Elaine. She saw your car, didn't she. But I don't understand about Eddie. What happened?'

'Eddie,' gasped David. 'That bastard.' His hands held Sam by the arm and the thigh. He kneaded her flesh like dough and his face worked. 'I went to talk to him. I wanted to give him a chance to make things up to me. I worked like a dog for him and I needed the fucking money, OK?' His voice rose to a hysterical shriek.

'OK,' Anderson said easily. 'It's OK, David. What happened?'

'He laughed at me,' David said. Tears spilled from his eyes and mixed with the sweat on his cheeks. 'He laughed. He said he'd fobbed me off for years and Dacre & Co. would get rid of me and why should he care? The bastard,' he sobbed, 'the bastard. What does he know? School fees and bloody negative equity?'

Was that a siren in the distance? Christ, they should have the sense to switch them off before they came! He knotted his hands into fists to contain his fear and said gently, 'What did you do? Did you hit him?'

David shook his head and laughed. 'Didn't need do, did I? I went to the bog and when I came back he was out like a light. Drunken bastard, asleep and snoring. And I –' He broke off and stared at Anderson as if he was suddenly very puzzled.

'You took your chance,' Anderson said. 'You put him in the Porsche.'

'It was better than he deserved,' David snarled. 'He should have died screaming! The bastard!'

Suddenly Sam stirred. Her limp head lifted and her eyelids fluttered. If she struggled she would fall. Anderson snapped, 'Sam, keep still! Don't move!'

'Fuck –' David turned to look at Sam and Anderson leapt. In two strides he was across the balcony and as David screamed and tried to push Sam into empty air Anderson caught hold of her arm and pulled her. For a moment she hung suspended between them, then David let go and Anderson dragged Sam to safety behind him.

'Bastard!' David shouted. As Anderson released Sam, David jumped for the balcony and climbed on to it. Anderson swore and reached for him and caught his arm and David fell into space and hung there, suspended from Anderson's hand and struggling like a hooked fish.

'Let me go,' David gasped.

Anderson's arm was creaking with the strain. He jammed his toes into a drainage hole to give himself extra purchase and brought his other hand down to catch David's elbow and pull. 'Hang on,' he managed to say. 'There'll be help here soon.'

Beneath him a police car screeched into the car park, followed by another. They looked a very long way down. His arms and shoulders began to shake convulsively and he closed his eyes against a rush of nausea. 'Get your feet against the wall,' he panted. 'Take the weight.'

'Fuck you.' David stretched up with his free arm to beat at Anderson's hands. 'Let go – you bastard –'

Then there was something beside Anderson, pushing against him. He glanced up and saw Sam, her face smeared with blood and white with rage, reaching down towards David. 'Bastard,' she shouted. Her fists pounded at David's head. 'Bastard!'

David grabbed at Sam's arm and pulled and she screamed as she slid forward. 'Bitch!' David shrieked, his voice thick with fury. 'You come too!'

Sam slipped. She screamed again and her hands made claws on David's arm. In a moment she would fall. Anderson couldn't hesitate. He hissed, 'Oh *shit*,' and let go of David and caught Sam by the waist. David hung from her arm, cursing her and struggling. Anderson gasped and staggered as he took the weight of two bodies. He wanted to move back, to drag them both to safety, but he couldn't. He tried again and moaned as his eyes blackened and blood rushed in his ears.

Then Sam screamed and was suddenly light. He lunged forward, reaching down, but too late. David had lost his grip.

Anderson tried to pull Sam towards him to hide her eyes, but she wrenched free and stared downwards. Together they watched the silent struggling fall, the sickeningly soft impact, the slow spill of blood and matter. Then Sam staggered up and let out an incoherent wail of fear and shock and he caught hold of her and pulled her into his arms and held her tightly.

'Sam,' he said softly, 'hush, hush, it's all right.'

She lifted her head and stared at him as if his comfort was the final straw. Then her face crumpled and she gave one huge sob and clung to him, burying her head in his shoulder, smearing his suit with blood and tears. He was conscious of it, but suddenly it didn't matter. He wrapped his arms more closely around Sam and stroked her hair. Her heaving breasts pressed against his chest.

Quick footsteps outside. Fielding's voice called, 'Sir!'

'It's OK, Pat,' he called back.

Sam freed herself from his embrace with a convulsive jerk

and stepped back, shivering and wiping her eyes. Her hand came away from her face red with her own blood. She stared at her fingers for a moment, trembling. Then Fielding hurled herself through the balcony door, and Sam lifted her puzzled eyes to Anderson's and fainted.

EPILOGUE
Sunday

Anderson slept late.

He woke at 9.30 and lay as if stunned, staring at the ceiling. His arms and back ached as if he had been beaten with sticks. He thought of going back to sleep, of getting up slowly and taking a hot bath. Then he shook his head and pushed himself out of bed.

The corpse of yesterday's suit lay on the floor by the laundry basket in his bedroom, like the discarded skin of a snake. He had shed it there when he returned home at one in the morning, exhausted after interminable hours dealing with the ramifications of David Thompson's death. He picked up the jacket and examined it. The front was dark with smears of Sam's blood. His fingers stroked the stain gently and a smile touched his face. Then he hung the suit in the dry cleaning cupboard and put on his running gear.

It was already hot. Running the two miles to the bridge was bad enough, and on the way back he needed all his determination to keep going. He pounded grimly onwards, his breath searing his lungs with every stride.

As he turned into the grounds of the mill he saw a little red sports car driving out of the car park. He stopped, panting, and stared after it. It looked like Sam's car. But it couldn't be Sam. She was in hospital, kept in for observation with concussion and a suspected fractured skull.

He made himself run the last few strides to the door. On the ground beside the entryphone lay six long white madonna lilies wrapped in cellophane. He looked down at the card on the wrapping and saw his own name.

He couldn't run up the stairs with an armful of flowers. In the lift on the way up to the flat he opened the card. It read, *To the HMP. Thank you. From Sam & Emma.*

He smiled and pulled back the wrapping to smell the lilies. They were just beginning to open, and their intense, sweet scent caressed his nostrils. He ran his finger along the smooth, cool surface of one flower. Thanks were rare, and thanks from someone like Sam were rarer still.

The lift hissed to a halt. He let himself into the flat and put the flowers into the sink while he found a tall vase in cobalt blue glass. It was important that they were looked after before he went to have his shower. He filled the vase with water and was about to strip the leaves from the lilies when the telephone rang.

He picked up the portable and tucked it under his chin. 'Anderson.'

'John,' purred a familiar voice.

He raised his eyebrows and went on with what he was doing. How had she got his number? The leaves pulled from the stiff stems with a satisfying rip. 'John,' said Julia Bond's voice in his ear, 'I heard about David. I hope you realise you've made things very difficult for me.'

'Yes, I believe I do.' His tone did not reveal the intense irritation that the sound of her voice inspired in him.

Irony didn't put her off. 'John, you remember what we talked about when we last met. You were saying that you wanted to make love to me.'

'No,' he corrected her coolly, 'you were saying that I wanted to make love to you. I don't.'

She hesitated. Then she said, 'Well, that's a disappointment.'

'No, it isn't.' Contradicting her was as pleasant as a cool drink on a hot day. He had put up with her games for long enough. 'You weren't interested in me. You were just being obstructive.'

'Possibly. But didn't you think it was rather entertaining?'

'No,' he said.

'I felt that by the end you were beginning to get a bit of a kick out of it. I certainly was. Perhaps we could meet, just to see if there are any areas of mutual interest worth discussing.'

'I have no areas of mutual interest with you.'

'If you don't meet me, you'll never know whether I'm serious.'

He didn't care whether she was serious. 'Goodbye.'

He put the phone down. In a few moments it rang again. He ignored it and continued to deal with the flowers. After ten rings the answerphone cut in. Julia's voice said, 'Well, *Anderson.*' It was the tone she had employed on their first encounter, arrogant and superior. 'There's more to negotiation than putting the phone down. One day perhaps I'll have the chance to demonstrate how it should be done.'

The machine bleeped. He put the lilies in the vase, contemplated them for a moment with quiet pleasure and went to have his shower.

By lunchtime he had finished the Sunday paper. He made himself a salad and ate it on the balcony, then stretched out on his teak and brass deckchair with a book. It was Flaubert's *Salammbô,* in French. The place was marked with a silk bookmark. He opened the book, took a long breath of pleasure and read.

> *The white light seemed to envelop her like a silver mist, stars shimmered in the depths of the water; the snake tightened round her its black coils striped with golden patches. Salammbô gasped beneath this weight, too heavy for her, her back bent, she felt she was dying; with the tip of its tail it gently flicked her thigh.*

The entryphone rang. He glanced up with a frown. That, too, might be Julia: if she had found his telephone number she might also have found out where he lived. He could ignore it, but then it could be Patricia Fielding, come to discuss what they should do about Sam. He sighed and pushed himself to his feet.

'Hello,' he said into the entryphone.

'John?' said a diffident voice. 'John, it's Catherine.'

'Catherine.' His heart lifted. 'Come up.' He pressed the button.

He went to open the door and wait for her. Soon the lift arrived and she was there, pale and apprehensive. She was wearing a loose sleeveless dress of white crinkled cotton which clung to the curves of her body. She stopped a little way from him, pushed her hand through her dishevelled hair and said, 'I have to talk to you.' As if she wanted to forestall him, she added quickly, 'Just talk, John.'

'Come in,' he said, holding the door for her. 'Have a drink.'

She shook her head. 'I'm driving.' She shrank away from him as she passed him, as if she was afraid of his touch. Her fear moved him. He wanted to hold her and stroke her hair, but he knew better than to try to approach her now. He let her go ahead of him into the living room. She stood on the tree-of-Paradise carpet twisting her hands. 'John, Penny Thompson called me this morning.'

He hadn't realised that she had known. Was she distressed or angry? He couldn't tell, so he said nothing.

'She –' Catherine hesitated and looked away from him. 'She told me what happened.' Her head lifted and suddenly her hazel eyes were very soft. 'Are you all right? I mean, are you hurt?'

He shifted his shoulders, exploring the aches. 'Nothing serious,' he said.

She watched him for a moment in silence. Then she said, 'I came round rather than ringing because I owe you an apology. About David, I mean. It seems that – that I was wrong.'

'It's all right.' He liked her more because she thought well of people. He was cynical enough for two.

'Penny called because –' She hesitated. A spot of colour appeared on her pale cheeks. 'She called about David's insurance.'

'His insurance.' Anderson barely restrained a disbelieving shake of the head. He had been right when he told Fielding that there was no love in this case, only loathing, lucre and lust. Even David Thompson's wife had her eye on the money.

'Yes. He was well covered. I mean, there was his employment insurance, and the mortgage cover, and he had a school fee policy. But if he –' she swallowed hard '– if he killed himself, they won't all pay out.' She lifted her head and faced him. 'I thought you'd know the situation.'

Anderson nodded. Perhaps David had known what he was doing when he fought to fall. He certainly seemed to have comprehensively solved his money worries. 'Yes. I see. I imagine that it will be death by misadventure. I –' He thought back to that moment when he had let go of David and caught hold of Sam. It wouldn't be possible for a coroner's jury to say that David had deliberately dropped to his death. 'I tried to hold him. It was – unfortunate.'

Catherine let out a long sigh and closed her eyes briefly. 'Penny will be so relieved.' She looked at him with a wry smile hovering around her lips. 'As will Julia Bond. This will be the second key man payout in a month for Drax & Bond.'

Another £5m for Drax & Bond? He raised his eyebrows thoughtfully. He ought by rights to bring charges against Sam for fraud, but he was already in two minds about it and this made it even easier. Anything she had taken from the company would be more than made up for by the profits on David's death. The irony of the situation made him smile. It was only a pity that the main beneficiary was Julia Bond.

Catherine turned towards the door. 'I'm sorry to disturb your day. You must be exhausted. Thank you for your help.'

He was by her side at once. 'Catherine, don't go.'

She stepped quickly away from him, holding up her hands. 'Don't. Don't, John. Please. I can't.'

Her face was full of fear. He did not attempt to touch her. Gently he said, 'Come to dinner with me tonight.'

She shook her head, over and over again. 'No. I'm sorry. I can't. I daren't.'

Without another word she turned and ran to the door. She was in such a hurry to escape. He followed her and watched her stab the button for the lift and wait, tapping her foot, not looking at him.

The lift doors opened and she went in. Just before she pressed the button to descend her eyes met his. Her lips were parted, her face tense with longing, her pupils wide and dark with desire.

'Call me,' he said, and then the lift doors slid shut.

He went back into the flat and gazed at the lilies in their tall blue vase. They were opening, casting the invisible net of their scent through the warm air.

There was no rush. She would come back when she was ready.

CRIME & PASSION

A MOMENT OF MADNESS
by
Pan Pantziarka
ISBN: 0 7535 0024 8
Publication date: 17 April 1997

Tom Ryder is the charismatic head of the Ryder Forum – an organisation teaching slick management techniques to business people. Sarah Fairfax is investigating current management theories for a television programme called *Insight* and is attending a course at the Ryder Hall. All the women on the course think Ryder is dynamic, powerful and extremely attractive. Sarah agrees, but this doesn't mean that she's won over by his evangelical spiel; in fact, she's rather cynical about the whole thing.

When one of the course attendees – a high-ranking civil servant – is found dead in his room from a drugs overdose, Detective Chief Inspector Anthony Vallance is called in to investigate. Everyone has something to hide, except for Sarah Fairfax who is also keen to find out the truth about this suspicious death. As the mystery deepens and another death occurs, Fairfax and Vallance compete to unearth the truth. They discover dark, erotic secrets, lethal dangers and, to their mutual irritation, each other.

This is the first in a series of Fairfax and Vallance mysteries.

INTIMATE ENEMIES

by Juliet Hastings

ISBN: 0 7535 0155 4

Publication date: 15 May 1997

Francesca Lyons is found dead in her art gallery. The cause of death isn't obvious but her bound hands suggest foul play. The previous evening she had an argument with her husband, she had sex with someone, and two men left messages on the gallery's answering machine. Detective Chief Inspector Anderson has plenty of suspects but can't find anyone with a motive.

When Stephanie Pinkney, an art researcher, is found dead in similar circumstances, Anderson's colleagues are sure the culprit is a serial killer. But Anderson is convinced that the murders are connected with something else entirely. Unravelling the threads leads him to Andrea Maguire, a vulnerable, sensuous art dealer with a quick-tempered husband and unsatisfied desires. Anderson can prove Andrea isn't the killer and finds himself strongly attracted to her. Is he making an untypical and dangerous mistake?

Intimate Enemies **is the second in the series of John Anderson mysteries.**

A TANGLED WEB

by Pan Pantziarka

ISBN: 0 7535 0156 2

Publication date: 19 June 1997

Michael Cunliffe was ordinary. He was an accountant for a small charity. He had a pretty wife and an executive home in a leafy estate. Now he's been found dead: shot in the back of the head at close range. The murder bears the hallmark of a gangland execution.

DCI Vallance soon discovers Cunliffe wasn't ordinary at all. The police investigation lifts the veneer of suburban respectability to reveal blackmail, extortion, embezzlement, and a network of sexual intrigue. One of Cunliffe's businesses has been the subject to an investigation by the television programme, *Insight*, which means that Vallance has an excuse to get in touch again with Sarah Fairfax. Soon they're getting on each other's nerves and in each other's way, but they cannot help working well together.

A Tangled Web **is the second in the series of Fairfax and Vallance mysteries.**

A Blakes Cottage for Only £5* per person, per night when you buy any two Crime & Passion books

Offer is open to UK residents aged 18 and over. Offer closes 12th December 1997.

Booking your Blakes Cottage is easy. Just follow the step-by-step instructions listed below:

1. To book your Blakes Cottage for only £5* per person, per night, simply call 01282 445056, quote the Crime & Passion £5 per person, per night offer and reference MPJ702.

2. The Blakes Holiday Adviser will ask you for the following:
   * the number of adults and children in the party
   * your preferred holiday dates (the duration must be a minimum of one week)
   * you preferred holiday area

3. You will then be offered a choice of selected properties and provided with details of price, location, facilities and accommodation.

4. To confirm the booking you will be asked for full payment by credit card or cheque.

5. Send the completed application form show below, together with two Blakes Cottages/Crime & Passion tokens and a till receipt highlighting your purchase to: Blakes Cottages, The Crime & Passion Offer, Stoney Bank, Earby, Colne, Lancs BB8 6PR.

Application Form

Title   Mr/Mrs/Ms ....

First Name(s) ....

Surname ....

Address ....

....

....

Postcode ....

Telephone Number ....

> C & P
>
> *One Token*
>
> Deadly Affairs

If you do not wish to receive further information and special offers from Virgin Publishing or Blakes Cottages you should write to Blakes Cottages, Dept. DPA, Stoney Bank Road, Earby, Colne, Lancs, BB8 6PR